REQUIEM OF SILENCE

THE FAMINE CYCLE: BOOK THREE

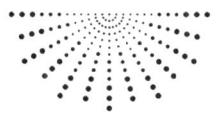

J.D.L. ROSELL

RUNE & REQUIEM PRESS

Illustration © 2022 by René Aigner
Book design by J.D.L. Rosell
Maps by Kaitlyn Clark

Published by Rune & Requiem Press
runeandrequiempress.com

CONTENTS

Maps   v

Prologue   1
1. Assassin   3
2. Blood and Wine   12
3. Reckless   20
4. Dishonorable   28
5. His Most Loyal Servant   37
6. Secrets of the Serpent   45
7. Summons   55
8. Old Enemies   65
9. Sacrifice   77
10. The Right Moment   85
11. A Choice   92
12. Deserters   97
13. The Tarnished Pearl   107
Interlude I   116
14. Through Foreign Lands   120
15. Homecoming   126
16. An Exile's Welcome   136
17. The Red Lake   143
18. An Offering of Blood   151
Interlude II   157
19. The Third Fold   163
20. The Final Solution   174
21. Principle   179
22. Whirling World   185
23. The Only Way   194
24. The Fires Below   201
25. Rage, Hope, Despair   211
26. The Endless Stair   223
27. Catalyst   232
28. To the Last Breath   240

29. Chaos   246
30. Requiem   251
31. Zenith   258
32. Beauty in the Broken   264
33. From a Seed   270
    Epilogue   282

    Glossary   286
    Guide to Oedijan Society   293
    Acknowledgments   295
    Books by J.D.L. Rosell   297
    About the Author   299

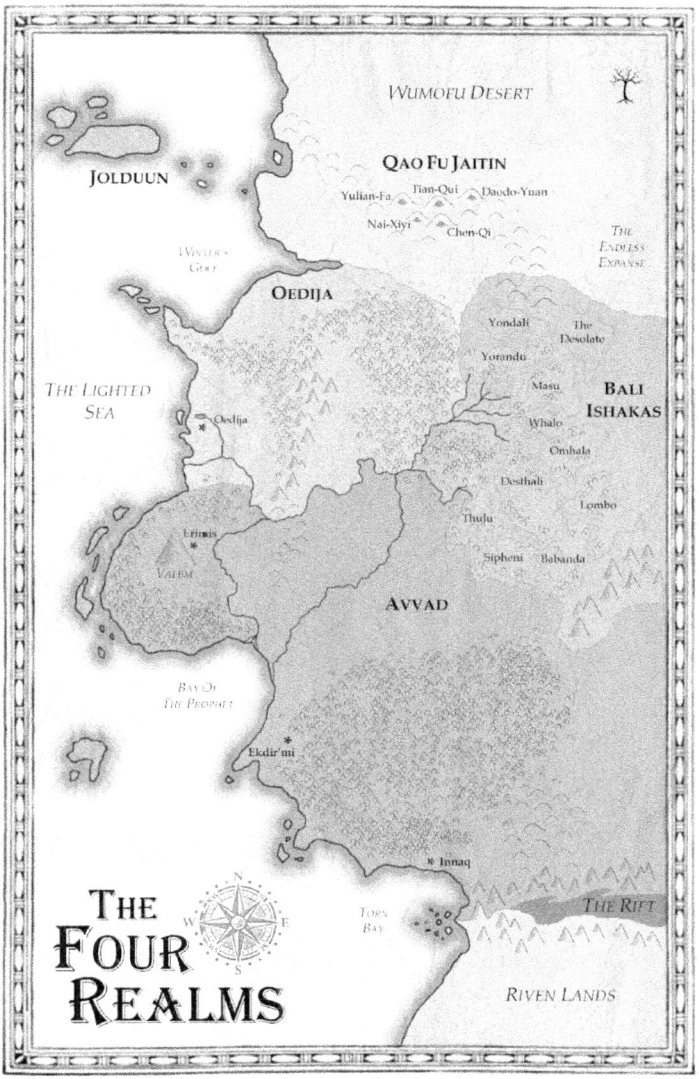

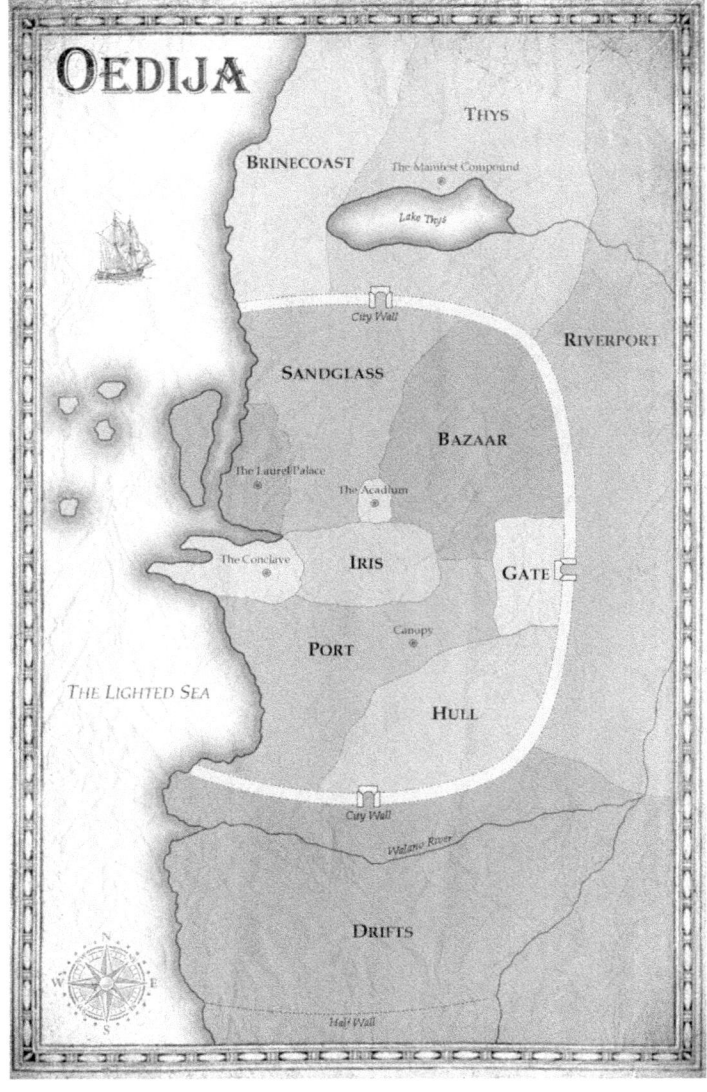

OEDIJA

THYS

BRINECOAST

The Manifest Compound

Lake Thys

City Wall

RIVERPORT

SANDGLASS

BAZAAR

The Laurel Palace

The Acadlum

The Conclave

IRIS

GATE

PORT

Canopy

THE LIGHTED SEA

HULL

City Wall

Walano River

DRIFTS

Halt Wall

PROLOGUE

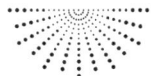

Secrets have governed my life. As surely as the tides of fate, my hunt for them has molded me, become my identity. Their allure drove me into a long-dead profession, and their capriciousness haunted me with the tragedies of my brothers. The pursuit of them has endangered my life more times than I can count.

I have always believed in the power of secrets. But I could never have known they would hold the key to caging a god.

Famine is real. It took me a long time to accept what that means. But now I must.

He will consume my world. I alone stand in his way.

Why me? — the self-pitying question has occurred to me many times during this ruinous journey. *Why must I bear this burden?* I have mulled over the matter during many sleepless nights, listening to the monsoon rains patter on the windows of the Laurel Palace.

There are a few answers. In part, influences beyond my control put me here. In part, my own actions and mistakes were responsible.

But there is no doubt that it is true, that I must be the one to stop the daemon god. If only for the secrets I alone understand.

The true power in secrets has always been in how they are wielded. I must use mine perfectly if I am to succeed.

I will be the Sacrifice.

This dragon, this daemon god — he has plagued us for too long. I will end the cycle if I can. But even if all I can do is delay his return, it will be enough.

Famine must be stopped. No matter the cost. No matter the sacrifice I must make.

Even if there is little of the world left to save.

1

ASSASSIN

Any fool can spill blood if you put iron in their hands. The true
soldier is the man or woman who knows when and how to use it.

- On the formation of a standing army; by Stratechon Bion,
1086 SLP

I drifted into the Pyrthae.

If anything could have focused my mind, it was the
Council's discussion playing out in high drama before me.
Tempers had long since flown out the window. Kyros had
bellowed his piece and stood in the corner of Jaxas's solar,
stewing and staring over the cityscape, though the view was
obscured by rain and smoke. Feiyan looked at each of us, a
small smile turning her lips even now, waiting for her
moment to claw still more power to herself. Jaxas, wan with
dark circles under his eyes, and wearing a green crown that
seemed to weigh as heavily as gold, leaned onto the table and
stared at his steepled hands, as if hoping to find answers
between them.

I blinked away my double-vision of the city and sat up in
my chair. Nomusa glanced at me from where she sat at

Jaxas's left, and Xaron's brow creased with concern as he watched me from across the round table.

I gave a small shake of my head. My problems could wait. These were proceedings I wouldn't interrupt if I could help it.

"And the casualties were high," Kelena was saying. "Scores died, perhaps hundreds."

"How many were guards?" asked Feiyan, smug as a fed cat.

Kelena's jaw worked silently for a moment. I could guess what she was thinking. Being an honor herself, she was keenly aware of how little the loss of her people's lives mattered to the First Consul.

"Three," she said at last.

Feiyan smiled and leaned back. "Well, that's more than a fair trade, wouldn't you say? Three lives for a hundred traitors dead."

Silence filled Jaxas's solar. I stared around the room, hoping someone would speak out. Nomusa, the new Archon. Xaron, the First Warden. Isidora, the First Watcher, leader of the new division of battle wardens under Jaxas's command. Kyros, of course, remained the Archmaster. Kelena was now the sole First Verifier. Even Shaka-Heir Komo, though not an official part of the Council, had the right to speak, for he and his people were critical allies of Oedija.

And then there was Feiyan. The sly minx had worked her way into Jaxas's good graces to become his First Consul, his closest advisor and second-in-command. Only Jaxas, the Despot of Oedija and sole ruler of the nation, possessed more power.

All present had titles, had the right to make their opinions heard. All except for me, as Feiyan reminded me at every meeting.

Two spans before, it had seemed reasonable, even noble, to refuse a formal position from Jaxas. Then, I'd been sick of failing my duties as a First Verifier. I'd thought I could best oppose Famine by having no distractions and operating from the shadows. A good part of me still believed that. But in these Council meetings, though Jaxas continued to invite me, my words carried no more weight than a finch's chirp.

At times like these, I sorely regretted that decision.

The Manifest Massacre, people were already calling it. So many dead in a riot that had emerged from nowhere and accomplished nothing. It had begun with a simple gathering. Then, as city guards flooded the scene, they fanned the sparks into flame. Even an angry mob stood little chance against trained and armed men.

For all the titles at this Council, none here knew how to deal with the issue before them. I couldn't remain silent any longer.

I felt dizzy from my 'Thae-drift, yet still, I stood. "Jaxas, if I may speak."

His hollowed eyes found mine. "Yes, Airene. Of course."

I looked around the room. "We all know what's coming. Who's at our doorstep. The reports have the Avvadin vanguard arriving within the span, with the rest of the armies following a span after. We cannot still be waging war on another front when they arrive."

"Are we at war with the Manifest?" Feiyan asked with a small smile. "I believe we just slaughtered their followers, or so the people say."

"But that's just it. The city guard didn't just kill Seekers; they killed our own citizens. The very people we need to support Oedija if we're to come through this."

"The very people who now support the Manifest!" Kyros broke in. "They're traitors! Unquestionably traitors!"

I clenched my jaw and held my tongue. There was no winning a shouting match with the Archmaster.

Jaxas turned from Kyros to me. "I believe a proposal was forthcoming."

The rest of the Council looked back to me as well, their

expressions a mix of apprehension, scorn, and hope. I wondered which was predominant, if my idea was doomed to flounder from the start.

"Yes," I said, "there is. I propose we strike at the heart of the Manifest. If we gut their leadership, we can unravel them from within."

"Assassination." Feiyan's lips curled. "We've discussed and dismissed this before. We have no assassins, nor can we spare any Watchers to pretend to be one. Where, then, would this killer come from?"

I took a breath, wondering if I'd really thought this plan through, if it didn't spawn from the same madness that tightened its grip on me each day. Nomusa and Xaron stared at me, horror quickly settling in.

Unwilling to meet their eyes, I looked at Jaxas. "I believe I have someone, Your Radiance. If I have your permission to proceed, I will inform them of it."

Jaxas's dark eyes had become as hard as flint. The Council fell silent as he considered my words, though Xaron looked as if he might burst forth at any moment.

"Yes," the Despot said at length. "You have my permission. When will it be done?"

I pushed down my fear long enough to speak. "Tomorrow night."

WHEN THE COUNCIL session broke shortly after, Nomusa and Xaron pulled me aside in the hallway outside Jaxas's solar. Isidora lingered just out of earshot as she waited for Xaron, their romance somehow continuing to flourish even as the world came to an end.

"You can't mean what I think you did," Xaron muttered.

"I did."

"You'd better be planning to send Talan." Nomusa looked

me up and down. "Because *you* would be dead at the entrance."

I chose to play it coy. "Maybe."

Neither of them were fooled. Xaron shook his head. "Aire, I know Avvad is almost here, and the Manifest Massacre just happened at the worst of times. I know you feel Famine feasting and growing more powerful by the day. But this... this is throwing your life away."

"It's not, Xaron. It's doing what must be done." I leaned in closer. "Ariston the Dishonored holds information, information I need. Vusu told me to find his honor, Seda, to understand all he's done, and Ariston has Seda. Go to him, and I can finally reach her."

Nomusa straightened. "You can't be sure she's in the Brinecoast compound. Ariston might be, but he may keep Seda somewhere else entirely."

"But I do know. I saw her there."

They shared a look. I knew what they were thinking even before they spoke.

"'Thae-drifting again?" Xaron asked quietly. "Airene, you shouldn't. You've not even been a warden for a season."

"And yet I'm doing things you've never attempted."

Nomusa seized my arm. "Because you're reckless!" she hissed. "Don't do this, Airene. Please!"

I almost gave in. Seeing their looks, the desperate love in them, I almost said the words they wanted so badly to hear. Instead, I lowered my head and spoke to the floor.

"I have to. Or Famine wins."

The hallway fell silent when the door to Jaxas's solar opened, revealing Feiyan. Her violet robes lined with silver swished as she strode toward us.

"So here's our little assassin. Trying to talk her out of it? I wouldn't bother." She reached out and put a hand to my cheek. I flinched from her clammy touch, but just managed not to draw away.

"You always were a finch flying too close to the sun," she cooed softly. "Always destined to destroy yourself."

I acted without thinking. My locus opened; the power of the Pyrthae came within reach.

I channeled.

Feiyan yelped and withdrew her hand, staring at it. The skin on it had reddened as if burned. When she looked up, her smile was gone.

Only then did I realize the significance of what I'd done. It was more than that I'd used radiance without channeling it through the shifts on my fingertips and toes, though that was extraordinary enough. Feiyan was the First Consul now. She could order me killed if she wanted to. I didn't think Jaxas would allow it, but what if he didn't find out in time?

Still, as Nomusa had noted, I'd always been reckless. Instead of apologizing, I pasted on a smile of my own. "I almost hope this is goodbye."

"It will be, if you dare to use magic against me again." Feiyan swept down the stairs without a backwards glance.

Xaron and Nomusa stared at me. "Did you just—?" Xaron started.

"Yes. I did." I closed my locus and felt weariness seep into my bones.

Nomusa shook her head. "Airene, I love you; you know I do. Which is why you should listen when I say you're not well."

"No one is well. Our city is about to be under siege."

"But not everyone is losing their minds."

I looked her squarely in the eyes, a touch of my temper returning. "I'm not mad, Nomu. Not yet. Believe it or not, but I've thought this through. It's the only way I can get what we need. The only way to help Oedija."

Jaxas's door opened again, but this time, it was the Despot himself who stepped out. He walked with renewed vigor these days, ever since he'd overthrown the Conclave and seized power exclusively for the Laurel Palace. Though all the cares of the realm weighed on his thin shoulders, though the circles under his eyes darkened with each passing night, he'd never seemed so full of life. As if this were what he'd been born to do.

I wished I felt half as prepared for my tasks.

He nodded to us, and we gave deep bows in return. I wondered if we ought to kneel, as had been the custom of old, but Jaxas — or, more to the point, Nikias — hadn't yet demanded it.

The Despot's gaze found and held me. "Airene. Do you still mean to do this?"

I hesitated, but there was little point in denying it. He knew whom I meant to be the assassin. "I must."

His eyes flickered to my friends. "And will anyone accompany you?"

"No." I said it firmly before either of my friends could speak up.

"We'll see about that," Xaron amended with a rebellious look.

"No, First Warden Xaron; I agree with her. This is not your task. I need you for the war to come." The Despot looked back at me. "Airene walks a different path."

I looked away, unable to meet his gaze. If anyone knew the road I traveled now, it was Jaxas.

"But don't go alone," he continued. "Find that Guilder friend of yours — Talan Wraithsbane. From what I have heard, he sounds like the right man for the job."

I winced. "He is." *Or was.* I wondered if he would be now, but kept my expression blank. Xaron and Nomusa didn't bother hiding their doubts.

If Jaxas noticed, he didn't show it. "Then it's settled. Eleven blessings, Airene. Our hopes go with you."

With that, the Despot and his ever-present shadow of

Nikias walked past us, the steward with a lingering skeptical look.

Nomusa waited until they were out of earshot before speaking. "The Manifest aren't supposed to be your concern, Airene. Not even Oedija can be, no matter what Jaxas says."

"You're a Seed of Famine, right?" Xaron's eyes darted around to make sure no one but Isidora was near enough to overhear, though the words would be gibberish to most. "Just you and Linos. You two are the only ones who can stop that daemon god. And at the moment, I don't think your brother is up to the task."

"Not stop him," I said softly. "Repress him. And only for a little while."

They exchanged glances. All of us knew what that meant for me.

"Still" — Nomusa's voice trembled, then steadied — "still, you cannot throw your life away on some pyr hunt. We'll sort out the Manifest another way."

I shook my head. "It's not about that. I need Seda, remember? She's my key to defeating Famine." Or so I hoped. Part of me wondered if I went down this road just to delay the inevitable. If this was, as Nomusa put it, a pyr hunt.

She sighed. "Fine. But at least do as Jaxas asked and bring Talan."

A bitter laugh escaped me. "I doubt he'll want to go."

"Try. He might surprise you."

Xaron snorted. "I wouldn't go that far. But even if he's an ass, he's loyal and competent."

I looked down the staircase, hiding the emotions I couldn't repress. "Even after the Silvencrest?"

An awkward silence fell, punctuated by the bustling steps of honors hurrying past.

Nomusa's answer came in a murmur. "It was a panicked decision. And you've been busy since, understandably so. He can't expect you to make time for dalliances."

"Even if *you* have," Xaron said with a sly look her way. "Many times."

"Not now, Xaron," she snapped. "Airene, he's a grown man. He'll understand if you just go talk to him."

"Maybe," I hedged. "Maybe not."

Either way, I had little choice. Without Talan, this excursion stood an even scanter chance of success, and there wasn't much hope for it to begin with.

But, despite my wishes otherwise, I didn't know that the Talan I needed was still with us.

2

BLOOD AND WINE

"Above all else, two appetites infect our men: one for spilling blood, and the second for overflowing wine."

- Father Tarik, a priest of Valem; date unknown

I fell to brooding as I left through the northern Laurel gate and traveled through Sandglass. I'd had brief contact with Talan since that day I'd left him at the Silvencrest two spans before, the same evening as Famine's return from wherever Vusu had briefly imprisoned him. Only one note had found me — a few lines devoid of affection telling where I could find him, ending with a barb: *In case you have time for me.*

I hadn't had the stomach to visit.

With an effort, I pushed the gloomy thoughts from my mind and focused on my surroundings. Oedija was suffering a calm after the storm for the moment, but danger still abounded. The massacre at Brinecoast had come as a shock, but I doubted it would tamp down the violence permanently. Too much fear and anger filled the air. Death was on the horizon, and Avvad's armies brought it ever closer.

But though vagrants lurked in most of the alleys I passed, their eyes glimmering as they watched me, none tried to assault me. Perhaps it was the bald confidence with which I walked, even if half of that confidence was faked. I could channel well for my limited experience, but even wardens were vulnerable to knives and arrows.

The place I sought was close to the border along Bazaar. Muttering Talan's directions to myself under my breath, I strolled along the street until I found it. A cellar door to a butcher shop, tucked just inside a shadowed alcove. No one lingered nearby, and I wondered if that was coincidence or if knowledge of its inhabitants kept people away.

Shrugging off my fear, I approached the door and, finding it unlatched, hauled it open. The stench of rotting flesh wafted up from the dark entrance, and I gagged, swallowing back bile as it hit the back of my throat. Bitterly, I wondered if Talan pointed me to this entrance for petty revenge as I climbed down into the reeking cellar, closing the hatch behind me.

The darkness became nearly complete, and my heart hammered in my chest. I hadn't brought a pyr lamp, yet I was loath to channel my own light. Even here, at the beginning of what should be an abandoned tunnel, I didn't want to risk someone finding me. But it was the least of the risks I'd taken lately.

Opening my locus, a pleasant heat swelled in my belly and spread throughout my body. Holding up a hand, I allowed a sliver of the energy to flare onto my fingertips. I held the potential for an inferno inside me, and part of me ached to release it, but I pushed the wild desire down and pressed on through the cellar.

After some searching, I found a rotting animal skin that hid a damp tunnel, moisture from the monsoons finding their way into it. Each splashing footfall echoed down the path. There'd be no disguising my approach.

But as I exited the tunnel into a wider cavern, no one appeared. I brightened my light and looked around the chamber. Its walls were covered in mud, but I glimpsed underneath the muck faded etchings, masterful works lost to time. This wasn't just some smuggler's den; this had once been an important building, either to my ancestors or those of the honors. *We're always looking to the Pyrthae and sky above for great things, and forget the hidden wonders lying below,* Talan had once said to me. The truth was spread out before me.

I walked across the chamber to a broad entrance that led to a larger corridor, this one immune from the damp. There, I paused. The glow of pyrkin lay ahead, escaping from a small door along the side of the tunnel. I extinguished my light and crept forward. I couldn't yet soften my footsteps like Xaron, but I'd had enough practice sneaking around in my Finching days that my approach was nearly silent. Reaching the edge of the doorway, I peered around.

And found the point of a knife leveled at my eye.

A strangled gasp escaped me as I flooded my body with radiance and kinesis. I barely kept from striking out, even as I looked beyond the knife to the man who held it. Power birthed of the god who had attuned me raged within.

"You," the man growled. He withdrew the knife, tucked it into his ragged clothes, then turned away without another word.

I hesitated at the doorway, breath still coming quick and heart pounding. With an effort, I dismissed my magic and closed my locus. The tunnels seemed especially dun and dank without the Pyrthae's touch upon me. Or perhaps the cold came from Talan's expression.

I set my jaw. Time to set aside the past and do what had to be done. Feelings didn't matter in the face of Telae's destruction.

Not much did, when it came to it.

I followed him into a dark hall. On the other side opened

up a small chamber. Perhaps, in another time, it had been a gathering room, a place to entertain guests. Stone benches ran along the curved walls, likely set before tables that had long ago rotted away and never been replaced. The flickering light illuminating the room came from the far end. There, Talan's silhouette crouched, his back to me. I put one foot in front of the other, forcing myself to approach.

Even when I stood behind him, he didn't turn around. I stared into his small fire burning on the stone floor. On top of what looked to be broken timbers, strips of cloth twisted as they burned. It was the only fuel he could find in the Underguild's old haunts, I guessed.

I worked myself up to ask the question. "Is Sule here?"

"Was she the reason?" Talan half-turned toward me, unkempt hair falling before his eyes. In his hand, he clutched a flask.

I averted my gaze. "My request is sensitive. I just wanted to be sure we were alone."

Abruptly, he stood and faced me, breath hot against my face, the sickly sweet stench of wine wafting over me. "I have to know, Airene. It's been two spans since you left me at the Silvencrest. I've tried to talk to you and you've refused me. So answer me now: why didn't you come that night?"

I couldn't meet his eyes, afraid of what I'd find in them. Of what he would see in mine. "I told you. Famine" — I winced, the name burning on my tongue — "he returned as I crossed the bridge. I couldn't go to our rendezvous after that."

"Yes, you could have."

He reached for my hand, and I didn't have the strength to refuse him. Even grimy and stinking of liquor, his touch sent fire racing through me with far more urgency than radiance ever did.

"You could have," he repeated. "We could have faced that bastard together, could have stolen a little piece of happiness

15

to spite him. After the moment we shared, I thought we were finally getting our chance. But then..."

His gaze was hard on me, amber eyes glinting in the firelight, and suddenly, I couldn't take it any longer. I swallowed back the sobs threatening to rise in my throat, swallowed all the bitter disappointment and rage at the unfairness of it all. Only when I had felt the caustic solution settle back in my stomach did I turn my gaze up to his.

"I promised Jaxas I'd kill Ariston the Dishonored."

Talan blinked. "What?"

"I need to find the honor with him," I plowed on. "Seda, Vusu's personal honor. Vusu said before his death that she has everything I need to know. I saw her with him in... in the Pyrthae." Better to say that than a dream, though these days, the two were increasingly intertwined in my experience. "I will do what must be done."

His eyes grew harder with every word. Almost, I could have believed him sober, but for the slight sway in his stance.

"You want me to come with," he said quietly. "That's why you came here."

I clenched my jaw, then forced out the only word I could. "Yes."

He closed his eyes for a moment, then opened them again. I almost flinched at the fire in them.

"You say you'll kill Ariston. But you're no killer, Airene. You've only killed two people, and both in self-defense. You can't murder someone in cold blood."

Ice crept through my veins. I spoke through numb lips. "I have to. Someone has to."

Talan barked a harsh laugh. "I've struck down so many men and women I can't count them all. I didn't even see their faces, most of them. I've murdered with a knife, and Valem's curse. Even with my bare hands." He leaned toward me. "Who better than I to kill this unruly honor?"

I knew Talan, knew him down to his bones. I saw behind

the fury to the drowning pain, the guilt at all that blood on his hands. He wasn't a murderer either, no matter what he said. A soldier, yes, but always on the right side of the fight. A good man, down at his core, who did the best thing in the worst of situations.

But I still couldn't help a shiver of fear running through me at his stare.

"I'm not asking you to kill him," I muttered. "I'm asking you to help me get to him. That's all."

He broke eye contact first, turning to look into the dying flames. I stepped up beside him, wanting to put a hand on his shoulder, to lean into him, hold him, kiss him. But I couldn't, not now. Maybe not ever.

"When do we go?" he asked without turning around.

I felt something loosen inside me, knowing I wouldn't have to do this alone. Even as another part tightened with guilt that I'd roped him into danger once again.

"Tomorrow night. We'll meet at the Sandglass gate."

He nodded, then took a long pull from his flask. "If that's all, you can see I have a busy night to get back to." He spoke without turning around, wiping his mouth as he did.

I stared at him a moment longer, but he didn't glance back. I lowered my gaze. It was for the best. If he'd met my eyes, my resolve and better judgment would have crumbled.

"That's all," I murmured, then made my way back through the gloom.

At the end of the passage, I lifted the cellar door and stepped out into the dark alley. Instead of the roiling tumult in my belly settling after speaking with Talan, it had grown worse. I stiffened my trembling lips, latched the cellar door, and exited onto the main street.

Few people were around, but I spotted a knot of men loitering in an alcove. As I passed under a mounted pyr lamp, their eyes turned toward me.

"Oi, wench!" one of them called across the street. "Come here a moment! Come give Atlan a kiss!"

The others cackled, shadowed faces turned toward me, eyes glinting in the thin light.

I should have kept walking. Most likely, they would have left me be. I should have given them the chance.

But at their leers, something snapped in me. I spun toward them, body coursing with energy, fingers burning.

"Come here then," I said, my voice not seeming my own. "Come claim it."

The men shuffled back, faces startled in a sudden red glow. I looked down and saw flames crawling out from the tips of my gloves and over my hands. Even then, I couldn't hold back.

"Well?" I taunted. "I'm waiting!"

I could barely hear their responses as they backed away, though I picked up a few curses and mentions of "daemon." I smiled, cold and brittle, as they disappeared into the darkness.

As I released my hold on radiance and closed my locus, I felt even more deadened than before. Slapping my hands to dampen the lingering tongues of fire, I closed my eyes and tilted my head back, breathing in and out. I pictured Isidora's desert in my mind, hoping it would center me, that it would bring me back to myself again and out of the boiling rage that always seemed to be with me now.

When I opened my eyes, I found that, instead of clouds and the dull light of the moons, buildings hung overhead. I swiveled my gaze up and down the street and saw a mirror image of it above.

A spike of pleasure ran through me. Somewhere, far in the distance, Famine had feasted well, and felt for a moment his hunger abate.

But only for a moment.

I pulled myself back from the 'Thae-drift and into my

shivering body. As the vision of the mirror Oedija blew away like smoke, I gasped and doubled forward.

I'm losing it. Famine is growing stronger, and I'm losing myself.

Standing upright so quickly my vision fuzzed for a moment, I let out a low laugh. If I was our only hope, we had no hope at all.

But I'd never been one to give in. My legs wobbly beneath me, I made my way down the dark street back to the Laurel Palace.

3
RECKLESS

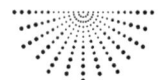

HIGH TRIBUNE: That was recklessly done, Veri-
    fier Jaxale. Much could have gone wrong in your
    investigation. Better to have waited for the
    proper authority before proceeding.
VERIFIER: With all respect, High Tribune, little is
    accomplished without being reckless.

  - Verifier Jaxale before High Tribune Krynollon;
    1067 SLP

I stared at the building across the canal and wondered if I'd already gone mad.

The warehouse rose from the gloomy night like a cliff, just as tall and impassable. Once, during the height of Salt-peter's wealth a century back, it had housed the salt for which the deme was named. Since then, it was slowly abandoned, its senescence mirroring the district's own. Vagrants and rats became more common than trading goods.

Now, the Manifest infested it.

Even with the cloud moon's violet light and the green radiant winds illuminating the cityscape, I couldn't see anyone standing watch. Yet Seekers had never been lax, nor had Ariston fallen so far as to lose all his followers. Much as I wished otherwise, there would be sentinels to reckon with.

I hoped they wouldn't spot us in return. Talan and I wore dark clothes, a hooded cloak thrown over to ward off the rain. Gloves covered my hands, and not only for the warmth. My shifts had continued to advance. Not content to remain at my fingers, all the skin up to my wrists moved in mesmerizing patterns now. I wore gloves as often as I could get away with it, and never showed my hands without good reason.

Soon, however, I would have to remove them. Channeling was required this night, and I'd already burned through one pair the night before.

I glanced at Talan, crouched beside me behind the canal wall opposite to the Manifest hideout. I was grateful for the salt stinging my nose from the incessant wind off the sea, for otherwise I would have smelled the stench of alcohol hanging about the former Guilder. Still, he reeked less than he had the previous night. Considering what I'd put him through, and what I expected of him now, I could hardly ask for more.

"See anyone?" I whispered, pitching my voice low though the gale would disguise any noise we made.

He shook his head. "Not see; sense." His lopsided smile materialized as his eyes slid over to me. "Can you not feel them?"

I only shrugged. Talan had always displayed a preternatural awareness of his surroundings. I suspected it was something to do with an unconscious use of quintessence, but if so, it was another of his secrets I had yet to uncover.

Yet I had my own methods. Trusting him to keep watch, I closed my eyes, opened my locus to the Pyrthae, and channeled.

The world changed around me as I drifted into the spirit realm. Though my eyes remained closed, I gained a different sort of vision as my soul peeled away from my body. The strange, shifting landscape of the Pyrthae was disorienting for a moment. The colors, kaleidoscopic and ever-changing, made my head spin if I studied them overlong, and distances fluctuated, the warehouse seeming within reach one moment, then far away the next. I quickly adjusted, having spent enough time in the pyr's plane to be used to the shift.

Refocusing, I confirmed Talan's declaration, counting the glowing flames that signified those attuned to the Pyrthae. There were eight Seekers in total: two on the warehouse roof, six within. *Only eight?* It was far fewer than I had expected and much fewer than I'd dared hope for. Xaron, Isidora, and their Watchers had whittled away their numbers, and Vusu's fall lost even more, but this force showed that desertion had become widespread within the Manifest.

But though eight made for better odds, Talan and I still numbered just two. We had to proceed carefully, lest we be the ones with knives in our backs.

I eased back out of the Pyrthae, but did not entirely reenter the material plane. Instead, I employed a trick I'd discovered in the spans since Famine's liberation: I hovered halfway between. Enough of me occupied my body to speak, hear, and even move if needed, yet I still saw within the Pyrthae. It was useful for keeping track of wardens.

I spoke to Talan, following the Seekers' flames as I did. "I see eight. Two above, six within."

"I sensed the same."

In his silence, I heard his unspoken question. I didn't offer an explanation; he didn't ask.

"Our approach then. From above?"

I balked at the idea. "And how do we reach the roof?"

I heard the smile in his voice. "Oh, my Finch. You're a warden now. Do you forget you can fly, if you only try?"

Ordinarily, his mockery would not have bothered me, for

Talan had always been gentle. Now, however, there was a bitter edge to it that could cut.

With little other recourse, I ignored the gibe. "I'm still clumsy with kinesis. I doubt I could make that leap."

"I could send down a rope. Or did you miss that I'd brought one?"

I had noticed it, but being treated like I was still unattuned was not something I wanted to perpetuate. I struggled to remain neutral. "Fine. You'll lower the rope. But let me ease the way."

"And how do you propose to do that from down here?"

It was my turn to smile. "Wait and see. But don't be surprised when the watchers no longer watch."

Leaving him with a taste of his own potion, I fully entered the Pyrthae once more. Instead of hovering above my body, I ventured forth, soaring through the law-defying realm. I drew close to the warehouse roof to the nearest of the two Seekers until I felt the heat of his flame. It was not the warmth of fire, but the strength of his quintessence. How brightly it burned in the Pyrthae was a sign of how much of his spirit entered this realm, and thus the depth of his attunement.

This Seeker appeared to be a four-shift. I debated attempting to snuff him out entirely, but quickly rejected the thought. Though I presently fashioned myself as an assassin, and these Seekers had chosen a faction opposing mine, I had no desire to sow more death than I had to.

I kept my approach slow but inexorable as I neared the Seeker. Pieces of his soul leaked out and threaded through my own the closer I came. I saw his thoughts and memories in fragments, a puzzle I did not try to piece together. Through them, I glimpsed his face, his friends, his family. I saw moments of hunger and despair. He was a thin man, desperate to survive as drought and war impoverished the realm.

J.D.L. ROSELL

I stifled my pity. When I had channeled quintessence before, I had used it clumsily and incompetently. These past few spans, I had trained myself hard to change that. When not poring over the tomes that might clue me into how to defeat Famine or searching for Vusu's servant Seda, I had devoted every free moment to comprehending and honing my newfound abilities. At the outset of my attunement, such time spent seemed an indulgence, a pastime unlikely to yield results, and every warden I knew reinforced this view. Now, however, I was a ten-shift and growing stronger every day. As Famine swelled in power, so did I.

If I was to be the Sacrifice and ensnare a dragon, I had to be as strong as possible.

During my training, I had learned more than one new skill. Now I used another of them as I pressed my quintessence into the Seeker's. He registered something was wrong at once and instinctively fought against my presence. I didn't resist, but instead emitted calming thoughts and words, backing them with the power my amplified spirit wielded.

Sleep, I told the sentinel. *Rest your eyes, only for a moment. Nothing moves through the dark.*

His resistance ceased. His spirit-flame dimmed. Like a cup set over a candle, the Seeker sputtered into unconsciousness.

I withdrew and waited. When he did not rouse, I smiled and moved to the next watcher on the opposite side of the roof. She resisted more than the first, her five-shift connection lending her increased strength, but it wasn't long before I'd lulled her into unawareness as well.

Had I been able to ambush the other six Seekers in the same way, I would have continued. But grouped as they were, even if I brought one down, the others would be alerted to our presence. We would have to handle them in a different way.

I returned to Telae. The world seemed to tremble beneath my feet, and for a moment, I thought I would sprawl on my rear. But a steadying hand on the canal wall proved sufficient to suffer through the vertigo until it dissipated.

"Back?" Talan muttered. He bent in close so that his breath puffed over me in a cloud of sour wine.

I leaned away. "The Seekers atop the roof are out cold. The others below are still alert, though."

By the faint illumination, I detected the smile curling his lips. "You astound me, Airene, truly. I would ask how you did it, but I have a feeling you'll withhold your secret."

I jerked my head toward the wall and the warehouse beyond it. "You'll just have to trust me."

The amusement faded from his expression, and I regretted my choice of words at once.

"Would that I could," he muttered. Before I could respond, he was rising and darting off toward the short bridge across the canal, then to the warehouse beyond it.

I watched him go, a shadow in the gloom, and tried to stifle the despondency welling up in me. *You had no choice,* I lectured my guilt. *Famine had returned. There's no time for anything between you and him.*

Yet none of the placations seemed to stick.

Talan reached the base of the nearest warehouse wall, then paused. A moment later, he flew up from the ground. Though it did not seem possible, he sailed smoothly to the top of the warehouse, then reached out and hauled himself over in one fluid motion.

But his kinesis-fueled leap was not entirely discreet, for a crack accompanied it that was audible even from where I crouched three dozen paces away. I winced and channeled quintessence to keep tabs on the Seekers within the warehouse. There was movement; they seemed to be heading toward where Talan had leaped from.

Profanities tumbled through my mind as I tried to figure

out what to do. Talan decided for me, tossing down his heavy length of rope so the end dangled a few cubits above the ground. Muttering curses aloud now, I rose and sprinted toward it, ignoring the groaning in my legs, stiff from crouching for so long.

Breath rasped in my throat as I reached for the rope and hauled myself up. My mind flashed back to when I'd done a similar thing when entering the Wyvern's Claw. Though I was now a warden, I hadn't learned to channel kinesis to fuel my body as Xaron and Talan could. My efforts were all my own, and it wasn't long before my arms and shoulders burned.

It seemed a long time later when I dragged myself over the lip and onto the flat roof. No sooner had I tumbled over than Talan hauled up the rope, grunting softly with each motion. The rope was thick and heavy, its kind typically used for hoisting sails on ships, and even for a warden who could channel kinesis effectively, it was an arduous task. Yet in moments, he had accomplished it and coiled the rope before crouching next to me.

"You alright?" he asked. He sounded more like himself than he had in a long while.

I nodded, but could spare no more thought for a response, for I channeled quintessence again. The situation was as I feared. The Seekers had noticed something, whether it was the flare of Talan's channeling or the sounds of our arrival. Their footsteps echoed up to us from below, as did their hushed, urgent voices.

"Damn," Talan muttered, peering at the edge of the roof as if expecting one of our enemies to come soaring over it at any moment. "Think they're coming?"

"Best not to wait and find out."

The former Guilder seemed to consider it for a moment before shaking his head. "Best *you* don't. You'll have a tricky time infiltrating while they hunt you, so I'll draw them off." A shadow of a smile touched his mouth. "I have a few ideas for how to make sure they can't ignore me."

I gripped his arm, fear causing me to squeeze harder than I intended. "Don't be a fool, Talan Wraithsbane."

His eyes found mine. "The same to you, Airene the Finch."

Then he was tearing free of my grasp and vaulting over the edge to a drop that should have broken his legs. The cries of surprise and pain that wafted up moments later told me his descent hadn't gone unnoticed.

I shook my head in disbelief. The man never did listen to me.

But I had my own task to be about. Praying for his safety to gods I only halfway believed in, I pressed on.

4

DISHONORABLE

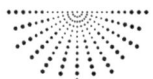

The Kalthuae were an accomplished people before the landing of the Lighted Passage. They raised marvelous temples of innovative architecture, designed to celebrate their many foreign gods. Some of these structures stretched toward the Pyrthae, while others dove deep underground.

The city is a mausoleum for these empty sanctuaries now, though many were torn down or lost to the centuries. We no longer know the names of these gods, nor what forms they took, for no records of them were kept. If they did once exist, they seem to have ceased to touch our world...

- Oedija: A History; by Acadian Helene, Master Historian; 1167 LP

A brief check on the two Seekers atop the warehouse assured me they remained unconscious. A proper assassin would have slit their throats; I indulged in mercy instead, creeping away from their prone bodies and hoping it wouldn't prove to be a fatal mistake.

The sounds of the clash below had faded away, the Seekers

taking off in pursuit of Talan. Trying to forget that he was running or fighting for his life, I set to searching for a way inside. The warehouse had fallen into disrepair along with Saltpeter, and in several locations, the timber had rotted and folded in. A drizzle pattered on my hood and the surrounding roof, a testament to where the building's ruin had originated.

Gingerly, I tested the boards with my foot, but dared not venture farther. If I fell, I doubted I'd be able to catch myself, magic notwithstanding.

So I tied Talan's heavy rope through a gap in the low wall edging the roof, tugged on it to see if it would hold, then began lowering myself down. The aperture was about twice as wide as my shoulders, but reaching splinters of wood snagged at my hair and clothes and scratched my skin as I went through. I gritted my teeth and endured it. With the ground far below and my feet scrabbling for a hold on the writhing rope, a few cuts and scrapes were the least of my concerns.

My stomach clenched tight the entire drop, until at last, my sandals touched the ground. Stifling a sigh of relief, I studied my surroundings. Illumination was scant, with little more than the light of the moons and radiant winds filtering in through the holes in the roof. Dark piles of refuse and abandoned crates huddled throughout the warehouse. The air had a thick scent of dust and disuse. Had someone stumbled upon this place, they would see few signs that it was occupied.

Yet this had to be where the Dishonored hid. For Talan's sake, I hoped I wasn't wrong.

I crouched behind the nearest pile of debris and channeled quintessence. A brief check ensured that the two Seekers above were the only attuned around. That did not, of course, guarantee there weren't unattuned guards posted throughout the warehouse, but I'd been listening and had heard nothing. Considering I had to see to search for my target, I would just have to take a gamble on light.

Exiting the Pyrthae and enduring the transition, I rose a moment later and pulled at radiance. Its warmth unfurled in my body as it streamed toward the shifts on my fingers. There, I gathered it into a small, glowing orb and lifted it to look at my surroundings.

The warehouse's size was intimidating. Mounds upon mounds of refuse littered the ground. I stepped over rusted nails, moldy boards, and smashed crates in my search, and more always lay ahead.

One area seemed to be where the Seekers had stationed themselves. It was marginally cleaner and boasted a small fire pit in its center, still smoking from recent use, as well as blanket rolls around it. I explored the area around the camp more thoroughly, but saw no sign of other occupants. If Ariston and Seda were here, they were likely secured underneath a hidden hatch somewhere.

Pausing at the Seeker camp, I reassessed my approach. I could search all night and still not find them in the chaotic, sprawling chamber. I had to be more focused. And I knew how I could do it.

Dismissing my hold on radiance, I closed my eyes, then dredged up from my memories a particular instance, when Xaron had sharpened my hearing to eavesdrop on distant conversations. I dissected the moment, trying to remember each thing he had done to augment my senses. It was little enough; his magic had mostly been beyond my awareness then. I cursed myself for not asking him about it and his other tricks since I'd begun to understand my attunement, but there'd been too little time, and I hadn't yet had a need for them. I'd been more focused on my own discoveries than anything other wardens might have to share.

I would just have to uncover this on my own as well.

I focused my hearing. On another occasion, Xaron had

explained that sound was just a natural variant of kinesis. Seeing this as a starting point, I drew in the element through my locus. My body buzzed with the fresh energy, but my hearing grew no more acute.

But it had not been kinesis alone that enabled this. Xaron had channeled quintessence, though he did not know it. Drawing on it now, part of my mind extended into the Pyrthae, but did not fully enter it. In that halfway space, I could both feel the kinesis in me and perceive it in my spirit-flame. If I could sense it, I reasoned, perhaps I could manipulate it.

I reached out with invisible hands and began to mold it. Kinesis was everywhere in the Pyrthae. If I changed it so that kinesis did not flow away from me, but *toward*...

Sound burst into my ears.

Before, it had been all but silent in the warehouse, only the occasional scratching to be heard, likely from a rodent or bird that had taken refuge here. Now, every noise clawed into my skull. I steadied myself against the ground and heard the scraping of my palms on the dust. If it had not been so excruciating to endure, I would have been fascinated.

But I still had a task ahead of me. Opening my eyes, I squinted and peered with hazy vision around the warehouse. As on the occasion with Xaron, wherever I looked, my hearing also honed in. I hoped that, by scanning the warehouse, I might locate a hatch beneath which Ariston and Seda hid.

Before I'd scanned half the chamber, an ache began throbbing in my head. I ground my teeth, then stopped as the noise irritated my ears further. I just had to press on. A little more, and—

My thoughts silenced as I heard something. It was not the shifting of debris or the scuttling of rats, but a swish that could only come from the movement of cloth, and the *pat-pat-pat* of feet on stone.

I noted the area, then released my grip on the elements and sighed with relief. My suffering had yielded results.

I rose, swayed for a moment as the disorientation seized me, then stumbled through it, weaving my way toward the place where I'd heard the promising sounds. As my balance returned, I slowed my approach, prudence winning out over urgency. I summoned radiance again to illuminate the rubbish. There were signs that objects had been moved in this area, the dust trampled by feet, and of something being dragged. A crate lay conspicuously at the end of these tracks.

A smile alighted on my lips. 'Thae above, I had them.

Being silent now would be nigh impossible, so I settled for swiftness. Gripping the edges of the crate, I heaved at it, grunting with the effort. Even empty and partially broken, the box was almost beyond my strength to move. I debated channeling kinesis to blast it out of the way, but settled for dragging it away myself. No need to stretch my abilities further than I had to.

At last, I moved the crate, then stepped back to wipe the sweat from my brow as I took in the result. As I'd hoped, a trapdoor lay beneath. A thrill went through me, intoxicating and terrifying. All that was left to do was open it and find out if my quarries truly were within.

I took a moment to settle my nerves, then drew in kinesis and radiance. I'd never used them to much effect in a fight, but even my clumsy wielding, backed by the power of my attunement, should be more than sufficient to take care of any opponent before me. So I hoped.

Drawing in a deep breath, I called fire to the fingertips of my right hand, then reached out for the leather strap serving as a handle on the hatch. Heaving it open, I saw a shadow moving below me and thrust my hand forward.

"Stop there!"

As the illumination from the flames leaking from my shift caught on the figure, however, I knew I was outmatched. An object pointed at me — a crossbow, loaded and drawn, and aimed at my chest.

I didn't lower my hand, though magic would not save me now. Vusu had eventually died in part because of the quarrel I had shot into him. Even wardens were not invulnerable to weapons, and I was mere feet from this bolt.

I looked at the face beyond the weapon and startled. The changes that had come over Ariston were shocking. His head, before shaved bald, had grown a layer of dark stubble. His face had been thin, but now verged upon skeletal, approaching how Vusu had appeared near the end of his life, or like Jaxas before he'd taken the Evergreen Wreath for his own.

The Dishonored seemed alarmed at seeing me as well, though a smile spoiled his lips a moment later. "Of course," he rasped, his rich voice flatter than the last time I'd heard him. "It would be you who found us."

I didn't move. Though the standoff wasn't in my favor, I couldn't risk trying to find a new balance, lest the former honor allow his hand to slip on the lever. All I could do was talk.

So I spoke.

"Ariston the Dishonored. I've been searching for you."

A laugh escaped his lips. "And you have found me. What will you do now, Airene the Finch? Or is it First Verifier these days? Perhaps 'murderer' would be more to the point."

That last title rankled me. How many times had I wondered it of myself? I tried not to let my guilt show, but kept my outstretched hand steady and my voice calm.

"We don't have to do this, Ariston. I just want to talk. Lower your weapon, and I won't harm you."

The crossbow, a heavy wooden piece that looked made for a laurel guard, shook slightly in the man's emaciated arms, but Ariston did not otherwise shift. "You kill my protectors, but merely wish to speak with me. Why, Finch, do I not believe you?"

Truth had a power that lies often did not. I searched for the slivers I could safely share with Ariston.

"I didn't kill those Seekers. Some, we drew off, while others are unconscious." All true, though if Talan still survived, I doubted all of them would live through the night.

The former honor frowned. "Even if that is true, I must assume you came here to kill me. I am what remains of the Manifest. While I live, I pose a threat."

I skirted around the issue. "Perhaps so. But my fight is with someone far more dangerous than you, Ariston. One who is enemy to us both."

His eyes flickered to the ceiling, and I knew he looked to the sky beyond. "You do not mean Avvad, do you?"

"You know I don't."

Ariston's gaze settled back on me. "Still, it does not answer why you are *here*."

I couldn't tell the full truth, so I settled for half. "I've come for Seda."

"Seda?" His eyebrows flew up. "Why her?"

"Despite being Avvadin, she acted as an honor to Vusu, as I'm sure you're aware. She knows what I require. The key to defeating Famine."

"Is that so?" Despite the skepticism in his voice, to my eye, the crossbow lowered a fraction. "Why should she?"

My hand trembled, yet I took the final leap. "Because Vusu told me she did."

Part of me expected Ariston to laugh. Instead, he grew graver. I couldn't tell if fear manipulated my senses, or if the crossbow raised once again.

"Vusu is dead, Finch. He has been for spans. He could not have told you anything, even if I believed he had."

My chest felt as if rope had been wound and pulled tight about it. I was losing him and coming closer to a confrontation I couldn't hope to survive. Words alone would not influence him. Ariston had suffered too much at my hands to believe me now.

So I drew upon the only resource left to me.

I channeled. It was not the radiance burning at my fingertips that I reached for, but quintessence. My soul split between the planes, material and spirit, and I stretched it blindly toward the man before me. He was no warden. He lacked attunement to the Pyrthae. By all rights, I should not be able to influence him.

My only hope was that, somehow, everything I had been taught about being a warden was wrong.

Where before, I had always used quintessence within the Pyrthae, now I tried to wield it in Telae. It pushed forward through my body to my fingertips, but there abruptly halted. My hopes faltered. In this realm, my spirit was trapped in my body. I couldn't do it.

I racked my head for other possibilities. If it could not reach beyond my flesh, was there another way it could spread? While I schemed, Ariston's eyes narrowed, and his body tightened, showing all the signs of preparing to fire.

Then it came to me: quintessence could be melded with other elements. I had just done so to augment my hearing, and how often had I seen Xaron manipulate radiance into illusions? It was quintessence made manifest — or so I hoped.

Drawing kinesis into my body, I spoke, this time projecting with both elements. "Ariston. Do not shoot. Our only hope of defeating Famine is by working together. Let me speak with Seda and discover what she knows. Then I will leave you to your fate, and I will go to mine."

It was nothing I hadn't said before, though I spoke now with finality. I could only hope the quintessence lacing the kinesis held the influence I tried to infuse into it.

The former honor's eyes crossed for a moment, then he

blinked rapidly. As he shifted the crossbow, I flinched, braced for the deadly impact of the bolt tearing through my flesh.

It never came. Instead, Ariston opened his mouth and spoke.

"I do not think I should believe you, Finch. Yet I find I do."

He raised the crossbow so the quarrel no longer aimed at me. My chest loosened a fraction. I repressed the radiance flickering at my fingertips and brushed back the sweat dripping into my eyes.

"Thank you, Ariston. You won't regret this."

The Dishonored's mouth twisted as he turned from the hatch door and stepped deeper within, allowing room for me to clamber down the short ladder. "If I do, I doubt I will be alive to regret it long."

I hid my expression by turning away and setting a foot to the top rung. That, at least, we agreed upon.

5

HIS MOST LOYAL SERVANT

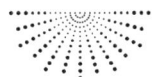

We were not always honors, we Kalthuae. Once, before the Lighted Passage that upended our world, to act as an honor was considered noble, the suppression of pride for the good of all. Many of the notable men and women of the old world could only accomplish what they did through the service of their honors.

Then Oedija's ancestors came across the water and conquered our people. They named us "honors," for it was a more palatable label than "slaves." Peaceful as we Kalthuae were then, we accepted our fate.

But it is not honorable to be what we are; it is unjust. And I dedicate my life to righting these wrongs, for our people now and forevermore.

- A Nation's Sins; by Ariston the Dishonored; date unknown

As I entered Ariston's cellar, I was reminded of Talan's many disreputable hideouts spread throughout Oedija. It had the same mildewy stench, though underlaid with urine, as well as similar cramped walls and the claustrophobia that accompanied them. Violet pyrkin was smeared over the dirt walls, casting the single chamber in an ethereal light not unlike the Pyrthae. Little occupied the space: two makeshift cots, a spattering of satchels, and in one corner, a small kitchen entailing a pot and a sparse collection of half-spoiled foodstuffs.

One of the sleeping areas was a neat rectangle of blankets. The other was occupied. Even in the odd light, I recognized Seda. Her head was bare, though scarred and pocked from clumsy shaves. Her face was downcast, seemingly disinterested in my appearance, as if she had given up on caring even about her own well-being. Like Ariston, she looked much thinner than the first time I'd seen her, a flower wilted from lack of sun and rain. As I watched, she gently rocked back and forth, her thin arms curled around her knees, her lips mouthing silent sentences. By all looks, she was madder than our former Despoina.

I couldn't help but pity her.

"She has become like this in the past span," Ariston spoke from behind me. "Barely eats. Barely sleeps. I do not know how much longer she will survive."

Privately, I agreed with his assessment. I had traveled the streets of Oedija all my life and seen my fair share of starving souls. They had that same skeletal frame, that feverish look in the eyes. Foreboding grew in me. I wanted to flee this scene of encroaching death. Only my purpose forced me to stay.

"Does she speak?" I asked in a hushed voice, partly afraid of her overhearing me, though it seemed like she paid us no heed.

"Yes. But only on her terms, and never for long."

It was troubling to put my back to Ariston, but I did so, maintaining a pretense of trust. As I looked upon Seda, I tried to harden myself to her plight. She had dedicated herself to serving the man who had caused the city so much anguish, the man who had hollowed out my brother's mind. As pathetic as she appeared now, she had chosen her fate.

Yet no matter how I had tried, mercy refused to die in me. So I adopted a different tact: wielding compassion as a weapon.

As I had once done with Asileia in her gardens, I put myself on level with Seda, sitting cross-legged on the ground before her. My hands rested on my knees, showing them to be empty. For several moments, I sat quietly, observing her while pretending to look elsewhere. I hoped to give her time to adjust to my presence.

If it made any difference, she didn't show it. Seda continued to rock back and forth, back and forth, as endless in her self-comforting movement as waves against a shore. My wariness outwore my patience, for I was keenly aware Ariston might still change his mind and shoot me in the back. Last that I'd looked, the crossbow remained drawn and loaded. Though urgency pulsed inside me, I kept my voice low and calm.

"Seda. Do you remember me?"

At her name, Seda paused. Her eyes did not lift from their spot on the ground, but her lips stopped moving. I took it as progress.

I placed a hand against my chest and forced a smile. "I'm Airene. We met once, spans ago. Your master sent me, Seda. Vusumuzi wanted me to find you."

The mention of Vusu was the key I'd searched for. Seda's head jerked up, her dark eyes chasms as they bore into my face. My expression grew rigid, the smile false, so I let it slip away and waited.

"My master?" Seda murmured at length, her words little more than a whisper.

I nodded. "I saw him before he… passed. He told me to find you, said you were the secret to defeating the enemy we hold in common. Famine — or Taozu, he might have called him. Do you know anything of this?"

Seda was shaking her head before I'd finished speaking. "The Other," she muttered. "The Corruptor. The Serpent."

By those titles, I knew we spoke of the same adversary. My gut tightened at the thought of Famine as I'd last seen him, and my violent desire to be consumed by him. With an effort, I pushed away the memory. I needed no more fear just then.

"Yes," I continued. "Though your master is gone, you can still be loyal to him. You can still serve."

My gut twisted as I uttered the words. Their relationship revolted me. I couldn't understand the willing subjugation of oneself to another, as Seda had done, nor the acceptance on Vusu's part. But I had to set my own biases aside to succeed here. Again, I forced myself to calm and spoke.

"Will you help me, Seda? Will you help me achieve your master's aim?"

The honor seemed to return somewhat to her senses. There was a spark in her eyes that had nothing to do with the lavender light of the pyrkin as she stared unblinkingly at me.

"How?" she asked quietly. "How did he ask this of you?"

My mind whirred. I hadn't expected her to question anything that came from her master. But I'd gambled this far. I had to believe what I could reveal of the truth would prove sufficient.

"As he lay dying, I was there with him, Seda." I raised my hand slowly, holding it palm up, fingertips extended. "I'm a warden, just like your master. We were in the Pyrthae together when Famine was breaking free of him. He caged him a little longer, though his strength was nearly at its end. I've never seen such power before."

That much was true. Though I reviled the man, I couldn't help but admire Vusu's fortitude.

"But before he descended," I continued, "he told me I would have to be the one to defeat the daemon god now. And that I must find you to do it."

A lump formed in my throat. Not from sorrow, no — I wasn't sorry to see the end of Vusu. It was terror at what his expiry meant for me. It was the impossible burden of my task, resting on my shoulders alone.

The weight of the world — I couldn't bear it all. Yet I had to.

Seda hadn't looked away from me the entire time I spoke, unnerving in her focus. I tried not to let it show while I listened for any sign of Ariston's betrayal.

Then she moved. I flinched as Seda reached under her pile of fraying blankets, but didn't shift away as she extracted her hands to reveal what she sought. My shoulders lowered as my curiosity was piqued. She didn't hold a knife, but a small, leather-bound book. Its face was plain and dyed a deep scarlet, and the ends of the pages looked worn and frayed. Though I burned to know what it portended, I kept my hands still.

Her voice was scratchy and quiet when she spoke, but Seda seemed to have found some hidden measure of resolve, for fresh certainty underlay her words. "This is my master's journal. He asked me to keep it safe before he left. I know little of the daemon that haunted him, and I would never reveal his secrets. Never." Her eyes drifted down to the book. "But he told me one would come seeking it after he was gone. I did not know what he meant. Now I do." Her gaze lifted, and there seemed a desperate hunger in her as she lifted the book toward me. "Take it. Fight the *sheytin*. My master was a good man, a very good man... Let his death not be in vain."

On our sentiments toward her master, we couldn't be further from agreement. But I nodded as I took Vusu's journal in hand. "I'll do all I can," I said, knowing it was all I could promise.

I longed to open the diary then and there and discover the secrets of my enemy within its pages, but I wasn't yet out of danger. Murmuring thanks to Seda, I stood and turned back to Ariston. He still cradled the crossbow in his arms, but he didn't look inclined to raise it, his posture weary as he slumped against one of the dilapidated walls. His eyes, tracing the purple pyrkin on the wall opposite him, lazily came back to rest on mine.

"I hope you do as you say," he said. "This is not a nemesis who allows mistakes."

"I know."

Both of us seemed to be waiting for something. My stated purpose in coming accomplished, there was little reason for me to stay. But I hadn't forgotten my promise to Jaxas. Nor had I forgiven Ariston's hand in Linos's ruination. He was lax and unprepared, and apparently coming to trust me.

I could kill him.

And yet, I couldn't. I could not raise my hand or draw on the elements to do it. I'd claimed to be an assassin, but I was wrong. There was good in Ariston; I'd glimpsed that this night. Even for his sins, I could not stamp that out.

"Go," I told him. "Leave the city. Don't return."

He stiffened, and seeming to become more alert. The Dishonored glanced toward the exit, perhaps wondering if my intentions were as honest as they had first appeared.

"What do you mean?" he asked slowly.

"Leave now — you won't have another chance. The Manifest is all but dismantled, but the Despot will not overlook your hand in creating it. He will hunt you down if you remain in Oedija."

I must have instilled more into my words than I meant. Ariston's next words captured and held me.

"You came here to kill me."

I stiffened. How could I answer that? If I lied, would he know? If I told the truth, would he strike before I could explain?

Before I could decide, the hatch was wrenched open. At once, I drew upon my magic and whirled toward it with hands raised. Ariston reacted, too — by pointing his crossbow at me.

"Dishonored!" an unfamiliar voice shouted through the portal. "Are you hurt?"

Curses jostled in my head. My heart seemed to beat against my temples. I had delayed too long, and Seekers had come. Now, I would pay dearly for the mistake.

Before anyone could speak or move, a shriek came from behind me.

"Do not harm her!"

I was as startled by Seda's outburst as Ariston. His eyes darted toward the Avvadin honor for a moment before settling back on me. I didn't dare move, though my skin crawled as I stared down the tip of the crossbow.

Once more, Ariston lowered it, the quarrel aiming at the ground.

Breath whooshed back in my lungs, and relief made my knees weak. I lowered my hands, but not my guard as I waited for Ariston to speak.

"Seda is right," he said. "You should not be harmed. If everything I suspect about you is true, you must survive. You have a purpose to fulfill, do you not?"

I nodded, my throat gone too dry for words.

Ariston cocked his head slightly. "I will heed your words, Finch. Though once my ancestors ruled these lands, I, their descendant and heir, am forced to flee them. Yet we all must make sacrifices, must we not?"

Was that use of the word "sacrifice" intentional, or mere coincidence? Did he know my purpose? Now was not the time to inquire further. I had to take my exit and hope he wouldn't change his mind.

"Yes," I muttered. "We must."

The Dishonored smiled, the expression ghastly on his thin face. "Let her pass," he commanded the Seekers above. "And as Seda bids, do not harm her."

"Dishonored—"

"Do not," Ariston pressed, and received grudging assents.

At the incline of his head, I made for the ladder. My palms were sweaty on the rungs, and not only from the radiance still pouring through me. It went against every instinct I had to leave myself so vulnerable as I climbed out of the cellar past the Seekers. Yet I was lucky just to be alive; I didn't push it further.

The Seekers cast me hard glares as I rose to my feet between them. Despite their leader's command, their hands were raised toward me, distortions around their fingers telling of the energetic elements held at the ready. I only glanced at each, then strode quickly for where I saw the door cracked open at the far end of the warehouse.

I didn't slow until long after their stares left my back.

6

SECRETS OF THE SERPENT

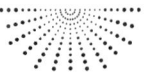

Power was to be paid for in blood. Though no words were spoken, Lophe and I understood the bargain. If we accepted the Serpent's offer, we would sacrifice unto it souls in return.

It was an exchange I made gladly, great spirits help me.

- The journal of Vusumuzi; date unknown

Talan found me as I reached the edge of Saltpeter.

I kept a careful watch as I hurried away from the Manifest bastion, even occasionally flitting into the Pyrthae to keep tabs on any nearby wardens. Still, he managed to surprise me. Flames flickered at my fingertips before I recognized him emerging from a nearby alley. I lowered my arm with a relieved sigh.

"Talan. You survived."

He flashed a smile as he closed the distance between us. "Takes more than a few half-trained ferals to kill me."

"Not much more." I looked him up and down. Burns blackened his vest and tunic, and blood stained his trousers. Even in the shrouded night, I detected purpling on his face telling of fresh bruises. Unkempt to start with, he appeared little better than a beggar now, and one who had recently received a beating. I wondered if any had survived his retribution, then decided it was better not to ask.

Talan shrugged. "One or two got a hit in." He gestured to the burden I carried. "Your mission was successful?"

I glanced down at Vusu's journal, which I'd compulsively checked to be sure I still had throughout the walk. Even clutched in my hands, its importance made it seem as if it might slip away at any moment.

"Mostly. I found Seda. She gave me this."

"This?"

"Vusu's journal."

He raised an eyebrow at that. "Perhaps this was worth it then."

"We'll see." I thought again of those he'd likely killed and struggled not to picture him doing it. My gut churned anew.

Talan seemed to see something was wrong, for he bent forward to peer into my downcast eyes. "But you said you were 'mostly' successful. What happened?"

I couldn't say what made it hard to confess. Part of me felt ashamed I couldn't kill, even when it might be for the best, especially when Talan seemed to do it so easily. Another part was angry at my shame. But I had always been honest with Talan. I didn't want that to change now.

"It's Ariston... I couldn't do it, Talan. I let him go, told him to flee."

His expression made me regret ever doubting him. Talan reached toward me, then seemed to notice how grimy his hands were and only lowered them again. His eyes caught mine.

"You're not an assassin, Airene — and that's a good thing. I wouldn't want you to be. Besides, things might be better this way. The Manifest aren't much of a threat anymore."

"No. Not much."

"Put it from your mind." But as Talan smiled, he must have remembered what lay between us, for it slipped away. "But we should get you back. With Avvad nearing, you need all the sleep you can get."

"And you?" The words came out like a challenge.

The smile was back, but it failed to touch his eyes. "I have my own appointments to keep."

I suspected those would be the same wine bottles keeping him company — and perhaps Sule and her Qarin. I turned away, trying to hide the envy and disgust I couldn't repress.

"Then let's go." I walked away without seeing if he followed.

WE PARTED at the Laurel Palace with barely a farewell. I spoke greetings to the guards on watch, but ignored their raised eyebrows as I strode between them and up to the golden castle. It took the entire walk to the doors to pull my stewing thoughts away from the former Guilder. My head throbbed with exhaustion, for dawn was not far off now, yet I could not sleep. Secrets simmered beneath my fingertips, secrets I needed to learn if I was to have any chance against Famine.

Instead of my bed, I sought the kitchens. There, a drowsy servant brewed me a carafe of coffee, which I took to the feast hall to drink along with yesterday's bread while I read. My stomach roiled, upset by the long night, yet I was always ravenous. Famine's touch pressed on me, body and soul.

I forgot my discomforts as I examined the journal open before me. I'd feared it would be written in Vusu's native language, but instead found it in our modern sea-tongue. I wondered why. Almost, it seemed he had expected an

Oedijan to one day read it. Perhaps that was why he kept the journal in the first place.

His words were sometimes difficult to read, jotted down with splashed ink and in a cramped and hurried scrawl, and my eyes strained with the effort. Yet I managed it, and soon, the mind of the man who had brought so much turmoil to Oedija unfolded before me.

He began with his first encounter with Famine. I suspected he had composed this journal after he had already come to Oedija, for its perspective was of an older man regretting his younger self's actions. He told of his ishaka, the Zakale, and how he and his brother had sought divine intervention when his tribe suffered during a terrible drought. A great spirit found him, one taking the form of a vast serpent, and offered them the sorcery to save their people.

> *Power was to be paid for in blood. Though no words were spoken, Lophe and I understood the bargain. If we accepted the Serpent's offer, we would sacrifice unto it souls in return.*
>
> *It was an exchange I made gladly, great spirits help me.*

My skin erupted into gooseflesh. It was an arrangement I would never make, yet having seen Oedija suffer, I could all too easily understand how Vusu had. *Tales of the Desolate*, which recounted these same events from a different perspective, had made Vusu — Yama, he'd been then — and his brother Lophe seem monsters in service of their Serpent God. Now, I wondered if they'd had much of a choice in the matter.

I had felt Famine's hunger. If I thought about it, I could feel it then. How much worse would it be when the dragon god was bound to them, starving and insistent, not free to feast on his own?

Could Vusu have been less of a villain than I suspected?

I pushed the uncomfortable thought away and kept reading, paging through Vusu's account of the Bali war. He kept it brief, shame lacing each word, and only made minimal mentions of the atrocities for which he was responsible. Instead, he focused on how Famine feasted on those they slew, and their corresponding growth in power.

We believed ourselves immortal, for a time. That we had ascended to become gods. Foolish, when we served a god ourselves. But we were young, lusting for blood, yearning for justice. And power fueled our arrogance.

Then came the day I lost my brother.

My resolve broke with his soul's departure, my belief in our cause breaking with it. The loss of him, by my side since birth... For a time, I believe I truly went mad. I did not know how to understand his absence. And so I refused to believe it.

I spoke to him all throughout the day for longer than I care to admit. I confided in him, commiserated with his troubles, joked and laughed.

But I was alone. It was only to the ghost in my head that I spoke to.

Grief was not the only thing responsible for my madness, I think. With my brother gone and our followers scattered, the Serpent's focus fell entirely on me. His hunger tormented me no matter how much I ate, nor how much I fed him. Lophe had shouldered more of that burden than I knew, and my mind buckled beneath it.

How he came out of his madness, Vusu didn't specify. I detected dark depths into which he refused to delve.

Soon, he moved on to his realizations around his relationship with Famine.

I had made a deal with a daemon, and now I understood what that meant. So awakened my resolve to win free of it.

I searched the Four Realms for answers. For decades, this hunt consumed me. I stole into the archives of the Kahin-Shah in Erimis, defying soul-stealing spirits and mind-yoked guards to do so. I pored over the knowledge there, the greatest collected in the known world.

And I discovered nothing.

Slowly, I puzzled out why. Avvad had never suffered an attack by the Serpent. I had to search in places that had. So I returned to where I had first encountered the god: my home ishaka. And there, I followed its trail to the Qao Fu jaitin.

Finally, my search bore fruit. Much of what I learned was too warped in myth to be of use, but there were some treasures. I discovered that an empire had once sprawled across the Wumofu Desert, an empire whose descendants became the Qao Fu people. I learned of a ritual just over a century faded that involved sending a child as a "savior" to a white tree whose boughs pierced the sky itself — the Chains, it was known.

And I heard of the terrible spirit — Taozu the Corrupted — once trapped within that tree, but who had been freed when the ritual was sabotaged.

Tradition muddled the meanings, but I parsed out the truth. My Serpent — Taozu, Famine — had once been caged, but won his freedom a hundred and twenty years before. What he had done in the intervening time before finding me, I could only speculate, though I guessed by his hunger it was to hunt and grow stronger. But even more than discovering his immediate origins, I reveled in one other fact.

If the Serpent had been imprisoned once, he could be imprisoned again.

The means by which this could occur, too, revealed itself. Involved in the ritual was a scepter, what they called a "ruyi," one as white as the vast tree. But it had been lost to the sands when the ritual failed.

This scepter seemed key in defying my god. So I set out into the wasteland to find it.

My heart beat a little faster at that. It was a matching description to Aika's knife, the artifact the ancient girl had used to become a Sacrifice. Aika had speared Famine upon the branches of a tree in the Hunger War my ancestors fought long ago across the Lighted Sea.

Pressing aside my horror at the ritual that would sacrifice children, I read on.

> *For how large the tree was said to be, it was difficult to find, for it was distant, and the sky was often obscured by dust. Yet at last, I saw it looming out of the distance, as tall and thick-limbed as the Qao Fu had spoken, though gray where it was said to be white. It would have been a wonder had it not failed in its purpose, to the ruin of my life and the world.*

I tried to imagine such a tree and failed. The Pillars scattered about Oedija were the tallest things I knew, and they did not come close to such a height. I decided to reserve judgment until I'd read further.

I poured more coffee, careful not to splash on the pages, intending to press on. But the feast hall had populated during my reading, and noise rose with others' arrival. Dawn must have broken and gone. Eyes gritty, mood sour, I tried to concentrate through the conversations springing up around me. Eventually, I would have to go someplace else, but I couldn't yet muster the energy to move.

I soon regretted it when a familiar voice spoke. "Airene."

Curbing my impatience, I looked up at Corin, readying a weary explanation for why I couldn't chat, but the words stuck in my throat. The former cartwoman wasn't alone. A young woman stood beside her, with pale skin and blonde hair that marked her as an outlander of Jolduun, as did her strange clothes, all fur and coarse leather and pilled wool.

Clues abounded as to the newcomer's identity, yet I

couldn't turn the tired cogs of my mind to come to a conclusion. Corin provided the answer a moment later as she held up one of her calloused hands to gesture toward the young woman.

"This is my sister, Kari."

Her sister — the resemblance was unmistakable once she pointed it out. Though Corin's features were blunter and rounder, and her brow more pronounced, their noses possessed the same petiteness, and their ears were inordinately small.

And there was the matter that the entirety of Corin's life had been bent toward bringing this very sister to Oedija to escape the persecution back in their homeland.

"Kari." My voice came out faint, so I cleared my throat and tried again. "It's good to meet you after all these years."

Only after I'd spoken did I wonder if she understood the sea-tongue. Corin had possessed only a rudimentary grasp of Oedija's language when she first moved to the mainland. Kari's response, however, put my mind at ease. Though her words were heavily accented, her diction was clear enough to understand.

"I thank you, Airene Finch. For taking care of Sister." Kari grinned. She had a toothy smile, one that seemed almost childish in its exuberance.

I returned it hesitantly. "She's taken care of me as well."

Corin nodded gravely. "We are family. We watch out for one another."

Family. That she would apply that word to me when her sister stood next to her, the sister for whom she had sacrificed all other happiness, caught me by the throat. I blinked rapidly to keep my eyes dry.

"Thank you, Corin. Of course we are."

Kari startled me by reaching across the table and seizing my hand. "We are sisters!"

But as soon as we touched, Corin's sister froze. Her eyes

seemed to grow distant, and she clutched my hand tightly enough to hurt. I tried to hide my wince as I wondered what was happening.

Then I remembered.

Corin had named her sister a witch. Likely, it meant she was attuned. As her trance went on, a horrible suspicion rose in me. I tried to pull away, but she held fast. Only by slipping off my glove could I escape her, and I would thereby expose my expanding shifts. Fortunately, Corin intervened before I was forced to.

"Kari! *Seska!*" The former cartwoman seized her sister by the shoulders and brought her upright. Kari spasmed, her eyelids fluttering, before she seemed to come to. Her eyes traveled to the ceiling for a long moment before they settled back on me. No hint of a smile remained, but only a haggard stare.

"You are *pilsaam*," she said. "Tainted. Beware the bone, Airene Finch; it traps you."

The hairs rose on the nape of my neck. I couldn't precisely understand her words, yet they didn't seem idle ravings. They flirted around ideas I had been reading about, secrets which I desperately needed to know — and those I wished to hide.

I tried to disguise my feelings behind a kindly smile. "Thank you, Kari. I'll take your words to heart."

I had no desire to remain in the feast hall then. Gathering my possessions as hurriedly as I dared, I rose from the table. Corin watched me silently, her sister still held close with one hand.

"You are going?" my former loftmate asked quietly.

"Afraid so. This book — I have to keep reading it. I'm sorry, I don't mean to rush off, I just…"

My words trailed off. We both knew the true reason I fled. Yet I saw only acceptance in my friend's eyes.

"If you need anything, Airene," Corin said, "ask. I will do it."

My throat tightened again, so I merely nodded, then turned and fled, Kari's words chasing me to my room.

7

SUMMONS

Daemon possessions have long been a tradition among our people. How often it has actually occurred, I cannot say, yet I suspect it is less frequent than claimed. For some, it has provided a convenient excuse for improper behavior. A dalliance done under a spirit's influence, after all, can hardly be one's own fault.

But there is undoubtedly some truth behind the more reputable claims. Avvad is suspected of knowingly possessing their own people. Incidents in Oedija have no explanation as well. Persons whose personalities change overnight. Deeds done with seemingly no rationale.

Maybe there is another explanation. But for want of one, we must fear the pyr who might wish us harm.

- Tales of Wardens: A brief study of Oedijan folk stories; by Acadian Helene, Master Historian; 1160 SLP

With Vusu's journal clutched in one hand and my heel of stale bread in the other, I sought Linos's room. Perhaps it was Corin's reminder of family, or seeing her with her sister, but when I was forced from the feast hall, the urge to visit him arose in me.

My younger brother had shown no will in the spans since his harrowing escape from the end of Vusu's knife. Still, I made it a point to visit him each day and spend a little time with him. I hoped my presence might eventually coax out the part of his spirit that lingered.

Kyros Brighteyed had said something remained of Linos, though tenuously connected. I had to believe there was enough that he would once again be the life-filled young man I remembered.

The healing ward was at the opposite end of the palace from the feast hall. Linos's room was one of four available. Plain, almost austere in its adornment, it boasted little more than a bed, a washing basin, and a small cabinet.

My brother lay in the bed, never seeming to blink as he stared up at the ceiling. I could only look at him for a moment before I turned back to fetch one of the honors monitoring the sick ward, asking them for a tray of food and broth. Though Linos sometimes fed himself, when he was in his more apathetic states, broth was the simplest for me to give him. It wasn't necessary; his attendants took good care of all his needs. Yet the elder sister in me always felt the inclination to look after him.

I fetched a chair and dragged it next to his bed, then sat heavily in it while I waited for the food. Vusu's journal hung unopened in my hand as I stared out the window over my brother's bed. I often found it difficult to look directly at him. The mauve scars around his eyes, resembling the last clawing of the damned, reminded me too much of what he'd suffered.

I entered briefly into the Pyrthae. Each time I indulged the inclination, I hoped I would see a change in his spirit, but there was only a glimmer of a flame, and I felt no recognition from it as I neared.

Returning to my body, I leaned back and finally cracked open the book. It took my weary eyes a long while to focus, then longer still to find where I'd left off. At last, I picked it up: Vusu was drawing conclusions for his visit to the Qao Fu.

> *This substance, whether it was stone or bark or something not of this world, I could not tell, even having touched the trunk of the Chains. But that it had held Famine once, and only failed when the wrong sacrificial boy was sent for the duty, was too tantalizing an idea to dismiss.*

The idea, with its echoes to Aika and her tale, intrigued me as well. My interest hooked once more, I began to read faster.

> *Having learned all I could among the Qao Fu, I ventured south-west to a different land. From the jaitin's elders, I had heard rumors of another appearance of the Serpent, long ago and in a land far across the western seas. I set out for Oedija, hoping to hear more of the "Hunger War" that led to their immigration to these lands.*
>
> *Through forests and across plains, around the mountains guarding the nation's northern front, I finally arrived at the so-called "Pearl of the Four Realms," and found the title to be only slightly aggrandized. Oedija was a true city, with all its flaws and marvels. The poor littered the streets, while the rich lived in pala-tial manors. Merchants flung every good imaginable from across the known world at me, each slavering for a bit of coin.*
>
> *Yet there were rumblings of unease. Despoina Zalfene was building what would become known as the Half-Wall, an incom-plete defense against Avvad to the south. And word of the conflict among my people, the war I had begun, had long ago traveled across the miles. I hid my identity with magic, pretending to belong to a neighboring ishaka, the Yorandu, and changed my name to the one I bear now. Though forty years had passed since my uprising, I feared someone might guess I was the Yama who had spilled so much blood.*

The names and events Vusu referenced were strange to see, for it was still difficult to imagine the length of his life. He had seen over a century, and yet had still possessed a vitality befitting a man of Xaron's years.

I wondered if I would inherit Famine's strength as well. I doubted I would live long enough to find out.

Without my name and station, the knowledge I sought was barred to me. But for a warden of my power, nothing was beyond my reach for long. In the dead of night, I stole into the library at the heart of the Acadium and delved into the depths of its lore. I learned of their absent gods, the Eidola, and the name by which they knew my Serpent: Famine. I read of the Hunger War, the conflict between the deities, and how it had ended with a girl, who had killed the daemon god upon the branches of a white tree.

No doubt the scholars believed it to be myth, as I once would have. But I suspected the stories were quite real, at least at their core. The tree in the Wumofu was proof alone. But for all I learned of the Serpent's nature, and how I saw patterns emerging as to how I might one day be rid of him, no immediate solution revealed itself.

The two god-binding trees, Aika's knife and the Qao Fu scepter — there were connections that I could not yet untangle, clues that might help me in my present quandary if I could only understand them. Too tired for speculation, I resolved to finish my reading before I attempted to draw any conclusions. *And get sleep,* I amended as I turned back to the pages.

Like myself, Vusu wondered about Harvest and her role in Aika's story:

In the years that followed, I questioned the truth of the Oedijan stories. What was real and what was not? Was this Harvest any more material than the other absent gods? Yet Famine exists, and though he is a god confined by my blood and flesh, he seems too immortal and pervasive to be named anything else.

I required the scepter or the knife, but knew not where either lay. Yet even with them, I was beginning to understand that, if I wished to truly be rid of the daemon plaguing me, and to rid the world of him besides, it would require more than myself.

I needed a sacrifice; better yet, the right sacrifice. It seemed likely a child would be required, or a youth, for both stories had involved the young. They likely had to have some influence of a god, of Harvest or Famine. But it would take years to discover what would do.

So I realized I must establish myself here in Oedija, become more than a pathetic vagrant living among paupers. I needed influence, resources, access. And, most important of all, I needed people upon which to experiment.

For only with all the world behind me could anyone hope to survive. And survival is worth any sacrifice.

At this, I leaned in, wondering if, at last, I might discover the secrets to my brother's condition. But before I could read further, the door to Linos's room opened. The honor had returned, balancing a heavy tray of food as she came over to the bed. I thanked her, then looked away until she'd gone. After Kelena's revelations of what an honor's life was like, I hadn't felt comfortable requesting their services. Still, my task was too urgent to do otherwise.

Still famished, I scarfed down half the tray before I attended to Linos. Broth dribbled out of the corners of his mouth and down his chin as I unsuccessfully tried to feed him. Making him sit up worked better, but he failed to rouse and take the spoon himself. I fought down my disappointment, but soon grew too discouraged to continue. I finished the meal myself.

Satiated for the moment, I set the tray on Linos's side table and settled back into my chair. The need for sleep was catching up to me. I opened the journal to where I'd last read, but at once began nodding off. I leaned on Linos's bed, trying to prop myself up and persist a little longer.

As my head rested on the covers, my resolve melted away.

It wasn't a restful sleep. I dreamed of my mother, slinking off into the night when she thought no one else was awake, to attend one of her various liaisons throughout the years. In the dream, I was a child again, listening to her footsteps. She'd always believed herself stealthy, yet I'd heard her every departure. Not for the first time, I wondered if my brothers and I shared the same father. If the man I called father was, in truth, my own blood.

But I didn't mull over the memory for long. As often happened since Famine's reemergence, I drifted into the Pyrthae.

The landscape was not the parallel mirrorscape I was used to seeing while awake, but the sandy wasteland it had been when I fought against Vusu. I was sand in a gale, spinning in a torrent through the dusky sky. A glow settled over the city, as if the very buildings themselves emitted light. I roamed, looking over Oedija, this city I called home, and how it had been ravaged.

Was this what it would soon be reduced to? I feared the dangers facing it were too great to overcome. Famine, Avvad, rioting from our own people — the Manifest's fall was a minor victory. I still had only the slightest idea of how to deal with the daemon god. I feared I would only gain days of reprieve for Telae. Vusu had only held on for a few turns, and even half-dead, he'd been far stronger. As I looked down, it seemed the winds in that phantasmal place would pull me apart, grain by grain, until there was nothing left.

A part of me thought that might not be so bad. Then, at least, I wouldn't have to struggle any longer.

It is not the only way.

I gathered the strands of myself as I flinched away from

the voice. A moment later, I recognized it, even as I saw the stray swirl of sand filtering toward me like a serpent through water.

The boy in the whisper finch, I thought back.

Yes. The boy moved closer, then reshaped himself, the sand coalescing into the approximation of a child. With dun lips, he formed a smile. I found it more haunting than reassuring, yet the boy had helped me often enough that I didn't flee.

You're a pyr? I queried him.

He nodded, the movement not quite natural to his sandy flesh. *As you have long suspected.*

Why are you helping me? It was the question that had always kept me from fully trusting him. Motivations were far more telling than oaths.

The boy gestured with one hand, his fingers fraying even as they flexed. *To right old wrongs. To mend the world. To stop Taozu.*

Taozu. An old Qao Fu name, and one I now recognized well. *Famine.*

The boy drifted closer. *The Corrupted stole everything from me. My life. My honor. My family. I will not let him take my world. So I intend to aid you, Airene the Finch, if you let me. I will help you cage him once again.*

How do you know my name? Why won't you tell me yours? My frustration mounted. Though I appreciated allies, I liked ones I could rely upon more.

His shoulders rose and fell. *My name is no secret. I am Azhi; Xian Azhi, once.*

Azhi. A Qao Fu name, too. *How have you survived? You're only a boy.*

The pyr smiled again. *Though young, before I died, I was a talented weaver, as we called our attuned, one of the best in my jaitin. My ability made me reckless. I craved eternal honor and earned immortal shame. So I have endured, hoping to right my wrongs.*

His words didn't add up in my mind. *Your wrongs... what wrong could a boy have done?*

The sand spirit slowly spun, tendrils of his body breaking off to curl around him, like the strands of a Silk's bonds.

I appear as a child to you, Airene, but I am older than any alive. My existence reaches back centuries, and my sins as well. The boy bowed his head and continued to turn. *I am to blame for Taozu's return. I am the one who freed him.*

My thoughts were frozen for a moment. Then, as the pieces fell into place, my mind raced.

How? When? Why?

They were only the first of the many questions assaulting me. Answers tried to crowd in next to them. Hadn't I just read something of the like in Vusu's journal? Could it possibly be referencing the boy before me?

Azhi stopped his revolution and raised his hands as if in surrender. *I will tell you all, Airene. I will guide you as best I can. But to explain the rest, you must meet me.*

That threw me off-kilter. *What do you mean? We can talk now.*

No. He shook his head. *In the flesh. In Telae.*

But you're a pyr!

In part, yes. But I wear a face you will recognize. Do not fear me, Airene. And remember: I am ever your friend. If we are to defeat Famine, we must do so together.

Those claiming to be friends had tricked me before, and I wasn't trusting to begin with. Yet Azhi had assisted me many times and never asked for anything in return. Without his interventions, I doubted I would still be breathing.

I made my decision.

Where will we meet?

The pyr's relief washed out from him. Apparently, he

hadn't been sure what I would do, either. *The Pillar in the Conclave. I will be there as soon as the sun has set this night.*

How will you enter? I wondered whose face he would wear. Then it occurred to me how a pyr might wear any face, and fear struck through me. *Wait! Will you—?*

At dusk!

Azhi fled. His body splintered, bursting out in a hundred different directions, and I watched as the Pyrthaen winds carried him away. Foreboding filled me as surely as the plane's energy, and I hadn't shrugged it off when I emerged from sleep's clutches.

Awake, I raised my head and clutched it with a groan. My neck was horribly sore, my skull pounded, and my limbs dragged with exhaustion. Yet a feverish energy filled me as well. I didn't know if it was born of the need for answers or Famine's connection to me, augmenting my attunement and flooding me with power. I wouldn't get any more rest now, not until after the meeting this evening.

I would go. Against my better judgment, despite the knowledge of what Azhi likely was, I would go to the Conclave Pillar. The pyr held back many secrets, but I believed him when he said he had information I required to cage Famine.

No matter how foolish and desperate it seemed, I had to grasp at every chance. There was little hope of success as it was. If it took a few risks to further it, then I would gladly accept them.

I rose, stretched, and stared out the window. The sun was already falling toward the horizon past the Lighted Sea. I had to go now if I meant to meet Azhi in time. My stomach, grumbling already, would have to wait.

My gaze fell to my brother, still lying in the same position. I was racked by guilt again, but I hardened myself to it.

"This is the only way, Linos," I whispered to him and

pressed his hand. "Azhi might be a Qarin, but he has the answers I need."

I feared that the pyr was the kind of abomination I hated most, a spirit who occupied a human body to once again exist in Telae. It was the same kind as had haunted Linos and sometimes possessed him.

But I would go. I would overcome my prejudice and listen. I had no other choice.

I straightened, adjusted my disheveled clothes, still the same as I'd worn to infiltrate the Manifest warehouse. Then I strode down the hallway toward the Conclave.

8
OLD ENEMIES

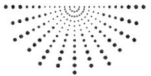

There is comfort in seeing the face of an enemy. When they stand
there before you, you know they do not plot behind your back.

- The journal of Vusumuzi; date unknown

I reached the Conclave Pillar as the sun touched the
horizon.

I absently followed the sunset's progression as my mind
sorted through what to expect from the coming conversation. The clouds crowding the sky caught the light, glowing
crimson for miles in either direction. It would have made me
smile under other circumstances.

Now, all I could see was the angry color of blood, waiting
to be spilled.

Though my eyes were distracted, I kept watch in the
Pyrthae. As a pyr — and Qarin, I suspected — Azhi would
leave a mark I could not miss. Yet for all my caution, I saw no
sign of him coming.

The Conclave had often been bustling during previous
visits, but now, the courtyard lay quiet. Even if its authority
had been stripped with Jaxas's seizure of the city, its offices

remained open to conduct the administrative affairs of the city. Oedija needed its bureaucracy, with its expertise and competence, now more than ever. Stability was sorely lacking in our nation.

With the courtyard empty, it would be impossible for Azhi to evade me no matter the body he wore. Yet still, I remained uneasy. I didn't have to reach far to realize why.

I wear a face you will recognize.

Which face? Whose body had he seized? I feared for my friends. I knew little of how daemons took their hosts, but Talan had once said they must be attuned to become so. Nomusa would be safe, as would my family far away on the Wreath estate. But Xaron and Talan were at risk, as were Isidora and her Watchers.

And so was Linos.

My heart raced. Could he be the one Azhi occupied? Vusu had once named him Vessel. A daemon had already possessed him before. Why not again? He had little resistance to offer.

No sooner had I resolved to run back to my brother than the Pillar began to change.

I stared as the dull gray stone swiftly gathered light of its own making. I channeled quintessence on instinct and sensed it was not just a trick of reflections. Something was channeling through the stone.

Something — or someone.

A further baffling sight appeared. Where no one had stood before, a man took shape. The Pillar in the Pyrthae vibrated, and a flame with a long tether emerged. In Telae, the light coalesced into a man's shape, then slowly stripped away, like the unrolling of a tapestry. Underneath, the man looked very much real, his flesh unblemished by his peculiar method of travel.

So bewildered was I by this entrance that, for a moment, I

did not recognize him. When I did, I flinched back, an arm raised as animal fear flooded through me.

Eazal smiled at me, the corners of his eyes crinkling.

"Hello, Airene. I am sorry to startle you."

I couldn't respond. My heart battered at my chest. I wanted to run, run anywhere, even off the edge of the cliff. My terror was irrational; part of me remained dispassionate enough to realize that. I was ten times the warden Eazal had revealed himself to be before he fled.

But he'd nearly killed me. And now he'd returned to finish the job.

I lowered my arm and clenched my hands into fists. My fingertips burned with radiance against my palms, blistering the skin, but I couldn't stop it.

"Don't come near me." My voice came out strained and weaker than I wanted, but my intent was clear. After how we'd parted, he had to know I was a warden.

The man raised his hands. As he had once been an apothecary, they were calloused and marred from contact with hazardous elements. He was gaunt, his eyes hollowed and his lips thin, and aged years beyond when I'd last seen him. Yet there burned in his eyes a vitality he lacked before.

"Airene," he spoke in a low voice. "I warned you I would come bearing a familiar face."

His words rang in my head, and I stared at him in disbelief. They too closely matched Azhi's earlier statement. But it was possible Eazal had been spying on us in the Pyrthae. He could know which words to say to gain my trust.

I channeled quintessence and peered into the realm above, and there saw the telltale connection of a Qarin and their host, as I'd viewed with Talan's companion Sule several times before. Eazal was not alone in his body any longer.

Though the man had tried to murder me, it still repulsed me.

"Tell me your name," I demanded.

"Xian Azhi. As I told you in the Higher Plane."

I could barely relax my jaw enough to speak. It was all the confirmation I could hope for, yet it wasn't enough. I needed answers.

"How?" There were too many questions to sort through. "How did you come through the Pillar? How did you possess *him*?"

Eazal — or rather, Azhi — shrugged. "I know you believe him evil, Airene. But remember him when you first met. Eazal of Sandglass was a wretched man, not a wicked one. He tried to kill you because his wife and daughter were threatened by a Valemish priest. When he failed, he was desperate enough to entrust his life to me."

"So he chose this, did he?" I shot back. "He wanted to be possessed?"

"Of course not. But, in time, he will grow to understand." Azhi's expression darkened. "So I must hope."

It seemed an honest answer, but I found little reassurance in it. "And how did you come to be here?"

"To explain that would take more time than we can spare. I will say this: matter and energy are two sides of a coin. They share more in common than you might think. How did you suppose you first entered the Pyrthae, a realm of pure energy, then returned in the flesh?"

It was a fair question, and one which I'd had too little time to consider. But doubt would show a fissure in my armor; I intended to keep as strong a defense as I could.

"And what does that have to do with the Pillar?"

"They are not mere stone, Airene. The Pillars are connected; not in this world, but in the other. Have you never noticed how their points bend toward one another, as if to touch? They are passages, ways of traveling quickly about the city. I suspect they were once commonly used, before magic became seen here as wicked."

I looked up in the Pyrthae and saw on that point, at least,

he spoke truly. The Pillars arced like the talons of the Wyvern's Claw, back before it had burned down. The very tips of their peaks touched together.

Passages? I wondered how such a thing could be constructed, and to span both Telae and the Pyrthae. Another reminder of just how little I knew of my powers.

In the flesh, my gaze remained steady on Azhi. "Fine. I'll take your word on it. But I cannot trust you now, Azhi. Not while you wear his face."

Azhi grimaced. "I must keep it. To do what must be done, I must have a body. But if you cannot trust me, Airene, at least listen. We have precious little time, and there is much to be done."

I knew that as well as he, felt the urgency throbbing in my bones. I refused to let it rush me into a fatal decision.

"Speak, then. I will listen, but I don't promise to believe."

Azhi nodded. "That is all I ask. But if I might sit. This body... I am still unused to how it tires."

His words made my skin crawl, yet I nodded and skirted out of the way as he went to a nearby stone bench. A sigh escaped his lips as he sat, and he stretched and rolled his limbs as if to relieve lingering pains.

"Some things, I have missed," Azhi murmured, almost to himself. "Others, I have not."

He seemed to come back to himself a moment later, for his eyes found me as I moved to stand in front of him, a dozen cubits away.

"I will start, briefly, at the beginning of my knowledge," he said. "A thousand years ago, my people claimed, the god we named Taozu was confined within a cage called *Liantao* — the Chains, in your sea-tongue. This prison, deep within the Wumofu Desert, manifested as an impossibly large tree with bark as hard as stone and as white as the sun. Its branches reached to the stars themselves, and through all the planes spiritual and material."

The Chains. Vusu had written of the large tree in his journal, though it had been gray when he visited it. Having heard of it from two sources, I no longer doubted it existed.

"Every generation, a child was chosen from among the jaitin to go to the Chains and renew the bonds." Azhi's eyes fell to his hands, clutching at each other as if they wrestled. "We knew it as walking the Ancestors' Path, for their spirits sang the way to us, their bones buried deep beneath the sands to guide the chosen child. Anyone who walked it would not return, for the only way to strengthen the cage was through sacrifice."

This story, too, Vusu had addressed. I tried to hide my distaste and suspected I did it poorly. Azhi had only to glance up to see it.

"I know — it must seem strange and barbaric to you. But among my people, it was a great honor, one envied by all the other children. I was the most jealous of all, so much so that I did what no other had done before: I stole the duty for myself."

"You what?" I could scarcely believe it. Not only had children been sacrificed decade after decade, but they *longed* to be killed?

Azhi smiled, his expression drenched in regret. "A foolish act with a foolish end. I was tricked into believing I was truly the one who must go by a spirit. Afterward, I came to understand they longed only to consume my soul for their own survival. But at the time, I thought it another sign that I was blessed, that I must go on my journey."

His head fell again, and he stared at the ground. "But excuses grow flimsier each year. Suffice it to say, I failed in my mission. Instead of feeding my spirit to the Chains, I gave Taozu my blood. And thus, at last, he broke free of his bonds."

Something about his story didn't add up. "But Famine was

bound by Vusu. He hasn't been free since… when did you free him?"

Azhi met my eyes. "Two centuries ago."

Two hundred years. I tried to imagine such an existence. Azhi had seen generations born and buried while he lived on. Was it for this purpose alone? For the day he knew Famine would threaten the world once more? Or was he now like the greedy spirit he'd once been tricked by?

He seemed to sense the war inside my head. "Considering all that Taozu has wrought in the past season, I can understand why you would be skeptical. But you must understand that when the Corrupted first won free of his cage, he was shriveled and weak, starved of the spirit for which he hungered. It took him years to harvest and grow to a vestige of his former might, and then he could only prey upon those spirits he could catch. I watched him on his hunt for years before he found a new way to obtain the essence he craved."

I guessed what he alluded to, but remained silent. No need to give him words to twist to his own purpose.

Azhi confirmed my suspicions aloud. "He sought those reckless enough to accept his bargain: the power of the Higher Plane in exchange for souls sacrificed to him. He bonded himself with two young Bali men from an outcast ishaka, and by them harvested the essence of humans and animals common to the Mortal Plane. And thus he grew and grew, biding his time until he could break free."

"Yama and Lophe," I murmured, lulled into speaking. "But Vusu didn't let him break free for decades after their crusade failed. He held him."

Azhi flashed me a wan smile. "He did, for far longer than I thought possible. I began to believe he would find a way to imprison the great spirit, as the Chains once had. But as every Seed before him, his strength eventually faded, and his despair grew."

A realization struck me. "You knew what he did," I said slowly. "Yet you didn't intervene. You didn't stop him from..."

I couldn't say it; fury choked out the rest of my words.

Azhi winced and looked away. "I did not have the power to. Only through other beings was I able to assist you, Airene, and then only at great risk. Taozu is a jealous being. He always watched for prey, and on several occasions, he nearly caught me. Only now that he has gone am I safe here — or, at least, safer than before."

I shook my head. My eyes felt swollen in their sockets. I badly needed sleep, but even more, I needed answers. Not daring to let the Qarin and his host out of my sight for a moment, I tried to reason through what else I needed to know.

"You hoped Vusu had a way to contain him," I said. "To cage Famine. That must mean you don't know how yourself."

Azhi sighed and stretched again. Evidently, his body was chafing at him once more, aged joints and muscles aching. When he finished, he leaned his elbows onto his knees.

"In one sense, you are correct: I do not know precisely how it is done. With a few exceptions, no being in existence has witnessed Taozu's capture, for a millennia is a long time for even a spirit to survive."

My thoughts caught on his words. "Exceptions? What exceptions?"

His eyebrows drew together. "Surely, you know. Their influence lingers upon you. They have intervened in your life and Oedija's fate more thoroughly than I have."

Only then did it occur to me. "Clepsammia," I breathed.

"Yes. She and some of the other great spirits have always interacted with the Mortal Plane. Too few remain now. Yet though they cannot, or will not, tell their secrets, I believe they are the key to defeating our enemy."

I wanted to tear Azhi's knowledge from Eazal's head, yet I tried to hide my eagerness. Though the daemon seemed to speak truthfully, I didn't want to introduce any sign of weakness, lest he take advantage.

So I only cocked an eyebrow. "Go on."

Azhi glanced toward the horizon. The sun's glow was fading, leaving the sky blue with touches of green from the radiant winds. "There are items in Telae that relate to the great spirits," he said, eyes sliding back to me. "Artifacts forged by or from their essence. One of these was used in the ritual that caged Taozu for hundreds of years. We called it the Binding Ruyi, and it appeared to be made of the same substance as the Chains."

The possessed man straightened, then reached a hand down to his waist. At once, I raised a hand, radiance flickering at the tips of my fingers. Azhi did not startle, but only looked up with a small smile.

"Still, you do not trust me," he murmured. "Yet you must, Airene, if we are to defeat our enemy."

I was in no mood for a lecture. "What were you reaching for?"

"The thing of which I spoke. The Binding Ruyi."

My breath caught. Though he hadn't said a false word that I knew of, I couldn't believe him.

"The Quintyr artifact. You have it here?"

"Yes. Would you like to see it?"

It shamed me, but I nodded. Even if it exposed a vulnerability, I had to see.

Azhi gave me another smile, then reached again for the cloth-wrapped object hanging from the sash wound around his middle. It seemed a peculiar shape, now that I looked closer at it. He slipped it free, unwrapped it, then held it up.

The artifact was a short scepter, no longer than my arm. Its shape was of a snake or a dragon, the head of it open-mouthed as if it meant to lash out. It appeared smooth in texture, and from top to bottom, it was as white as bone.

It had been mentioned in Vusu's journal, this scepter, or

one very much like it. Even more, it was not the only object I'd seen of its kind. Though I'd held neither item, I knew it would be the same material as Aika's knife, which Vusu had used to become a Sacrifice and bind Famine for those brief turns.

Artifacts of the Quintyr. My head spun to think of what it might mean.

Azhi watched me carefully, judging my reactions. As silence stretched on, he finally broke it. "You recognize something in this ruyi, do you not?"

I debated the wisdom of revealing anything, then nodded. The pyr had extended a measure of trust to me. I could give that much back.

"It resembles an object I've seen, one Vusu used to end his life, and another I've heard tell of. But tell me, daemon — what do you plan to do with it?"

He laid the ruyi on his lap. "As I said, I do not know precisely how to use the Binding Ruyi to ensnare Taozu once again. But we will not discover it here, away from him." His eyes rose to meet mine once more. "We must go to him, Airene. We must pursue Taozu and bind him. He grows stronger by the day, by the turn. Already, he can again consume the other great spirits. Soon, he will challenge the mightiest among them. I have seen what has happened through his supremacy. The wastelands across the breadth of the world. Only here, in the Four Realms, and a few pockets in other lands remain. Only here does civilization remain intact."

Azhi looked aside, and I couldn't deny the passion in his voice. Hadn't Eltris once said the same of the world? But to think that only in the Four Realms life remained, especially when we warred among ourselves... It was a terrible, bitter truth to swallow.

"If the other gods fall," he continued, softer now, "nothing will stand in the way of these lands becoming every bit as desolate as the Wumofu. All life will be consumed."

I remembered Oedija as I'd seen it in my dream, a sandy wasteland, and knew how close that vision was coming to pass. It struck terror through me that made my legs feel like straw and my head faint. Only by force of will did I remain upright.

"You would have me abandon Oedija?" I had to force out the words, for my throat tried to clamp shut. "Leave my friends and family to face Avvad on their own?"

Even as I said it, I wondered what I could do by remaining behind. I was no warrior. I had a unique capacity for channeling quintessence, but it would do little good against an army. And what use would it be to defeat the Imperium if Famine still destroyed Telae?

Still, I couldn't go. Not on Azhi's word and my suspicions alone. This was too much for my weary mind. I needed to think things over. I needed time.

Though I had none to spare.

Azhi seemed to weigh his words before responding. "I realize this must seem like a great gamble, trusting me. Leaving behind everything you know to venture into the unknown. But you can sense Taozu, can you not? You feel how he grows; your connection to the Pyrthae grows with him. I see it, even if I did not already know it."

His words struck too close to the mark. "What do you mean?"

Eazal's eyes contained the centuries of Azhi's life within them. "You are the last of the Seeds, Airene, now that Vusumuzi is dead. You are the only one who can bind him now."

It wasn't anything I didn't already know. Still, it broke me. I stumbled back a step, staring at the possessed man like he'd struck me. My mind was numb with panic.

"I must go," I managed to say before turning away.

"We must leave soon, Airene!" Azhi shouted after me. "I will return here tomorrow. Be ready, or we may be too late."

I only stumbled away from him, then nearly ran back to the Laurel Palace.

It wasn't fast enough to outrun the thoughts that haunted me.

9

SACRIFICE

There is, I know well, only one end to this struggle. There must be a sacrifice: of blood, of body, of soul. Someone must pay the price for the world's reprieve.

   Best if it is not me.

- The journal of Vusumuzi; date unknown

The night pressed in thick by the time I returned to my room. Golden pyr lamps illuminated the palace halls, and I flitted from one pool of light to the next. Though I was as safe as I could be within the Laurel Palace walls, it felt as if a specter stalked me and would seize me the moment I stopped moving.

I reached my room without incident, shut the door, and leaned against it. My eyelids drifted closed. For a moment, it was all I could do to simply breathe. I felt too tired to stand, yet too anxious to lie down. My head was full to bursting with all the knowledge I had gained and all I must do.

Yet my immediate duty was clear: I couldn't make any decision before I finished reading Vusu's journal. Already, a confluence between his thoughts and Azhi's proclamations had appeared, and I was only halfway through. I still hoped to discover the answers that plagued me, greatest of all how one committed oneself as a Sacrifice to Famine.

Only, didn't I already know how? I'd witnessed Vusu doing it, saw its results. Perhaps there were nuances I'd missed in the rush of the moment, but I suspected fear was what truly held me back. Fear, and a desperate hope that I might not have to die, no matter all the evidence mounting to the contrary.

I knew the truth. The best I could do was become a Sacrifice and hold Famine at bay. If we were lucky, I would imprison him for centuries. If we weren't... I couldn't consider what would happen then.

So I read, though my eyes crossed and my head ached and my neck sent shooting pains into my shoulders. I read as Vusu detailed his experiments in how he might more permanently confine the daemon god.

A vessel, a human vessel, is what is required. I have served as such for decades, but perhaps it is not necessary for me to be the Sacrifice. Perhaps another might be used in my place, and thus become a permanent prison.

My skin crawled, though I could muster little more reaction than that. Here was where the idea had begun for what he had done to Linos. What he had attempted on Thero and failed. Painful as it was to follow the man's twisted thoughts, I forced myself to read on. It was the only way I could make my brothers' sacrifices mean something.

After failing to make ready many for the Serpent, I have noticed a pattern in those who seem more suitable. This tendency runs in families, in bloodlines, as if it is a trait passed down. What it might be, I cannot say, yet it is my best lead yet.

And there, at last, it had come from nowhere: the explanation I'd long been searching for. I stared at the words, my mind slow to unravel their portent. What had happened to Linos hadn't been an accident. He'd been targeted as Thero's younger brother, who must have been more promising than most.

It also meant Vusu's interest in me hadn't stopped at how my profession as a Finch might benefit him. He'd been interested in my entire family and something in our blood, something that made us ideal for his experiments.

I'd been pacing my room in order to stay awake while I read, but now I collapsed onto the bed. My body felt numb, my mind empty. I wondered what it meant, this trait that ran through my family. It had brought us so much pain and misery. How could it be anything but evil?

I buried my face in my hands. My eyes felt feverish against my palms. I would have cried had I had the tears, but I was dry, empty. There was no venting the misery that filled me.

Yet only a few moments passed before a glimmering thought lifted it, if slightly. I raised my head and stared at the journal on my desk, my mind slowly chewing through the realization.

Perhaps whatever ran in my family's blood could be used for good. Perhaps it was a certain kind of fate that this duty of ensnaring Famine should fall to me. For if the trait made us ideal cages for the daemon god, I might be the perfect Sacrifice.

Maybe I would stop him for good. Maybe I could be enough — if I could catch him.

But Famine was far to the east; I could feel him, as I always could, feasting and reveling in it. It would take spans, if not seasons, to reach him, and that was only if he didn't move farther away. Besides, Avvad could arrive any day at Oedija's walls, and their scouts no doubt patrolled the surrounding lands. Then there would be no departure for anyone.

I covered the pyr lamp I'd been reading by and lay again on my bed with a soft groan. I would rest and decide come morning. For now, it was all I could do.

My mind wasn't content to stop just yet. Even as I drifted into sleep's clutches, a remembered fragment from an old tome floated through my mind:

How are we to know the Seed of Harvest has planted within you? Agmon Brandheart, the First of the Wardens, had asked Aika of the Green.

No words can tell; only my actions will, she'd responded. *Take me before Famine and I will show you.*

The thought lingered for a moment, caught by idle curiosity — then it passed on, and I fell away.

I STARTLED AWAKE, only realizing after I'd sat up that a knock had awoken me.

Combing my fingers through my tangled hair, I stumbled over to the door, then hesitated. I was dressed, a precaution against just such rude awakenings, though my appearance was still far from presentable. But it wasn't that thought that stopped me but of Shepherds, who had once come calling on Xaron and forced him to flee for his life. I doubted such a thing would happen to me, but caution bade me to crack open the door and peer out at my visitor.

Then I saw who it was. I hastily pulled the door open and bowed.

The Despot of Oedija was not to be kept waiting.

Jaxas was as thin as ever, yet stood more erect and with more vigor than I'd ever seen before he wore the Evergreen Wreath. His robes were the deep green of winter moss, and a golden stole hung about his neck. A few steps behind, Nikias and two guards waited, the steward staring at me with a baleful glare.

"Even for a man of my resources," Jaxas said in his mild manner, "you are a difficult woman to track down, Airene."

Had I not still been so weary, I might have flushed. "Sorry. I didn't mean to evade you."

"I'm sure." Without waiting for an invitation, he strode inside, forcing me to back out of his way. The Despot scanned my room, his expression hiding what he made of its disarray, before turning back to me. Nikias and the guards remained in the hall.

"You have missed my council two evenings in a row," Jaxas said, as dispassionate as if observing the weather.

I wasn't fooled. This was a reprimand, and I would take it as such. It was safer to take a monarch too seriously than not at all — even a man with whom I'd shared much.

I bowed again. "I apologize once more. My duties have kept me away."

"Duties." Jaxas spoke the word as if it were new to him. "Such as reporting your mission's results, you mean."

I winced. "That is one."

Jaxas did not smile; he rarely smiled these days. Ruling had changed him, molded him into the man Oedija needed him to be. I wasn't sure I preferred the Despot to who he had been before.

"Well then," he prompted after a moment's silence. "Tell me: were you successful?"

I debated how to answer that. But as hesitation might be interpreted poorly, I didn't pause long.

"Ariston has been taken care of. And I found Seda, Vusu's honor. After some convincing, she gave me his journal. Reading it has been preoccupying me since."

None of it was an outright lie, though the truth was certainly veiled. Yet I'd told Jaxas I would assassinate Ariston, and I had not. The man I'd known before would understand.

But the Despot he was now? His reaction, I couldn't predict.

Jaxas's hooded eyes were unshifting on me for a long moment. When he spoke, his tone hadn't shifted, yet his words chilled me through.

"Kelena's network gave me an interesting report. That a man of Ariston's description fled north from the city, and a bald Avvadin woman traveled with him. Unless they saw a ghost, I cannot see how this aligns with your story."

My heart pounded hard in my chest. I kept my chin high. I could only hope that the soundness of our partnership thus far would keep me safe. Since he knew the truth, my best policy now was to abandon all deceit.

"I didn't say I killed him, Jaxas. The Manifest is all but dismantled, and with him gone, it lacks a leader. Killing him would have done no good, and perhaps cost me my chance to get the journal from Seda."

"Seda," Jaxas repeated. "Vusu's honor."

I nodded. "I have to think about our greater enemy. It was a gamble I don't regret."

The Despot stared at me a moment longer, then turned and began to pace my chamber. I watched him, his movements making me nervous. Yet with as uncertain of ground as I stood upon, I held my tongue.

At last, he turned back to me. "I had hoped it might be otherwise. Now I see the truth plain before me. You are no assassin, Airene. Yet you must harden your heart all the same. An army is at our doorstep, an army we cannot hope to defeat without substantial losses. But no war is ever won without sacrifice."

I couldn't help it; a bitter smile worked its way onto my lips. "You think I don't know that? That I haven't already made sacrifices to get as far as we have?"

He cut me off before my self-pity could carry on further.

"We all have. I betrayed ideals I have believed in my entire life to do what must be done. I betrayed my uncle and my cousin and seized a crown that was not mine. Yet I accepted my burden of guilt, and I bear it, just as you must carry yours."

Yours does not require you to die!

I wanted to shout the words at him and barely bit them back. Turning my head aside, I hid the resentment that boiled inside me. It surprised me with its vehemence. I had mourned all that occurred, yet I hadn't known the sense of injustice I felt until Jaxas unlocked it.

Perhaps he sensed it, for the Despot pivoted the conversation. "You say you recovered Vusu's journal. Does it have the answers you seek? The key to stopping Famine?"

Since he'd made a concession, I had no choice but to do the same. "I'm not sure. It explains much of his motivations and actions, but I've found little that will turn the tide. I'm only part of the way through, however. The last pages will likely reveal the most."

Jaxas nodded and turned to the door. He paused before exiting, his gaze tilting back toward me.

"Read. That is your only duty, Airene. The Four Realms have little time — and Oedija even less."

With that, the Despot strode from my room and shut my door behind him.

I stared at the wood, but my thoughts had already flitted back to my last thought before sleep. I'd remembered a passage, one from my days spent down in the Acadium's archives. It had seemed significant when suspended halfway between consciousness, but now…

How are we to know the Seed of Harvest has planted within you?

I shook my head. *Harvest.* Perhaps some version of Clepsammia existed, and Famine as well, but it didn't mean all of the Eidolan deities existed. And if she did, what of it? Harvest was a minor goddess of no import. She bore no relevance in this war.

But why, then, did both Aika and Agmon believe her to be so crucial?

With no ready conclusion, I pushed the thought from my mind. I had to dress, eat, and fetch coffee, then finish Vusu's journal. Then I had to decide if I would take up Azhi on his offer. I had no time for stray fantasies.

Yet I'd never been good at letting go of curiosities. Even as I went about my tasks, I knew the thought would linger.

10
THE RIGHT MOMENT

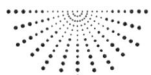

All has changed in a moment. Oedija, the Four Realms — perhaps even lands beyond ours will feel the reverberations of what happens here.

A moment was all it took. But perhaps all it will take is one more moment, the right one, to change things for the better.

- A Modern History of Oedija (in composition); by Acadian Helene, Master Historian; 1171 LP

As Jaxas commanded, I finished Vusu's journal that morning.

I had fewer pages to read than I'd initially thought, for many of the leaves, almost a quarter of the journal, were left blank. Even those filled held few revelations. Vusu detailed the reasons for his actions, for fomenting unrest and founding the Manifest. He'd believed the only way to defeat Famine was to rally the entire world, to produce such a state of alarm that everyone in the Four Realms would rise against him and the daemon god within him.

But it seemed a madman's plan. Why foment divisions rather than forge alliances? He could have sought help instead of enemies to destroy him, and the threat could have been overcome without such bloodshed.

Yet from all I'd seen of Vusu, I thought I understood his reasoning. Long ago, as a young man of a fading ishaka, he'd chosen to make war on his kinsmen. Conflict had long simmered within Vusu, and Famine's inhabitance of his soul likely expanded it.

Understanding brought no further notion of how to proceed, however. Journal clutched in my hands, I paced my room for so long it seemed I must wear a line into the stone floor. I had to make a move, but I didn't know which way to go. Each trail branching before me led to the same result, one I couldn't accept.

Only one avenue had opened before me that held even a chance of defeating Famine. Yet how could I trust Azhi, a Qarin occupying the body of my would-be assassin?

So I paced, racking my brain for another way, and each time coming up short.

Half a turn into my fretting, I realized I wouldn't be able to decide on my own. But who could I turn to? Nomusa and Xaron were needed here in Oedija; their positions were too important to vacate. And I guessed at the first insinuation of trusting Azhi, they'd tie me up to keep me from acting rashly. Talan was likely too deep into his cups for me to trust his judgment.

The next person I thought of surprised me. *Eltris.* The spans had cooled my anger toward her, though I hadn't recovered my opinion of the Master Augur. She'd been willing to let Vusu make Linos his Sacrifice; after that, I doubted I could ever trust her again. Still, either she or Kyros had taken Aika's knife, and if Azhi had spoken the truth, I would need the artifact no matter which path I traveled.

So it was that I set off for the Acadium.

The air was oppressive as I strode down the streets, and the guards who let me out of the gate stared at me like I were mad. Perhaps I was. The city guard had all but abandoned control over the revolting population, marshaling the walls' defenses against Avvad instead. Likewise, the taxoi Jaxas had ordered into being were occupied with drilling intensely so they wouldn't fold at the first charge — though that seemed a distinctive possibility regardless, considering the Avvadin forces had been trained from the cradle.

But I wasn't defenseless any longer. When a group of three men leered at me, I scared them off with a flare of radiance. It was unwise to advertise my attunement, yet I doubted word would reach back to anyone who would move against me. Jaxas knew and let me roam free. Of those in power, only Feiyan was vindictive enough to attempt something, but she seemed too distracted by her newfound position to mind me much.

The Acadium was near to the Laurel Palace, and I returned without further incident. The guards hesitated to admit me, for I had no official authority, but I had only to remind them I had the Despot's ear for them to relent. I went quickly through before they changed their minds.

The city's mania had infected the campus as well. Acadians bustled to and fro, heads bowed and eyes darting, constantly watching for threats. I ignored the passersby and headed straight for the squat tower where the old augur resided. If I knew Eltris, she wouldn't have vacated her decrepit accommodations even now.

Reaching her door, I pounded thrice on the weathered wood. Several minutes passed before I grew suspicious. The Master Augur had always been fond of petty retribution. After the way I'd left things between us, it was no surprise she sought to punish me now.

Just as I thought I might actually attempt to climb through her window, as I'd once fantasized doing, she opened the door. Her yellow eyes peered out from the gloom beyond the cracked door, like a cat ready to pounce.

"You," was all she said.

I forced a smile. "Hello, Eltris. Mind letting me in?"

The augur scoffed. "I doubt you'd give me a choice."

The aged woman turned and shuffled back inside. I kept my temper leashed and followed her in, sealing the door behind me and trying not to be uneasy at the darkness. Whatever the conflicts between us, Eltris meant me no harm.

Or so I hoped.

"Up here," she ordered from ahead, and I saw her ascending the stairs. I meekly trailed behind, a firm hold on my tongue.

The chamber upstairs was much the same as I remembered it. Finches fluttered among the rafters, their feathers red and yellow and green, chirping to each other as they danced. The same musty carpet was rolled out over the length of stone floor, pocked with stray radiant flares. Flames burned high in the braziers, filling the place with stifling heat.

Eltris stalked to the middle of the room before turning to face me. Her face, always wrinkled, seemed to have gathered a few more lines, and her gray hair was turning white. In just a season, Eltris had gained decades.

But aging did nothing to moderate her temper.

"Well?" she snapped when I didn't immediately speak. "Say what you want, or do you have the time for social visits?"

Despite my better judgment, my muscles tightened, readying for an assault. I'd come to mend bridges, but my resolve was quickly fading.

"I won't be long," I said. "I came for the knife." I didn't explain which one; there was no need.

If my request surprised the augur, she didn't show it. "And what would you want that for?"

"It's Aika's knife, an artifact used to cage Famine. And I'm the one who must imprison him now."

I longed to shake answers out of the aged woman. My fists clenched and my fingernails dug into my palms as I stared at her, daring her to deny me. As the silence stretched, I told myself I would wait her out.

As usual, impatience won the argument.

"Will you always stand by and watch the world burn?" I demanded, taking a step forward. "Will you let Famine consume everything before you act? I don't ask you to risk your neck — Eidola know you won't do that. All I ask is that you give me the knife. Then we never need see each other again."

The old woman sneered, and my fury grew to towering heights. Before I could invent a proper insult that would slap the amusement from her face, however, the Master Augur responded.

"You believe doing anything is better than nothing. But that is how we've come to where we are now. Vusu dead. Famine free—"

I interrupted her. "And that's my fault, is that right?"

"Yes," Eltris answered at once. "Undoubtedly."

I could barely think through the haze over my thoughts. Part of me wanted to tear her apart and burn her to the bones. Yet even if I could have managed it, I never would. If she infuriated me, it was only because I knew how much more Eltris could accomplish if she acted. That she did nothing but wait was a stance I couldn't sympathize with.

"When?" My tone was measured, my fury cold. "When will you act?"

"When it is time."

I smiled, but there was no joy in it. "By then, it will be too late."

I had little hope I would convince her. Eltris was the most stubborn woman I had met, and that included Nomusa, Feiyan, and my mother. Yet I couldn't leave without that knife. That was how I would offer myself as

Famine's Sacrifice. Without it, there was no point in pursuing the dragon.

There would be little I could do at all.

So I took a deep breath and imagined the desert Isidora had once illustrated for me in a meditation practice, and I found calm there. When my heart slowed, I looked up at the aged woman, whose eyes had never shifted from me, and held her gaze.

"I must be the Sacrifice, Eltris. I am the only Seed of Famine—"

"Not the only one," she interrupted.

I held my anger in check this time. Linos was another reason I couldn't leave without taking Aika's knife. If Eltris had been willing to sacrifice him once, I doubted she'd hesitate again.

"I am the only one still awake," I amended. "If Linos was..." The suggestion was too painful to consider, so I skipped past it. "We don't know what would happen. Would he contain Famine without his will behind it? Or would he only be consumed?" I swallowed, again pushing away images of that occurrence. "I know which possibility I think is more likely, and which I would rely upon."

I expected Eltris to have a snippy reply, perhaps how I was the least reliable woman in Oedija. If she had, I might not have been able to contain myself any longer.

She didn't speak for several long moments. As I stared into her eyes, I was surprised to find shrewd evaluation there instead of the usual disdain.

"You've learned," she said at last. "You've gained some control over that temper of yours."

I gave no reply. Her observation irritated me, but I refused to show it, knowing she goaded me. So I waited.

Eltris nodded sharply, then approached. I stiffened as she did. It wasn't that I feared an attack. Eltris had only ever touched me in the Pyrthae, first when she'd saved me, and then when she'd tried to obstruct me. Her nearness made me nervous in a way I didn't entirely understand.

She stopped several paces away and put her hands to her waist. Her fingers pressed through her billow of robes for several moments before appearing again, a cubit-long wrapped object in her hands.

My breath caught. I didn't dare speak, hardly daring breathe lest it change her mind.

"You are wrong about many things," the augur said. "Most things, in fact. But in this, you are right. You are the Sacrifice. It will be by your hand that Famine is trapped, or not. Much as I wish it otherwise, I cannot change that it will be your decision when and where to use this. Just swear to me, girl, that you will choose the right moment."

Eltris held out the wrapped parcel. I advanced slowly and took it, then unfurled it enough to glimpse the bone-white material beneath.

Aika's knife. She'd given it to me after all.

I replaced the cloth. "Thank you," I murmured, my anger abruptly gone. "I will use it correctly. I will choose the right moment."

The augur snorted and turned her back on me. "Don't you have some other place to be?" she said pointedly over her shoulder.

Just like that, all my dislike returned. But I'd done what I'd come to do. Firming my jaw, I turned and left without a farewell.

As I closed the tower door behind me and made for the end of the alley, part of me wondered if I would ever see the old woman again.

11

A CHOICE

I must make a choice. I have come to many crossroads in my unnatural lifespan. I have not always made the right turn. But this is the most damning.

How can I choose between paths when both end in my death?

- *The journal of Vusumuzi; date unknown*

I almost made it back to the Laurel Palace without trouble. With my channeling dissuading likely assailants, I fled along the main roads from the Acadium. I witnessed several fights breaking out: once between the city watch and commoners, another among drunken scoundrels. All ended with blood spraying and yells filling the hazy air. I increased my pace, nearly running, breath rattling and heart pumping at the violence.

I was in a state by the time the bastion came into sight. So as someone stepped out from the alley next to me, I whipped up both hands and drew on radiance until it burned.

Talan held up his hands, his smile never shifting.

Exhaling shakily, I lowered mine. "Do you have to do that?"

"How else would you have me approach? Waving my hands and shouting?" The former Guilder looked around with raised eyebrows. "Subtlety suits me, and I believe our surroundings call for it."

Though I repressed the radiance back through my locus, I kept a watchful eye on Talan. He seemed to stand straighter than before, though he'd always moved with a slouch, and to swagger more than sway. Standing a couple of paces apart, I couldn't detect the stench of stale wine about him.

Almost, I dared to hope the man I'd once known might be returning to me. But I didn't push my good fortune that far.

He smiled wider at my scrutiny and spread his arms. "Do I have pyrkin in my hair?"

A sigh escaped me, and with it left the tension I'd been clinging to. "It's good to see you out and about, even considering the times."

He advanced slowly, arms falling back to his sides. Every movement was deliberate, like I were a cat he might scare off.

"I had to find you," he spoke softly. His eyes flitted about us for a moment before they settled back on me. "The journal. Have you read it?"

I nodded.

"And?"

What could I say? "It explained much about Vusu. But..."

"...it didn't give the answers you sought," Talan finished.

The truth escaped me then. "I have a path forward, Talan. But I'm afraid to take it. That it's not what I hope it is. That I won't return."

I looked aside, my eyes burning, when Talan surprised me by seizing my hands. His skin was warm to the touch, as it always had been before. I didn't pull away.

"Is it the right path?" he murmured.

"I think so."

He squeezed my hands. "Then you'll have the courage to

take it. Trust me — courage is one thing you've never lacked. Common sense, on the other hand..."

A laugh burst from me, half-choked by a sob. I hadn't thought I could laugh then, and it took me by surprise. I extracted one of my hands to wipe across my eyes and nose. Talan smiled all the while, but amusement faded from his eyes.

"Airene, if you plan to do something rash, I only ask one thing: don't exclude me. Always, you have asked my aid before. Don't change that now."

My throat was dry, the words the wrong shape to fit through it, so I nodded and smiled. Given the circumstances, it was as close to an apology as I could have hoped for.

"I will," I finally managed.

He flashed me a lopsided grin, and again looked like the man I'd once known. "You know where to find me."

As suddenly as he'd appeared, Talan dissolved back into the shadows.

~

I PACED the length of Linos's room. Window, door, window, door — they were the guideposts of my walking. I wished I had such signs for my path. A choice lay before me, yet I did not know how to make it. It was a gamble to stay, an even greater one to leave.

Which was worth taking?

My gaze fell to my brother, lying on his side. His back was turned toward me, but I had seen his eyes open and unblinking. Leaving would mean abandoning him. I wouldn't be able to protect him from Eltris's designs.

At the thought of the augur, I drew out the enwrapped knife and held it in both hands before me. Aika's knife. If Azhi was telling the truth, between the two of us, we now possessed the two artifacts that could entrap Famine. It was as good a chance as we'd ever had.

I'd rarely hesitated to act before. Yet now, I couldn't make the only decision that seemed possible.

The door opened. Startled, I hid the dagger behind my back and readied magic in my other hand. As the visitors revealed themselves, however, I hastily closed my locus. My face burned, but I met Nomusa and Xaron's curious gazes straight on. By the flickering of their eyes, my reaction hadn't gone unnoticed.

"Airene?" Xaron said cautiously. "Are you well?"

I dredged up a smile. "Sorry. It's been a long couple of days."

He gave me a sympathetic look. "We figured as much. That's why we came."

Nomusa gestured toward the door. "All of us."

I tried not to startle again as Corin and Kari came through the doorway. "You two as well?" I said before I could rethink my words.

The former cartwoman nodded slowly. "We thought we would find you here," she said, her words soft as if speaking to spooked livestock.

I looked between my friends, trying to read in their expressions what was behind this appearance. "Well," I said at last. "You found me. But don't you have other things to do?"

Nomusa exchanged a glance with Xaron before speaking. "I wish we were only here for a visit. But the truth is we're worried, Airene. Worried about you."

It shouldn't have come as a surprise, yet it did.

"Worried?" A laugh bubbled up from me. "What is there to be worried about?"

Xaron grimaced as he edged forward. "If I wasn't before, I would be now. Aire, we've barely seen you the past few days. And the last time we did, you said you were going to, ah, kill someone."

"We want to know what you've been up to." Nomusa crossed her arms over her chest. "And what you're planning to do next."

I took them in with fresh eyes. Each was wearing the garb of their respective offices. Nomusa's peplos was the light green of the ocean's froth, in flattery of the royal family's colors. Xaron's clothes were just as fine, if more practical, jacket and trousers, both of dark violet and loose for effortless movement. Corin was in the plain but well-made clothes suitable for an Oedijan man, a tan tunic and dark pants, while Kari wore the bright clothes of her outlandish people, aqua and red and tan in reeling patterns.

My former Finches, at least, had places here. Responsibilities. If I told them what I'd learned and what I intended to do, was I afraid they would try to talk me out of it?

Or that they'd leave behind all they'd worked so hard to gain and join my foolhardy quest?

Corin had just as much to lose, if not more. She'd recovered her sister after years of separation, and with Kari under threat the entire time. Surely, she could least afford to come with me. Surely, she would not want to.

Yet I had long ago learned to trust my instincts. I didn't want them to sacrifice everything, but I feared I could not do this alone. If I was to succeed, I would need them, if only to carry me to my final destination.

I sighed, then spoke. "I have to leave Oedija. I have to hunt Famine."

12
DESERTERS

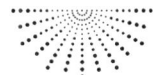

"To flee the defense of one's homeland in its time of need is a contemptible crime. Hence, the penalty for desertion, death, is well deserved."

- On the formation of a standing army; by Stratechon Bion, 1086 SLP

Deserters?" Xaron asked the same question he'd spoken twice already. "You'd have us be deserters?"

"And to follow the apothecary." Nomusa's nose wrinkled. Her carriage had become more erect with each of my conclusions. "Need I remind you that Eazal tried to kill you?"

"I know, I know. But can you see another way?" Exasperated as I was, I tried to hold back my temper. I'd expected every one of these objections as soon as I'd begun my confession, and I knew they were reasonable. It didn't change how wearisome it was to answer them not once, but repeatedly, as our arguments circled back over the same points.

"Many." Nomusa wore a heavy frown. "Of which we've already told you."

"Jaxas will never allow it." Xaron paced, plainly agitated.

"We'd never get past the city gates. They're closed to all traffic, you know. Fear of spies and deserters, I suppose — and apparently it's not unwarranted!"

"We're not deserters." I spoke the words through gritted teeth. Friends they might be, but I was coming dangerously close to wanting to strangle the both of them. "We're the damned opposite of deserters — martyrs, more like."

Xaron snorted a laugh, while Nomusa shook her head. Neither had budged an inch in all the time we'd spoken. Our discussion had lasted through the afternoon and bled into the evening. I kept a watchful eye for the sun's fall, knowing we had only so long to argue. If they weren't convinced by the time I had to meet Eazal, I would have to leave alone.

Alone with a Qarin and my would-be murderer. The thought sent a thrill of fear running through me. I hoped it wouldn't come to that.

Corin, who had remained silent beside her sister, now straightened from the wall she'd been leaning on. "Kari. What have you to say?"

All eyes turned to the young woman. She'd proved remarkably apt at sitting and waiting, but seemed as content to speak as well. Her gaze turned upon me, and I tried not to flinch before its intensity.

"He has his claws in you," she murmured.

The hair on my arms raised at her words, so similar to ones Azhi had once spoken to me. Did she know? How could she? The others seemed at as much of a loss as me, looking between each other.

Corin broke the silence. "Where Airene goes, I will too. If my sister is willing." She looked at Kari, who nodded at once.

I gave them both a grateful smile, then glanced at Xaron and Nomusa. Our former loftmate's words seemed to shame them, and they shared a look that told volumes. But still, I held my breath until they spoke.

"Of course we're with you, Airene," Xaron said. "We know what's at stake."

"We just wanted to make sure you're right." One of Nomusa's eyelids flickered, but she covered it well. "It's a big risk."

I wasn't irritated by their hesitancy now, only grateful they would come at all. "I know," I replied. "But we'll never be certain, not with how much time we have left. I think this is our best shot."

They hesitated a moment longer, then each nodded. I smiled at them, then included Corin and Kari in it.

"Thank you, everyone. I'm lucky to have friends like you. If I didn't…"

I was surprised as tears pricked my eyes. I turned my head aside. Someone reached out and squeezed my shoulder; Nomusa, I saw out of the corner of my eye.

"We're here with you, Airene. All the way."

All the way. I nodded, too choked up for words.

Xaron cleared his throat and sniffed. "Avvad is at our doorstep," he said, voice gruff with emotion. "If we leave now, I suppose we could be killed for it."

My tears dried at the stark reminder. Looking up, I saw my fear reflected in my friends' eyes.

"We must keep this from Jaxas." I glanced at the door. "And Kelena. And Feiyan, of course," I added as an afterthought.

Xaron looked aghast. "As if any of us would tell *her*."

The others nodded along.

"We'll begin gathering supplies," Nomusa offered. "Subtly."

"I will assist," Corin spoke up. "I know what is needed for traveling."

I nodded. "That's settled then. Guess I'd better let Talan know."

Xaron's eyebrows rose. "You two patch things up, then?"

"Enough." I withheld a grimace. "If not as much as I'd like."

Nomusa reached out and pressed my arm, but her smile was more teasing than sympathetic. "Don't worry. I'm sure it's a long way to wherever we're going. Plenty of time to become... reacquainted."

As the others laughed, I turned away to hide my flush and all but fled to the palace aviary.

∽

BEFORE WE LEFT, I returned to Linos's bedside.

I'd finished packing. Soon, dusk would fall and we would need to leave, but I couldn't do so without visiting my brother one last time. I stared at his still face, his open eyes, his too-thin body, its sharp angles apparent beneath his robe. Gently, I brushed a hand over his hair. It had lost much of its golden sheen, as if mirroring his soul's fading.

"They'll care for you here," I murmured. "Even if I don't come back, Jaxas will look after you. And Famine... I won't let anything happen to you, hear me? Your sister is still watching over you, Little Lion."

I waited for an answer, but of course, none came. There'd be no moment of closure, no strengthening of familial bonds. Pressing his hand one last time, I stood and left.

I met with the others outside my room. Isidora had joined us, too loyal to Xaron to not go. Talan would meet us where Azhi waited.

Once I gathered my pack from within my room, my friends and I went together to the Laurel bridge. We were burdened with what supplies we thought we might need. Nomusa guided this process, having once crossed the Four Realms to flee her ishaka, but Corin had given a surprising amount of input. I wondered at all I still didn't know of her past, even after all we'd shared together.

Though a pack animal would have been useful, we were gathering suspicion enough by readying for travel that we decided not to risk it. Judging from the strain on my shoulders and how my feet already ached with the weight, it was going to be a long journey.

Everything had gone smoothly to that point. I almost hoped we would escape unnoticed. But at the sight of the figures standing at the foot of the bridge, my hopes plummeted.

Feiyan and Kelena, surrounded by a contingent of soldiers, waited for us.

My gut tightened. I glanced at Xaron and Isidora and detected their attunements opened, their magic at the ready. A fight among Oedija's own was the last thing I wanted, yet I followed suit. Radiance burned brightly in me, making my skin itch.

As we neared, I saw Feiyan wore an infuriating smile. Kelena, on the other hand, was as somber as if she attended a funeral.

"My dear Finches!" Feiyan called out when we came within earshot. "I *am* so glad you came. I was beginning to think you'd disappoint me!"

It had started to rain, and the patter of water on the pavers made it so I almost had to shout to make myself heard. "We don't want trouble, Feiyan. Let us pass."

Her upper lip curled. "You are familiar with Oedijan law, are you not? Surely, you've skirted it often enough to know. What is the penalty for desertion, Airene?"

I knew. My hands clenched into fists. "Let us pass," I repeated, hoping she might relent, knowing she wouldn't.

But before Feiyan could speak again, Kelena took a step forward.

"Why?" she called across the cubits between us. "Why leave? I did not think you were cowards!"

Her words cut deeper than I'd expected. Nomusa answered before I could.

101

"We're not, Kelena. We're not fleeing. It's just that we're needed more elsewhere."

My friend glanced at me, as if unsure of how much more she should say. My thoughts had settled, however. I knew what must be said.

"We're facing Famine." I looked at Kelena first, then Feiyan. "He must be stopped at any cost."

"Even if your home will burn and your people become enslaved?" Feiyan mocked.

I didn't rise to the bait, but met her gaze with a steady one of my own. "Let us pass, Feiyan. You know you cannot stop us. And we shouldn't fight among ourselves. Tyurn knows we have enough enemies as it is."

The First Consul showed no sign of being swayed. The guards glanced at her. Their faces remained impassive, but their fear was clear. They knew they wouldn't stand long before wardens. Kelena, too, looked to Feiyan.

"If they wish to leave, let them," the First Verifier said. "We will find others to take their places."

Feiyan's lips twisted. "Very well. It shouldn't be difficult; they were never vitally important."

The comment stung. Hadn't I also wondered what I was doing in the Council? Yet there was nothing for it but to push down the shame along with the rest.

At a gesture from the First Consul, the laurel guards parted. I led my company forward, trying not to hunch over with my burdens before their watchful gaze. Feiyan's was hard to ignore; Kelena's was harder. Though she'd given her blessing, there was too much hurt in her eyes for my comfort.

I breathed easier when we were past, but only a little. It was just the first hurdle in fleeing the city.

I watched for Azhi as we approached the Conclave Pillar, but saw no sign of him. Worry gnawed at my belly. Had he played us false? I didn't know why he would do so, yet I couldn't banish my mistrust. Any delay cost us. I had little confidence Jaxas would allow us to leave as easily as his councilors had.

By their expressions, my companions felt the same pressure. "Where is he?" Nomusa asked as she looked around. "No place to hide here."

Isidora stared at Xaron, as if to say *What did I tell you?* Xaron wore a grimace, his hands clenching and unclenching as he peered around.

Then I noticed someone approaching from the nearest grove. I tensed, waiting to see who it was, but relaxed a moment later as Talan's features came into view.

"You," Xaron sneered. "Lurking in the shadows, as usual."

Talan looked at him sidelong. "I'm surprised. You've abandoned your usual garish outfits for a sensible one."

I intervened before things could get out of hand. "Thanks for coming, Talan."

His gaze traveled back to me. "Of course," he muttered, though he looked aside.

I tried to think of something else to say, but nothing came, so I contented myself with keeping watch for Azhi. When I saw no sign of the possessed apothecary, I invented a new plan for finding him. I channeled quintessence, and the world I knew became overlaid by the Pyrthae. Those of my companions who were wardens were dancing flames there in the gloom.

But no sooner had I entered than the Pillar glowed in both planes. I stared, suspecting who was coming, yet unsure if I was ready for his arrival.

I knew him by his Qarin's connection even before I released my hold on quintessence and saw him with my own eyes. Blinking away the Pyrthae, I stared at the face of my would-be murderer once more. My fear must have crossed my expression, for the apothecary winced.

"I did not mean to startle you," Azhi offered.

I shook my head and tried to even my breathing. The daemon-possessed man was certainly dressed for travel. He carried a smaller pack than ours, and it seemed better secured as well, hugging his back while the rest of ours dragged toward the pavers. He stood tall and seemed invigorated.

I knew that stance. He had purpose and direction once more. I hoped his was the same as ours.

I didn't make introductions; there would be time enough for it later, and I couldn't find any pleasantries in me. Instead, I asked him bluntly, "Why did we meet here? Every city exit is far."

Azhi gave me a tight smile. "We will not leave by a gate. Did you think we would spend spans on foot traveling through Oedija's wilderness?"

I kept my silence. What else could I have expected? But unless my intuition had dulled, I guessed another plan was forthcoming.

By the widening of Xaron's eyes, he'd divined it. "Gods," he breathed. "You mean for us to travel through the Pyrthae?"

It had come to me as soon as Xaron started speaking. I stared at Azhi, just as dumbfounded.

"How are we to know this isn't a trap?" I demanded. "That you don't mean to lure us to where you can take our quintessence?"

"How would those of us unattuned even reach it?" Nomusa wondered.

Azhi cast me a guarded look. "This is not a trick, Airene. I have dedicated my existence to rectifying my mistakes. If you still do not trust me, why did you come?" Without waiting for an answer, he turned to Nomusa. "And our means of travel are open to any, warden or not. After all, Airene entered the Pyrthae before she became attuned."

Amid everything else that had happened, I'd almost forgotten that had been my first experience with the Pyrthae.

What had occurred because of that experience did little to settle my fears.

Isidora spoke up, her eyes settled on me. "Even if it is a trap, we aren't helpless. Wardens have power in the Pyrthae. We can protect ourselves."

The resolve of the former Acadian decided me. I gave her a tight smile and a nod, then faced Azhi again.

"Fine. We'll do this your way. But if you betray us..."

"I know." For a moment, the apothecary looked as old as the pyr inhabiting him. "Watch as I open a portal. Then you can enter and leave the Pyrthae as you will."

I hardened myself to pity and observed him, channeling quintessence to be sure I missed nothing. Though my mistrust wounded the daemon, I wouldn't allow it to make me any less cautious.

Reaching to his belt, he withdrew an object there, white and long. The Binding Ruyi — I recognized the scepter from when he'd shown me it before. Extending it before him, he reached up into the air. I was aware of him channeling — was it quintessence?

Suddenly, he ripped down his arm, and the fabric of the world split apart.

I stared at the tear. It had opened as wide as my forearm, just enough that we might sidle through. Within, light shifted in ever-changing colors, as many and varied as any rainbow. The touch of every element I knew and more reached toward me, affecting both my body and being. The warmth of radiance; the vibrance of kinesis; the elation of magnesis.

As I looked into its depths, I tried to master my fear. I would enter it. I had to. It wasn't a rash error, not this time.

I hoped.

"Quickly!" Azhi urged.

I took a step forward, reached a hand up. The others followed me a step afterward, as reluctant as I to travel this way. But before any of us could take the last step, a familiar sound blared through the air.

As it swelled in the sky and cascaded down to us in the courtyard, I looked north toward its source. I could have died happy never hearing it again, but I wasn't that fortunate.

The shell horns of the Laurel Palace called once more.

I knew how many times they would blow. There were no signs of fire, and Jaxas wouldn't have died so soon after leaving him. And this was news we'd been expecting all season.

The horns trumpeted once, then twice. *War*, it meant. War had come to our walls.

Avvad had arrived at last. And we were fleeing.

Deserters, Feiyan had named us. Despite how I rationalized it before, I wasn't sure she was wrong. As much as I feared facing Famine, I had a method by which to battle him. Against the Imperium, I had no such comfort.

My city would fall, and I wouldn't be there to protect it.

"Now, Airene!"

I glanced at Azhi, then at the rest of my companions. Their faces mirrored all that I felt, yet determination was etched into every taut muscle.

I hardened my will and nodded, then stepped forward. Pushing aside my doubts and fears, I stepped up to the tear.

Extending a hand, I touched the Pyrthae, and it seized me and dragged me in.

13

THE TARNISHED PEARL

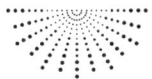

DESPOINA: *Accuse me of what you will! But you*
must acknowledge this: never did I allow the
Pearl of the Four Realms to be tarnished!

- *The Trial of Zalfene Wreath, from the records of*
the Confessionary Tribunal; 1087 SLP

T he world shifted and multiplied.

I hadn't fully inhabited the Pyrthae since I'd first become attuned. It was a different experience than channeling quintessence. I felt light and weightless then, like I could fly, and the landscape took on a different aspect than the real world. Now it was as a mirror image of the world we had left, albeit twisted and malformed. While I didn't carry the same burdens as I had back in Telae, and the rucksack lightened considerably, I didn't think I could lift off and soar as in my dreams.

We stood on solid ground exactly like the paving stones we had left behind, but for how the light distorted and changed hues. Looking up, I could see the mirror image of the Conclave above me, impossibly hanging upside down.

Around me, the whole of Oedija spread out, almost claustro-phobic in how it crowded out the sky. The air shifted with color and movement. Energy buzzed through me, urgent and dangerous.

I looked at my companions and found they'd also changed. Their bodies had lost their boundaries, their essence trailing away from them in thin mist. Their coloring, too, faded to shades of gray. Xaron was the light gray of morning fog, while Nomusa was the dark gray of storm clouds. The others were somewhere in between, each as distinctive in their tint as they were different in the material world. Though their bodies were amorphous, I found I could make out their facial features, though I knew their emotions by how they emanated from them.

Azhi took a similar shape as the others, but with a critical difference. Around Eazal's shadowed figure, the daemon appeared as a white glow. If I stared hard enough, I thought I could detect the boy he'd once been, lingering just beneath the man's face. I didn't look overlong; I needed no more reason to doubt him.

I looked down at myself and found I had become a shade as well. It was my body, and yet not. It was like looking at my reflection in a fountain's surface: the same, yet malleable. I tried to suck in a breath, but what is breathing without air?

That was not the sole change. I had the feeling that my present form was not the only possible shape I could take. That if I but imagined hard enough, I might become...

I shook my head, or what I thought of as my head. No — it *was* my head. I clung tightly to my belief.

Think otherwise, and I feared where it might lead.

As I drew out of my musings, I became aware that we weren't alone in this strange plane. Other beings flitted above us, as weightless as I was when I channeled quin-tessence. Their shapes weren't limited by what was possible, but by their imaginations and willpower. Pyr, I knew them to be; yet I hadn't realized how thickly they thronged the city. Their presence heightened my unease further still.

After exchanging looks with each member of my party, I turned to Azhi. "Where to now?"

Azhi glanced at me, then looked past. "Can you not feel him?"

With the mention, Famine's presence reasserted itself. The hunger pulled stronger now, an aching that began in my middle and spread through my limbs to touch every pore. I couldn't hide from it or distract myself with food here in the Pyrthae. I tried not to let show how deeply his influence had seeped.

"I do. He's still to the east. The Bali ishakas."

"Yes." Azhi's voice dropped to a murmur, yet it remained resonant in this uncanny plane. "He feasts now. Another spirit falls to his appetite."

I felt that, too. A wash of pleasure and satiation passed through me, so intense I almost smiled. But it didn't ease the hunger, only caused it to grow. I felt on the verge of tears with its agony, though I wasn't sure if I could cry here.

"Let's go," I spoke to the others, tone sharp. If anyone noticed, their shadowy faces gave no sign as they followed.

We made for the Conclave gate and exited onto the promenade. A glance up showed that, though time seemed to proceed at a normal pace here, it had slowed in the world suspended above us, which represented Telae. The few people we saw on the streets walked as if through honey, though their urgency was still apparent in their movements. They were ragged and thin and worn. I shifted my gaze back to my immediate surroundings. Spans of travel would take days in this realm with its peculiar sense of time. I had to keep that in mind, that enduring this would be worth it, in the end.

We proceeded through the city, heading for deme Gate. Though the journey was safer than traveling in Telae, particularly with the Avvadin army having arrived, anxiety threaded through me. I kept an eye out for the pyr flitting through the sky, wondering which were daemons and which were not. Was that distinction even relevant? Azhi had been helpful to me before inhabiting Eazal. Perhaps pyr weren't separate kinds after all, but only differentiated by their actions.

I wasn't alone in my wariness. I caught my companions glancing up, and though their expressions were lost on me, their auras provided signs of their thoughts. Xaron even seemed to channel, and I paused in astonishment at the sight. In the material world, I couldn't see when he exerted his will over the energetic elements, only feel it through my quintessence, or see the results. But here, I watched his quintessence as it molded radiance, kinesis, and magnesis into weapons. It was like liquid light, like fire turned to water, flowing around his body in an undulating swirl.

If he thought to deter the pyr, he was disappointed. A dozen of the nearest spirits drifted closer at this display. I braced myself, wondering if they were more like fish curious about something dropped in their pond, or hawks spying prey.

Azhi decided for me. "Cease!" he called to Xaron, worry pulsating from him. "Channeling attracts them. It shows them the essence they crave."

That you crave as well. I kept the thought to myself.

Xaron startled and released his hold on his magic, glancing at our guide before watching the daemons again. Despite this concession, they circled closer, ringing just a score of cubits overhead. I had to fight hard to keep from following Xaron's lead.

"They're too close," I called to Azhi. "We need to drive them off!"

"Leave them, and they may depart. If you attack—"

But the pyr's hopes were dashed as soon as he expressed them. As if on a signal, the spirits dove, all making for Xaron.

I shouted and reached for the elements. It was a similar mechanism as channeling in Telae, with my locus providing the anchor point for directing the magic, but the quintessence radiating from my skin told me it was a very different experience than expected.

But there was no time to dwell upon it. As the daemons reached my friends, I channeled radiance and kinesis. They shot forward in a roaring plume, fire churning in the battering waves of force. A handful of the pyr were caught in my assault and went spiraling away.

I didn't strike alone. Xaron and Isidora both channeled as well, their onslaught sending half a dozen more flying upward. Talan whirled bizarrely, yet he emitted a torrent of magic that scattered the rest of the pyr momentarily. Corin and Nomusa, devoid of magic, cowered before the phantoms. Kari might have helped, but she seemed lost in a daze as she stared up at the pyr. Azhi, too, didn't fight, but kept a wary distance.

I shoved down my thoughts. It didn't matter; we didn't need their help. We could handle these on our own.

Recovering from the initial assaults, three of the spirits turned midair and dove for me, while the others opted to attack against my attuned companions. They spread out so that I couldn't repeat the same tactic as before. Instead, I opened my hands before me and arced my magic. It only caught one of them, the other two spinning lithely out of the way.

I scrambled for a follow-up, sweeping my hands above me and sending a wave of kinesis cascading upward. This buffeted the pyr, delaying but not stopping them.

My frustration and fear mounted, and they weren't contained to my body. I felt them vibrating from me, infecting the surrounding air like a miasma.

Then it occurred to me. If energy didn't deter them, perhaps something else would.

I channeled quintessence, taking the shimmering white substance of my soul and forming it into a different shape. I finished my work just as the pyr reached me. They lacked bodies, but from their amorphous shapes reached appendages eerily similar to arms and hands.

But I had a weapon now. I'd formed my quintessence into a spear, one pulsating with light and infused with all my bleak emotions. I stabbed upward and pierced through one. Though its body seemed as insubstantial as a cloud, I felt resistance to the spearhead. A scream rent the air, and the pyr fled.

Two more remained. One, caught by my first attack, stayed at a distance, but the second caught me in its grip. It was my turn to shriek. A flood of fragmented emotions and memories poured through me, most of them not my own. I struggled to keep ahold of myself and raised my spear before I brought it stabbing down.

This pyr lasted no longer than the first. At the touch of the spear's point, the spirit released its hold and fled.

There was no time to celebrate, for the third remained undeterred. Before it could catch me, I stabbed upward and caught it like a fish on a harpoon. The sharp point cut into its substance, and it took off after the others, wailing without words.

My enemies driven off, I staggered back and let my spear fall to my side. My companions had all fared well; Talan was helping Xaron and Isidora drive off the last three. He, too, appeared to be channeling quintessence, but in a twister that banished rather than harmed the spirits. As the final pyr fled, the former Guilder glanced back at me and grinned. I returned the smile, wondering if he could see my gratitude wafting around me.

Then I remembered that not all had fought so valiantly to

protect us. Turning, I faced Azhi. The apothecary still glowed with his possession. His face appeared blank to me.

"Next time," I said, "I'd like to see you fight with us."

He nodded, though I wasn't sure it was the answer I was looking for. My anger grew tighter. Before I could think of what to say, however, our guide walked past me.

"Come quickly," he said. "We must flee the city before more find us."

Though I didn't breathe air in the Pyrthae, I exhaled my frustration. He was right; we needed to go, and not just to leave before the daemons regained their courage. Famine roared in the distant east. Though he was hundreds of miles away, I heard it and felt it in the pit of my stomach.

Grimacing, I followed our guide, hoping once more he wasn't leading us astray.

The buildings crowded close and dark around us. We hurried, as if thieves waited in every alley. I kept an eye on the world above us, watching for both daemons and for what occurred in the city we'd left behind. Some commonfolk appeared to be running, though with time slowed, every stride took several of ours to complete. I wondered what they sought to escape and feared for them.

The walls appeared ahead and above us as we reached the end of deme Gate. As expected, the portcullis was closed.

"What now?" I asked pointedly of Azhi. My temper hadn't cooled.

He didn't answer, but crouched slightly, then leaped into the air. Defying all natural laws, he kept ascending until he fell lightly on the top of the wall. There, he turned back and glanced down at us.

"You must learn how to move here if we are to make good time," he called. "Will yourself into the air. Believe, and it will be so."

My anger flared again. "And what about those who cannot channel?"

"Even they may defy their bodies' limitations."

I realized that must be true. Hadn't I done exactly that when I first came here through a rift? Yet now that I knew more of the Pyrthae and channeling, ignorance could no longer lend me a helping hand. I closed my eyes, forced away my doubts, and tried to believe as Azhi had instructed.

I can reach the top of the wall. I am weightless. I will rise.

I crouched, following our guide's example. I ignored the cries of dismay and joy from my companions, concentrating only on my own thoughts. Then, when my belief was iron-clad in my mind, I leaped.

When my feet had not touched the ground for several moments, I opened my eyes.

Oedija hung below as well as above me. I drifted upward, though with every passing second, my momentum slowed. The top of the wall was a dozen cubits below me and a score ahead.

My chest seized. I felt myself begin to drop as my belief in my buoyancy crumbled. Desperate, I tried to cling to it, but it had eroded too far.

I crashed to the ground.

The landing was painful, but much less than it would have been in Telae. I heard my companions crying out to me, but I couldn't attend to them. Clenching my jaw, I stood. My legs weren't broken; they didn't even seem capable of breaking here. If anything, it was my quintessence that had taken a hit, the glow emanating from my form dampened.

I waved to the others, some of who had already reached the wall, then readied a second attempt. Talan, Xaron, and Kari had achieved it, so I knew I could as well.

The belief came to me easier now. When I was ready, I made another leap, my eyes open all the while. I set my gaze upon the wall and willed myself toward it. To my surprise, I drifted upward — until my shock again began eroding my will. Ready for it, I managed to repair it enough to float toward the wall until, at last, I touched down.

Talan and Xaron were on either side of me as soon as I landed. "Are you hurt?" the former Guilder asked, even as Xaron exclaimed, "I'm surprised your legs aren't snapped in half!"

"I don't think we really have legs here," I noted wryly, then reached out to press Talan's hand. "I'm fine. Don't worry."

Touch was strange here in the Pyrthae, I now discovered. Just as the boundaries of our bodies had eroded, so had the distance between our souls. I was tempted to delve into him, as I once had. To see his memories, his thoughts, his feelings...

I jerked back and saw he looked as startled as me. We both turned our heads aside. I wondered if he had been as curious as I at that sharing. If a part of him had wanted to let down his guard and merge.

Azhi spoke, drawing my attention back to him. "The Pyrthae is not like your world. The material has been made spiritual; your flesh has become like your soul. They share more alike than you know." He paused, cocking his head to one side, then shook it and continued. "I will explain more later. For now, we must go, before we are attacked again."

I looked to the others to find them nodding before I inclined my own head. Nomusa and Corin were just reaching the top, both opting to climb rather than try to fly. For now, it seemed sufficient.

As Azhi turned away, I followed him and didn't look back at the city. We'd already abandoned Oedija to its fate. This was only the last step.

I couldn't cry here; my form had no tears or moisture. I was glad for it. I held my chin high as we headed east, the call of Famine's hunger pulsating ever within me, beckoning me onward to my inevitable end.

INTERLUDE I

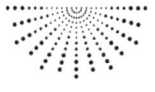

JAXAS

Jaxas Wreath, the Despot of Oedija, gazed over his city to those beyond the walls who would destroy it.

The fields had come alive with soldiers, blackening the landscape like an infestation of rats. It was only the vanguard of the Avvadin armies, yet already they were impressive to behold. Two thousand cavalry had led the way and begun cutting off trade routes and harrying any who had dared to remain outside the walls. The sky darkened with the smoke from the farmhouses they burned.

More intimidating still was the smaller regiment leading the horsemen. The Damask Esir, evident from their blood-red garb, had already proven their prowess in a skirmish with an Oedijan taxoi, killing two militiamen for every one of theirs who fell, even though they'd been outnumbered. They fought like devils possessed them — and if his intelligence was correct, they did.

But the worst was still to come.

The infantry. The siege weapons. The Silks and the Tefra. Enemies numerous as the stars in the sky. Jaxas had marshaled a force of eight thousand, but it wasn't nearly enough, nor were they trained half as well as the meanest member of the Kahin-Shah's military. And what could he do against spirits who couldn't be killed, who had magnetic allure and stole souls with a touch? Even his small battalion of Watchers possessed no weapon that could harm them.

He closed his skeletal hands into fists and shut his eyes. *We cannot match them.* He'd always known it. Yet, with the desperate optimism that had carried him through life, that had allowed him to believe in Asileia long after she'd gone mad, to seize the Evergreen Wreath without believing himself evil — still, he'd carried on. Though he would never say it aloud, Jaxas knew he was clever, even devious when need called for it. He'd hoped the seeds he'd planted in the people near him might bear fruit.

But now, Kelena reported they had abandoned him.

Airene. Nomusa. Xaron. Isidora. Four he had welcomed onto his Council, who had shown nothing but stout hearts and sound minds. Who had sacrificed everything to do what was right.

Or so he'd thought.

Now, he wondered if it had only been a desperate bid for their own gain. They'd been penniless and on the run when he swept them up. Xaron had been a feral warden evading the Shepherds, destined for execution. He'd thought being their savior would bind them to him.

It seemed he, however, had been the one taken advantage of.

Jaxas turned from the balcony and went inside his solar. He ignored Feiyan, who tried to engage him in a discussion, and strode down the hall toward a worn door at the end. Without knocking, he turned the key and stepped inside, closing the door behind him as he entered.

Myron Wreath looked over from where he'd been staring out the window.

Jaxas studied the changes in his uncle. He'd always had a generous head of hair, but now it thinned at his pate. His eyes, once incisive, were unfocused and wandering. He wondered what thoughts the former monarch had now, if he cursed his nephew in his moments of clarity. Though, to his knowledge, Myron had never come awake enough to comprehend the switch in stations.

"Uncle. How are you?"

Myron stared at Jaxas as he spoke, but turned away before replying. The aging man's gaze fell to his hands, which twitched now. That more than anything else placed a hard pit in Jaxas's stomach.

He walked up to stand next to his uncle. The man had all but raised him as a son.

Yet you betrayed him.

Jaxas tried not to listen to the whisper in the back of his head. What choice had he had? It was foolish to regret necessary actions.

"We're losing, Uncle," he murmured. "I am failing. How did you stand up under this burden?"

Even as he asked the question, he knew even the Myron of old would have no answers. He'd been the Despot in name only, never wielded the power and responsibility Jaxas did now.

He'd never faced their nation's annihilation.

"Oedija will starve, then be butchered. The people whose souls are not stolen will be enslaved. Our realm will fall."

He hadn't expected a response, and so was surprised when Myron looked up at him. Almost, the Despot's eyes seemed like they had of old.

"Do you believe that to be your destiny, Jaxas?" Myron's voice was pilled and worn now, but it retained some of the richness he had been known for. "Reach, and perhaps you will grasp what you seek. Clepsammia gives to those who strive."

The pit in Jaxas's gut grew larger. He was tired of hearing about Clepsammia, or any of the Eidola, for that matter.

"Of course, Uncle."

He left soon after. Yet as he closed Myron's door, Jaxas paused there, struck by a thought. Though the words had been flippant and disconnected from reality, they had contained a kernel of wisdom.

Reach.

Perhaps Oedija's fate was inevitable. Perhaps he would be the last Despot to fail their nation. But he refused to stop trying to save it until every avenue had been exhausted. No — he wouldn't stop even then.

Only death could conquer his will.

A grim smile stole over his lips as he entered back into his solar. Feiyan, who was bent over a correspondence, jerked her head up at his entrance, then seemed to notice his change in demeanor.

"Shall we continue?" she asked with an arched eyebrow.

Jaxas nodded, then set back to work.

14

THROUGH FOREIGN LANDS

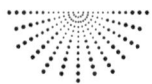

When traveling through foreign provinces, I am reminded of the comforts of home, and all the things taken for granted. From fare, to formalities, to even the flavor of the pests, there is much lost of one's native land.

Yet much is also gained. Wonder only exists in the foreign. I seek to claim it for my own.

- An Oedijan's Account of the Bali Ishakas; by Manenes of Gate, an itinerant scholar; 1140 SLP

We continued long into the night, only stopping when the glow of the Avvadin army's fires faded from view.

I was too burdened with emotion to be thankful when Azhi cut another rift out of the Pyrthae. My head felt numb; my body ached. My companions looked in much the same condition. The few conversations that started up had only to do with the logistics of setting up camp, and those were kept brief.

We had walked above the countless enemies facing our

homeland. We knew how little hope our people had of prevailing against them.

I at least had the comfort that most of my family was safe on a Wreath estate. Zipho, as good as kin to Nomusa, remained behind, as did Xaron's parents. I didn't know of Isidora's kin. For my part, Linos's fate weighed heavily on my mind.

I told myself we would return in time to help. It wasn't entirely out of the realm of possibility. We gained much time by traveling through the Pyrthae. If we only had to go to the Bali highlands and back, the siege might last long enough that we could return.

I tried not to think of how unlikely it was that I'd return at all.

Adding to my discomfiture was my lack of knowledge of the outdoors. I'd never spent a day outside of Oedija. A hum of anxiety threaded through me at the darkness that pressed in around us. Though Corin reassured us that wild animals would not disturb a party so large as ours, and Azhi suspected pyr wouldn't be an issue outside of Oedija, I still had the sense of being watched.

Making matters worse was the continual hunger filtering into me from my connection with Famine. As we ate our sparse meal of hardtack and salted fish, I kept my dissatisfaction to myself. I no longer dined at the Laurel Palace, able to feast any time of day that I wished.

Trying not to wallow in misery, I went to Azhi. The man didn't make for the best of conversationalists, yet there were many things left to discuss between us. The strangeness of the Pyrthae and the somberness of the siege had repressed my questions for a moment, but in the idleness of camp, they reemerged.

Our guide, however, evaded my queries once more. "We will discuss it in the morning," he begged off, and I reluctantly relented. His shoulders were slumped and his eyes hooded. Eazal was not a young man, nor had he ever looked strong. Whatever energy Azhi infused in him could not ward off his host's need for rest.

I volunteered for the first watch, knowing I would catch little sleep in my present mood. Soon I sat alone at the banked campfire, staring into the darkness. All three moons were out, but a layer of clouds, no doubt driven in by the monsoon winds, muted their light. I was swaddled in my chilling fears. My body throbbed from carrying my pack, and my head hurt from traveling through the Pyrthae.

The nightly sounds were foreign to me. The city was never quiet, but this was a different sort of cacophony. Bugs and birds called. Leaves and grasses shifted in the wind. I huddled my knees close to my chest and became marginally warmer. Perhaps they weren't malevolent sounds, but unfamiliar as they were, they might as well have been.

As much for a distraction as out of curiosity, I drew out the wrapped object I kept at my hip. Unwinding the cloth, I gripped Aika's knife by the hilt and held it up. Though it appeared orange from the dampened firelight, its glow betrayed how white it was. I tested its edge and found it sharp, gaining a slight cut on my finger for my interest. It was not as honed as steel, but felt more like bone, or perhaps wood.

I bent over it, examining it closer. Its texture was slightly porous and rough, like coral. What it was made of, I couldn't tell. A strange wood or stone from across the Lighted Sea? Or was it formed of the bones of some creature?

I let the knife fall back to my lap. I would not guess the answer. Perhaps it didn't even matter. I was grasping at straws, hoping one might be a rope that could enable me to escape the trap I found myself in.

Yet I had one avenue still left to explore. My locus was already open in case I needed to defend the camp, so it was simple enough to draw on quintessence. I emerged halfway into the Pyrthae again and marveled at the difference. When my body didn't enter it, but only my spirit, it was not nearly as disorienting, nor did I have the same strictures. Yet, remembering Azhi's earlier lesson on belief, I wondered how much of those differences were in my mind.

But that wasn't my concern now; I concentrated back on the task at hand. Staring down at the knife with Pyrthaen-vision, I nearly dropped it. A brilliant glow emanated from it, and while light could act peculiarly in the spirit realm, this was different.

Aika's knife gleamed like it contained quintessence. Like it was, in some way, alive.

I narrowed my focus, aware that I bent closer in the phys-ical world. My grasp on the nuances of quintessence was still elementary, knowing just enough to identify those wardens familiar to me by their distinct patterns. Yet there was some-thing to peering at the knife's quintessence that felt like staring at the surface of a well. I couldn't see beyond the surface, yet there seemed hidden depths to it... and some-thing familiar glimmering at the bottom.

"You make for a poor sentry, my Finch. Your eyes aren't even up."

I jerked upright and shut my locus as I whirled around. The abrupt changes disoriented me for a moment, but I already knew by the voice who had surprised me in the night.

"Talan," I greeted him softly.

The former Guilder folded with his easy grace onto the ground next to me, then leaned over to peer down at the artifact cradled in my hands. "The knife again?"

"With everything going on, I haven't really had a chance to look at it."

His smile told me he knew just how much that had grated on me. "And now?"

"Now, I was interrupted just as I found that chance."

Talan let out a low laugh. "Ah, Airene. You ever were a prickly rose."

My cheeks betrayed me, warming despite the chilly night. I ran a hand through my hair, suddenly aware of how disheveled it had become from our travels.

"You don't usually compare me to flowers," I said. The words sounded inane to my own ears.

For once, he didn't tease me about them. As I met his shadowed gaze, I found a stirring inside me I hadn't dared hope for again.

His words killed it.

"When you left me at the Silvencrest," said Talan, his voice gravelly and soft, "I thought you didn't want the same thing as I did. No, not thought — I *felt* it. My head knew your reasons were fair. My heart had different opinions. And with everything that happened in the Underguild..." He turned his head aside, and I saw by the firelight his jaw was clenched tight.

I repressed my fears and reached out to touch his hand, wrapping my fingers about it. I wished I didn't hold the knife just then, but I couldn't think of where else to put it. His gaze meeting mine pushed the distraction away.

Just when I needed them, words failed me. Then I realized I didn't need them after all.

I leaned forward and, closing my eyes, my lips found his.

We lingered there for several long moments, softly appreciating one another. I was suddenly warmed through. I longed to wrap my arms around him and kiss him deeper still.

He pulled away first, cupping my cheek with one hand. His callouses rubbed against my skin. I didn't mind.

"One of us must keep watch," Talan murmured. "And I fear I shall not be able to sleep now."

A laugh bubbled out of me. "And you think I will?"

For once, his smirk became a full-lipped grin. He jerked

his head toward the shelter where I was to sleep with Nomusa. "Best go, cr neither of us will."

Heart pattering, I rose before I lacked the strength to. Words swelled in my chest, but I could not say them.

"Good night," was all I murmured before fleeing, the artifact clutched in my hand all but forgotten.

15
HOMECOMING

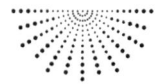

Though the Bali peoples are largely peaceful, they are not without their conflicts. Dynasties rise and fall with surprising regularity. As recently as ten years ago, the Yondali ishaka endured such an event, where all of the previous leader's family was killed, as is the tradition for such uprisings. Famously, half a century ago, the Zakale, now known as the Unnamed, also suffered such a change in leadership, when the twin brothers Yama and Lophe attempted to conquer all the highlands.

- An Oedijan's Account of the Bali Ishakas; by Manenes of Gate, an itinerant scholar; 1140 SLP

We entered the Pyrthae before dawn struck, and thus began our daily cycle.

The days blurred together, as did the dual planes of matter and spirit. After transitioning between Telae and Pyrthae repeatedly, I anticipated it would become easier. Once more, my hopes were thwarted. Every evening was spent in weary dissolution, vaguely ill from the day's travel. Our spirits dragged through deeper mires than those we were forced to camp in. Our appearances matched our internal states, becoming increasingly disheveled the longer we went without baths.

Yet there were brighter angles. Talan and I regained our warmth of the past, and added to it a fresh closeness. Sometimes, I felt like an adolescent again, burning with self-conscious desire. We had little time to make good on it, nor privacy.

But the kisses were all the sweeter for being stolen.

I tried not to think about what would come after we reached our destination. Tried not to feel the guilt I knew I should. I went to my death; no one had any delusions about that. Talan knew as well as anyone. He could make his own decisions.

But does he know it?

I tried to remember if I'd told him of my fate and couldn't recall any particular instance. Though I tried to dismiss the worry, it wouldn't keep quiet.

Shouldn't you protect him, if you can?

I had no answers. All I knew was I couldn't resist our daily dalliances, nor did I wish to.

A more ambiguous boon also affected me. Famine's hunger was growing stronger; whether from the closing distance or his waxing strength, I couldn't tell. Yet with it came an escalation of my vitality. The pack, which had cut into my shoulders and set my back aching, seemed lighter with each day. Even after the long marches, I could barely keep still, filled with an anxious energy like I were about to make a speech before a crowd. By the darting glances from the others, they noticed my agitation, but no one commented on it. Likely, they suspected the cause.

The landscapes of both planes shifted around us with our progress. Our route took us south of the Askorpi Range and through the Pagore Wilderness, places I'd seen on maps but never imagined I would visit. We reached a river, and I guessed it to be the source of the Walano River, which ran past Oedija, many miles away.

The more familiar land features shifted as we continued. The foliage grew thicker, the ground wetter, the land rising in cliffs and falling in canyons. Green dominated the world, though colors shifted in the Pyrthae. Water became almost a constant sound, whether from rain, rivers, or waterfalls. Though it seemed to flow, a touch revealed it to be nothing more than an imitation.

On the seventh day of our journey, we emerged from a dense thicket to see a rise in the land. At last, our destination was at hand. As we were in the Pyrthae, the landscape doubled and became even more impressive for it. I had always known great plateaus dominated the Bali highlands, but it was entirely different to experience it. Even more than the snow-capped mountains of the Askorpi had, they stole my breath away — or would have, had I the need to breathe in the spirit realm. Something about the domineering cliffs and the verdant landscape spoke of a paradise I'd never known existed.

I looked at Nomusa, and I saw in her expression my own feelings amplified. Underlying them was a deep sorrow, the fear and nostalgia of an exile's return. I ached for her, my Pyrthaen body almost vibrating with it.

"Home," she whispered.

I think our entire party heard, and most had the decency not to respond. Azhi, however, proved to be the exception.

"We will exit here and plan our approach. I trust we will have to go in secret." He looked at Nomusa now, not disguising his irritation.

His casual cruelty made me burn. While our guide tolerated everyone in our party, he'd never truly accepted them as necessary, believing they slowed us. Nomusa's situation, in his eyes, was evidence to support this belief.

But I knew better. Without my friends surrounding and supporting me, I wouldn't be able to do what I must. If the price was being a friend in return to them, it was one I would willingly pay.

"We will," I said shortly, then cut a path back to Telae. I'd practiced the technique as often as I could, enough to achieve a tear on the first attempt.

Exiting the Pyrthae always came as a relief. The moistness in the air surprised me, immediately beading on my skin. The day was bright even though there was a thin layer of clouds overhead. The weather and the sky had almost become strangers; I was growing used to having the ground doubled and suspended overhead.

We settled into our routines for setting up camp. I tried to ignore the small spats that inevitably started up. Though we mostly got along, Xaron and Talan often took issue with each other, and Nomusa was liable to be annoyed at anyone who got in her way.

Under other circumstances, I didn't doubt I would have joined in. But concerns about who carried their fair share of work seemed petty with death awaiting me.

When we gathered again and munched on our lackluster rations, I spoke. "He still lies eastward. North somewhat, too."

Azhi nodded. "That is what I sense as well. The distance is still significant, though closing. But I do not think he is on the Yorandu plateau."

"So we will bypass it." Nomusa's tone was carefully composed, a fact not lost on the others. Despite snapping at her earlier, Xaron cast her a sympathetic look. Even Talan's callous amusement seemed to lessen.

Azhi, on the other hand, remained merciless. "Yes. We will rest here, then travel until we reach the end of the plateau. It may take a full day's walk, but we cannot risk being delayed by being captured."

No one disagreed, and so the plan was set. The sun hung in the sky, yet under the thick canopy, it was almost dark. I lay down next to Nomusa, eyes drifting closed and thoughts dozing, when she spoke.

"I miss it. Home."

Sleepily, I reached out and took her hand. "I know."

We fell asleep that way, neither of us letting go.

~

WHEN A DEEPER GLOOM fell over our camp, Azhi woke us. Once more, we packed and entered the Pyrthae.

I was drowsy when I tottered under my pack through the rent in the material world. But as soon as I emerged into the Pyrthae, my body buzzed with fresh energy. Some of it was the mere feeling of the place. The greater part was the stronger pull of Famine. He was feasting again, and with each soul he consumed, a shiver of pleasure ran through me. I felt soiled for experiencing joy at such a horrid thing, though I knew the sin wasn't mine.

We hurried on, ascending the landscape in a way we never could have in Telae. Even those unattuned in our party formed their belief strong enough to at least scramble up the side of the cliffs. Corin struggled the most, her straightforward mind having difficulty contradicting the rules of Telae.

Nomusa had her own troubles. I tried to disguise my smugness at this, for much came easily to her in our former lives. By her sharp look my way, I did a poor job of hiding it.

True to Azhi's word, the journey went through the night and into the day. I wondered how much further the plateau could stretch when I saw signs of the trees thinning. Hopeful at any change, knowing the plateau beyond should be barren and arid, I peered closer at the sky to see what lay ahead and was surprised to find a city emerging from the wilderness. We had seen the occasional domicile, but nothing more.

Mtani, it was, the capital of the Yorandu ishaka, telling by our direction and its size. A glance at Nomusa showed her homesickness had worsened. I reached out to her, but in the Pyrthae, touch didn't hold the same comfort. I withdrew almost as soon as we made contact; her memories cut too deeply.

We traveled through the city, and I stared at the strange buildings surrounding us. They simultaneously seemed to battle against nature and integrate with it. Vines crept over thatched roofs and around circular walls, their leaves mostly green, but some in startling shades of red and violet. Most homes were single-storied chambers, but the larger ones sprawled in a series of connecting circles. The streets were paved with boards more often than stones. Feathers, horns, and beads hung from the eaves in homemade ornamentation.

A glance above showed the people to whom the city belonged. They thronged the streets, many laughing as they passed one another. Almost, it seemed like a village rather than a city. I smiled at the sight. If most were like Komo and Nomusa, I would have been glad to meet more of the Yorandu.

What could only be the Shaka's manor rose from the center of the city, the view of it clear from anywhere we walked. It sat atop a hill, and its compound sprawled across it. At the bottom, a fence with jagged metal atop it warned against intruders. I caught Nomusa's gaze drifting toward it often. When she didn't mention it, I judged it best to keep my peace. Some things were easiest to endure when kept unspoken.

Beyond the manor, we came to a fenced grove. As I observed the plants within it, I thought I understood what we looked upon. They were trees, but of a variety I'd never seen before. Their trunks split low upon them into a sphere of branches, and each was thorny like the stem of a rose, but at such a large scale that each thorn was the size of a dagger.

If they were what I thought they were, they made for a curious thing to consider holy.

I turned to Nomusa to confirm my suspicions, but paused at her expression. "What? What is it?"

The others had stopped and looked at her as well. Nomusa shook her head. "This is an *isikhayha* grove... but they're all dead."

Looking at the strange trees again, I saw at once what she meant. Their limbs were dun and leafless, mere replicas of our world. They had no magic of their own.

"They're supposed to be partly spirit, aren't they?" I asked. "That's why their pyrkin have such strange properties. Like stopping a warden from channeling."

Nomusa nodded, still seeming in a daze. "I don't understand how this happened."

"You know who is behind it."

Azhi had come up on us. I skirted a step away, never wanting to be too near to him.

"Famine," Talan murmured.

The daemon nodded. "He is strong now, strong enough to overcome their defenses. He has feasted on this grove and grown stronger still. I would be surprised if any of the *isikhayhas* have survived."

Nomusa stared at the dead holy trees a moment longer, then turned her head aside. "We should continue," she muttered, then set off without waiting for a reply.

I stared at my friend's back, helpless to understand what this meant to her. It was a loss that I had no similar experience to. But I hated to see her in pain. If my presence was all the comfort I could offer, so be it.

I caught up with her, and we walked side by side in silence.

THE LIGHT WAS FADING by the time we passed through the other side of Mtani, and our party's energy flagged. But we hadn't yet reached the end of the plateau, so we pressed on, walking by the ethereal light that permeated the spirit realm.

Kari seemed most exhausted, sometimes stumbling so her sister had to catch her. Even Azhi showed signs of strain. Sometimes, I wondered if Eazal fought against his daemon host, as the man twitched in unnatural ways. I was the freshest of our company, though I found little solace in it, knowing the reason for it.

At last, we reached a long bridge that spanned the final divide. At first appearance, it seemed a precariously built thing, composed of taut ropes and boards that swayed with the Pyrthae's mimicry of wind. We approached it cautiously and tested each board before putting our weight on it. A silly precaution, perhaps; in theory, we had only to believe we could float to stop a fall. Yet as I peered over the ropes suspended as railings into the dark chasm below, I couldn't quite kill my natural fear.

I sighed in relief when we made it to the other end. But though we'd reached the Zakale plateau, where I assumed Famine must be, the march was not yet done. So close to the bridge, we risked discovery by Yorandu patrols, or even those from the neighboring ishakas, Yondali and Masu. We had to venture in deeper, beyond the reach of the jungle, to be protected.

The next day had long risen by the time we found the end of the foliage. The changes had come upon the land swifter than I'd expected. Within a mile, it transitioned from thick forest to barren desert, with scarcely a tree to be seen. A deep sense of unease threaded through me as I looked around at the endless expanse. I knew what was behind it — or rather, who.

Then I saw him.

Distances had a way of shifting in the Pyrthae. My vision saw nothing but blank horizon one moment; the next, it seemed to have lengthened so even far-off objects appeared much closer than they should have. Famine had been nothing more than a speck floating through the air before the shift occurred. He seemed more defined even than the last time I'd seen him, and almost bloated in his middle, like he'd swallowed an entire herd of cattle at once. I wondered what source of quintessence he'd possibly found to feast on in this forbidding land. I wondered if I truly wanted to know.

But, whether or not I willed it, I would discover it soon.

I didn't mention what I'd seen as we stepped out of the Pyrthae and into the blinding sunlight. Though the whole of the spirit realm was filled with light, the sun bothered my eyes. In stark contrast to when we'd exited before, the air was hot and dry.

Between the light and heat, sleep seemed impossible, yet we set up camp all the same. I lay down next to Nomusa atop my bedroll and sweated through my clothes under the canvas tent. A nervous energy coursed through me, and my mind circled back to the deed I must soon perform.

The deed. I would have laughed if not for Nomusa sleeping. The term was wholly inadequate for what I would soon have to do.

Neither fear nor self-pity kept me up for long. I had drifted off to a dreamless sleep when a sound hooked me and dragged me back out. Groggy, it took me a moment to register what it meant. But as Nomusa shot upright and darted a startled look at me, it finally registered.

A man had shouted, and not in a tongue I knew.

"He says to come out," Nomusa whispered. Her eyes were wide, her nostrils flared. "Be ready."

I had no need for the warning; my locus was already open, and Pyrthaen energies pressed against my fingertips.

The man yelled again, and we heard the shuffling noises of our companions leaving their shelters.

"Let's go see," I said to Nomusa, then led the way out into the blinding sunlight.

16
AN EXILE'S WELCOME

"Never leave a rival alive, or you will forever be known as a usurper. Death is not fair, least of all for the innocent and the young. But blood on the father's hands is passed to the daughter. The price must be paid."

- Charratta Yorandu Ibubesi, Shaka of the Yorandu; 1162 SLP

I wasn't surprised to see Bali warriors surrounding our camp. Even less so that they had us entirely at their mercy.

As they glowered at us, I observed them in turn. Their features and the cerulean tatu on their arms resembled Nomusa's, but there, the similarities ended. Like Shaka-Heir Komo and his retinue had worn, bronze collars covered most of their chests, though their bellies were left bare, and leather skirts hung just above their knees. Each had half their face painted green; war paint, as I understood the custom. Most carried spears, and knives were secured at their hips. A few held no weapons at all, and these I feared most. If Komo represented the prowess of Bali wardens, they would be difficult to overcome, especially when we were outnumbered four to one.

It didn't help that we had chosen a poor location for a battle. Hoping to evade detection, Corin had advised that we take refuge at the bottom of a basin, a sandstone cliff sheltering our tents. That ridge was now occupied by archers, their arrows nocked, points trained at our hearts.

I glanced at Nomusa. Her face had transformed into hard planes as she stared up at her kinsmen, yet it seemed a shallow mask. I trembled to think about what lay beneath it. If she feared them, what chance did we have?

One of the Bali warriors spoke, and I realized I understood him. Though his sea-tongue was heavily accented, his meaning was clear.

"You are a strange group." He scanned us with a baleful gaze, his thick beard making his expression even more severe. "Oedijans, are you not?"

A moment of silence passed as we looked at each other. I expected Nomusa to answer, but when she only continued to stare, I spoke up.

"Yes. We're from Oedija."

The warrior didn't answer for a long moment, but only continued to study us. "And yet you are here," he said at last.

I opened my mouth, then hesitated. How much should I admit of our purpose? But the Yorandu were allied with Oedija now, and secrets wouldn't get us far. And Famine feasted; I felt it in my bones as his satiation fluttered through me. We couldn't afford any delay.

I swallowed before speaking. "We don't mean to intrude, but our mission is urgent. We're hunting something dangerous. A... daemon." *A god* seemed too grandiose to win us anything but laughter. "He's near, on this very plateau. We were going to reach him today to... handle him."

The warrior's expression did not change for all my farfetched words. His followers, however, exchanged looks with raised eyebrows. I kept my eyes on the leader, willing him to believe, wishing I could channel to convince him. But with their wardens possibly able to sense it, I didn't dare.

When the silence prolonged, and my companions glanced at me with increasing alarm, I spoke again. "What is your name?"

I didn't expect the warrior to answer and was surprised when he did.

"Khoda Yorandu Ayize."

Nomusa stirred. "Ayize," she murmured, as if in recognition.

Ayize looked at her again, eyes narrowed. I decided to head off any inconvenient questions. "Well met, Ayize. I'm Airene of Port." I wondered if I should introduce my party, then thought better of it. Best to avoid the matter than be forced to lie about Nomusa's identity. "We understand we are trespassing, and regret that we were forced to, but—"

Ayize cut off my babbling. "How did you come here? Our borders are guarded and patrolled, the bridge watched. If you are headed into the Desolate, you cannot have come from that way."

He waited, expectant. I wished someone would help me. It was perplexing that he deigned to speak to me at all. My experience with Bali showed them to speak to their kinsmen when present instead of addressing foreigners. But it was growing difficult to answer his questions. My gaze drifted to Talan, but he only shrugged.

Repressing a sigh, I resigned myself to the truth. "We came through the Pyrthae."

That finally provoked a reaction. Ayize's bushy eyebrows rose, and murmurs erupted from his followers. As the leader raised a hand, I flinched, fearing the worst, but it was only a gesture for silence.

"Oedija does not have wardens," the warrior said slowly. "Not ones without chains."

"It does." Talan finally came to my rescue, though I wasn't sure I wanted more attention drawn to his smirk. "Most of us before you are wardens, having hidden under the Shepherds' noses for years. But that has changed." The former Guilder jerked his head in Xaron and Isidora's direction. "They're both part of the warden division the new Despot's established. Even part of his inner Council, so I hear."

It took an effort not to chew my lip as I waited for Ayize's response. He looked over each of us again, as if hoping to see one of us break and expose what we'd said as a lie.

Then his eyes settled on Nomusa, and my stomach sank.

"You are familiar," he said. "You seem a kinswoman. You know our tongue. Yet you speak like an Oedijan."

Nomusa flinched. I knew how it must hurt to be seen as an outsider among her own people. Still, I pleaded silently for her to lie. *Don't make your stand. Not here. Not now.*

Her chin lifted high, and I knew what she would say before the words left her mouth.

"I am Eshalo Yorandu Nomusa. My father was the Shaka of our people before he was betrayed and murdered. I am the rightful Heir."

No one was silent then. Some warriors shouted, their weapons bristling. My locus had been open, and now I flooded my body with radiance and kinesis. Violence seemed inevitable now, little as any of us could afford it.

"*Silence!*" Ayize bellowed, and all fell quiet at once.

The leader gave his warriors one last hard look, then gazed back down on Nomusa. "So. You survived."

My friend was like a drawn bow herself, every muscle taut. "I alone did."

He nodded, as if it was the answer he expected. "I supported your father, Nomusa-sha. I grieved to see your family slain."

"And yet you serve the usurper."

I couldn't keep silent, not while she struck aside his

concession. "Of course he does, Nomusa. What would you have him do, die? Go into exile?"

She cast me as furious a glare as I'd ever seen from her. But I preferred her rage be directed at me than those who might kill us — or so I told myself, as I withered with hurt.

"No," said Ayize. "You are right to be angry, Heir Exile. You have been wronged by all Yorandu, even by those who do not wish it."

My surprise was almost sufficient for me to forget Nomusa's anger. Nomusa seemed just as astonished, her mouth parted as she stared up at the warrior.

The Bali muttered again, and more than one wore mutinous looks. Yet Ayize's authority had not eroded so much that they didn't fall silent at a gesture.

"But past wrongs do not change present duty. I must take you before Shaka Ibubesi to face his judgment. He rules the Yorandu and has for nearly two decades. I will not risk another war of succession."

"*Fareshi* coward," Nomusa hissed through clenched teeth.

Ayize flinched, but didn't rise to the goad. "But... for a time, our goals may align. You say you hunt a daemon."

My pulse quickened. "We do."

"In a sense, so do we. And as our quarry lies in the same direction as yours, I wonder if our enemies are not the same." Ayize turned his gaze aside then — toward Famine, I recognized.

My companions looked as confused as I was on this point. Then Kari murmured, just loud enough to catch, "The trees..."

The realization struck me. "The *isikhayhas*. You hunt the one responsible for their wilting."

Fresh mutters started up again, though of a different timbre than following Nomusa's revelation. My friend turned back to look at me, her stare a warning without the need for words. I only spared her a glance. I still held hope that the gamble would pay off.

Ayize frowned now. "How could you know this? It happened two days ago, and the news was kept quiet."

We had come this far, and the warrior seemed as reasonable a man as we could expect to get. I pressed further.

"It is as I said before: we came here through the Pyrthae. We saw the trees, dead and brown, as we passed. And we knew the daemon we hunt must be behind it."

The warriors had begun to yell in their tongue to Ayize, and by Nomusa's expression, they were not words of support. They did not entirely quiet as the leader gestured again for them to cease.

"This daemon," he said to me, the word seeming unfamiliar in his mouth. "Is it named?"

I swallowed and nodded. "Taozu, he is known to the Qao Fu. Famine, we call him. But here, he was once known as the Serpent God."

Pandemonium broke out. I braced to channel as Bali warriors shouted — to protest my assertions, I was certain. My companions flinched as well, and I sensed their readiness to fight by their stances: the flexing of their fingers and hands, the reaching for weapons.

"*Quiet, all of you!*"

I didn't think they would listen this time. As it was, it took them a lot longer to comply than duty dictated. But as each fell under their leader's glower, they lapsed into sullen silence.

"They speak the truth!" said Ayize, and relief flooded through me so powerfully my knees went weak. He continued speaking in our sea-tongue, though he addressed his warriors. "Their story stretches my understanding, yet I cannot fault a word. Are we so confident as to spurn allies? Do we know our enemy so well as to deafen our ears?"

Logic seemed to suffice where authority had floundered.

The warriors looked no happier, but most seemed placated, at least for the moment.

Ayize turned back to stare down at Nomusa. "We will join your hunt, for it is the same as ours." As we reeled from this inexplicable change of heart, he continued. "When it is finished, however, you must settle our other business. Nomusa-sha, you will come with us to be presented to Shaka Ibubesi and await his verdict."

I almost couldn't bring myself to look at Nomusa. Our lives and our mission were in her hands now, and she had shown little inclination to cooperate. I only breathed again as she nodded.

"Fine."

Ayize studied her a moment longer, then turned away. "Come. The hunt continues."

My head spun, but no more than the warriors' must. I firmed my will and looked at my companions, bafflement and relief battling for supremacy over their faces. I could only shrug.

"Guess we'd better follow," I said, and with that, we did.

17

THE RED LAKE

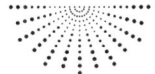

Our hands trembled, yet we made the cuts. Every man, woman, and child sent before us, we put to the knife.

How could we do otherwise? Our God demanded it. His thirst is slaked by blood; his hunger, by spirit.

He must be fed, lest he feasts upon us.

- *Tales of the Desolate, uncensored; 1092 SLP*

So it was that our strange company grew stranger as we joined forces with the Yorandu warriors.

We packed up our camp, but left our rucksacks there in the basin. Famine was not far ahead, and with the war party almost unladen, it was the only way we could keep up and be ready for a fight. Ayize waited until we came after him, then wordlessly turned away.

I puzzled over the warrior's change of heart for a long time before I mustered the courage to ask. Ignoring my companions' hushed questions, I wove between his scowling fighters and found my way to the man's side.

Ayize didn't seem one prone to preambles, so I gave him none. "What changed your mind?"

He glanced at me sidelong, but didn't answer until we began descending the next rocky slope. The land grew more foreboding with each step into it. I readily believed the fearsome reputation the Wumofu had gained for being entirely inhospitable to life.

"You know of the Serpent God," he said. "Do you know of its worshippers?"

I shrugged. "Some." A moment later, it occurred to me what he was saying. "But I thought they existed during the civil war."

"They have always existed in the shadows. Lophe and Yama showed that the" — Ayize struggled to find the right word — "the great spirit could confer great power, if it wished. Others have craved that, especially the desperate."

"But Famine has been caged since then. He..." I struggled to find a concise way to explain all I knew, then abandoned the attempt. "I don't think he's given many others power since."

"No," Ayize agreed. "But it does not keep the foolish from madness. And now that he reigns again, those who have clung to the beliefs have flocked back."

He paused, his jaw spasming. Knowing a hard confession when I saw one, I contented myself with waiting.

At last, he spoke. "They have been stealing people. Women and children mostly, but men as well. All who are vulnerable."

My stomach churned. "Why? You can't force people to believe in..." I trailed off, remembering something I had read in the book on the Bali civil war. "Tyurn's balls. They're sacrificing them, aren't they?"

Ayize's expression resembled a thundercloud. "We do not know; none have returned. But if they live, we will retrieve them."

Children. He'd said they took children. I had to swallow to keep the contents of my belly down, even as anger flared through me.

"How many cultists are there?"

"Not many. By their tracks, two dozen at most."

"Are they wardens?"

Ayize didn't answer, by which I guessed he didn't know this, either.

"The *isikhayhas* were the final sign," he said at last. "We knew it must be connected, for they have survived beyond our history." He paused, and I saw he was choked with emotion. I realized then just how little I understood of the Bali's relationship with their sacred trees. Their deaths were worse than their people's, as hard as it was for me to believe.

"We will make them pay," I said, hoping it was true.

I fell back soon after, though not before Ayize questioned me in turn. I explained what I could. That one who had kept Famine at bay had failed. That we had ways to stop the daemon god, if we could get to him before he broke into our world. Ayize didn't indicate if he believed me, but only nodded, a man taking in information to make his own judgments. I could respect that, as it had always been my practice as well. I only hoped our conclusions would align.

After filtering back through his warriors, who still had not warmed to me, I fell in line beside my companions. Nomusa, who kept as far from her kinsmen as she could, drifted close enough to hear, though not without a resentful look at the backs ahead of her.

In brief, I caught them up on what I'd gleaned. They had a dozen questions I couldn't answer: Were the cultists attuned to the Pyrthae? How were they armed? Would we attack with the Yorandu? When I threw up my hands time and again, they finally relented.

"Glad we're walking into a fight blind," Xaron muttered, loud enough for all to hear. I didn't rise to the bait, seeing his nervousness by the fluttering of his fingers, and Isidora's reassuring hand intertwining with his.

Talan sidled up next to me. "Stay close to me," he muttered. "Don't enter the fight unless you have to. Promise me, Airene."

I nodded, knowing he wouldn't be dissuaded, even as I churned with guilt. Only then did my part in the mission come back to me.

As if summoned by my thoughts, Azhi came up on my other side. Talan frowned, but moved away at my request. I glanced at the possessed man and felt I could almost see the boy spirit peering out of his eyes. I looked away again.

"It is almost time."

I didn't ask what he meant. We both knew.

"Yes," I whispered.

"You will still do it? Offer him your spirit and body, and so bind him?"

"Yes."

The word trembled as it left my lips. When the time had been far off, I'd kept the fear at bay. There had always been another leg of our journey to tackle, another distraction. Almost, I'd let myself forget the fate that awaited me when, at last, we caught up to Famine.

I couldn't forget it now.

Azhi's gaze was hard on me though, so I willed my expression to smoothness. "Just..." I didn't know quite what I wanted to say, only that I needed something, some assurance, from this ally I still did not entirely trust. "Don't make it a waste."

"I won't."

I glanced down at the sash around his middle, and the scepter tucked into it. How he would use it, I still didn't know. But I didn't even understand Aika's knife and how to be a Sacrifice with certainty. We were all flailing in the dark, hoping our attacks would land against the monster stalking us.

I forced my mind to other thoughts, lest my courage fail.

"Take care of them. Make sure they return home. And when it's over, you'll release Eazal, won't you?"

"Of course. I have always intended to."

Did he answer one question and not the other? I didn't have the heart to ask. With a tight nod, I branched my path from his.

Xaron swiftly closed in. "What does he want?"

"The same as all of us: to cage Famine."

I couldn't meet his eyes. Xaron knew, just as Nomusa and Azhi did. For once, he didn't speak, but only put an arm around my back.

It was enough to keep me going.

ONE OF THE scouts who had gone ahead returned, his expression grave.

The time had come.

Ayize ordered his warriors into formation, then turned to our company. "Nomusa-sha, I trust you and your companions know best how to use your strengths." His eyes slid over to me, then the others. "Be sure not to cross our line of fire, or I cannot protect you."

Nomusa answered something in their tongue, and Ayize's eyes narrowed. Suspecting her words to be less than kind, I hastened to say, "We won't interfere. We'll have our hands full with the Serpent."

The Bali warrior scrutinized me, no doubt wondering what we possibly intended to do to stop a deity. "Trees' blessing," was all he said before turning away.

Their warriors led the way. Daylight had begun to fail, so it was simple enough to identify where the cultists lay by the glow of their campfires. I opened myself to the Pyrthae and filled myself with the energetic elements, if only for the comfort of them. My companions might have been miles away for all the reassurance they brought me. I shivered, though I couldn't truly be cold when filled with radiance.

"Airene?"

So absorbed was I with my misery, I hadn't noticed Talan come close. I tried to muster a smile and failed.

He took my arm and pulled me to a stop, looking into my eyes one at a time. I was reminded of the intimacy we had shared and ached knowing we never would again. It made me want to turn aside from him, but stopped short, not wishing to arouse his suspicion.

Then he said the words I'd long feared. "You've told me everything, haven't you? About Famine?"

I desperately wanted to swallow, but he would notice the nervous gesture. My voice croaked as I spoke. "Yes. I'm just… afraid."

That much was true. His gaze softened, and he pulled me into a tight embrace.

"I won't let anything happen to you," he murmured, so certain I almost believed him.

The others had halted with us, and as Azhi neared, I knew we had to continue. "We're coming," I said, avoiding his studying gaze and following the war party.

Then all conversation ceased, for by a signal from one of the forward warriors, the final ridge was at hand. We passed by a still body; a cultist on watch, I guessed. A hint of blood lingered in the dry air, too pungent to belong to only one corpse. In complete silence, Ayize directed his warriors to line the ridge and ready their weapons. Over the hammering of my heart, I heard the people below, some laughing, others crying.

With my throat closed almost too much to breathe, I peered over the cliff to the basin below.

A rudimentary camp sprawled across the sandy ground. Tents nestled against the foot of the cliff and around it to where the ridge descended toward the basin in a crescent shape. There was a score of the shelters, and though the hour was growing late, their occupants appeared to all be outside of them.

The cultists were dressed like Ayize's warriors, but with horrifying changes. Some had barely healed scars and fresh cuts that seemed too measured to be accidentally accrued. Others had red tatu of serpents, dragons, and other terrifying creatures overlaying those of their original ishakas. Bones poked through their flesh in places, even on their faces, giving the sense that they were barely human at all. They leaped and danced and swayed, the many campfires at their backs casting dancing shadows across their bodies to make them appear more alien still.

But it was the pit around which they danced that terrified me most of all.

Bodies hung head-first off the edges of the pit. Their necks seemed to have been cut, for scarlet streaks leaked from them into the pit. Enough blood had collected to fill the bottom, the pool dark and still.

Dozens, maybe even a hundred, all dead and drained.

My stomach bucked and churned, and I had to swallow back my bile. What kind of people could do this? What evil possessed them? I felt Famine's influence; I was his gods-damned Seed. But never had I had an inclination to do *this*.

I hadn't come here to kill cultists. But if it came to that, I found myself more than willing.

Another feeling pulled at my attention. There was something else, something more than the horrors of the cultists below. A hidden presence that reveled in the atrocities.

I channeled quintessence and peered into the Pyrthae. And there he was.

Famine filled the sky, brilliant and pearlescent in his ink-dark, sinuous body. He seemed more distinct than before, the features sharper, like a painting twice drawn over. He had grown as well, swelling to double his size, and he'd never been small. If left to his own designs, he would soon stretch across all the city of Oedija.

He didn't seem to notice me, for he writhed around a thin, chalky cloud that filtered around him. *Quintessence.* I sensed it with the same revulsion that I'd smelled the blood. This was not only death, but eradication. Nothing would exist of those sacrificed once he consumed their spirits.

The thought awoke the anger I needed.

Though he didn't pay me heed, I felt him. His hunger and satiation wracked me, body and soul. The elation it filled me with sickened me. At least I didn't feel the wild abandon to give myself to him I had before.

A scream split the air.

As I oriented back to Telae, I saw the first arrow fly. More yells followed, both of pain and rage. Silhouettes seethed in the night all around me.

The violence had begun.

The end approached.

18

AN OFFERING OF BLOOD

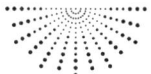

I must give to him what he seeks, but also the agent by which to bind him. Spirit, to placate his endless hunger; blood, to anchor him in our world; body, by which I gain power over him.

- The journal of Vusumuzi; date unknown

R adiance filled the sky.

I flinched as one of the nearby Yorandu warriors was blasted back, able to do nothing but watch as he fell to the ground, screaming and burning. Some of our enemies, at least, were wardens.

But this wasn't my fight. I had to live long enough to fulfill my purpose.

My companions shouted at me, but I ignored them and scampered along the ridge. I had to get closer, as close as I could to where Famine loomed, before I did what I had to do. I had to draw his attention. Or did I only have to say his name?

Do it! part of myself screamed. *Why do you wait?*

I ignored the voice and raced down the rise, tripping and only just keeping my feet under me. With kinesis at my toes, every step sprang me forward farther, and soon I neared the bottom.

Four figures emerged from around boulders before me; cultists, I saw at once. Their target was plain, for I'd left the Yorandu warriors behind. I barely had time to ready my sorcery before they struck.

I spun as flames scorched the air where I'd been. Gaining my feet, I threw up kinesis in a wave. I'd underestimated how much my strength had grown. The deluge crumbled the stone as it barreled forth and sent the cultists flying backwards a dozen paces. They screamed in the air, then fell abruptly silent as they landed with bone-crunching force on the hard ground.

I didn't wait to see if any would rise, but kept running, only glancing over my shoulder to ensure no one followed.

"Airene!"

Talan's cry cut through me. I staggered, then kept moving forward without looking back. My vision blurred as tears stung my eyes. I couldn't stop, couldn't hesitate, or I might never start again.

Fighting spread all around me. Wardens squared off against those attuned in Ayize's company. The cultists seemed to hold their own. There were more than Ayize had reported, many more — maybe fifty at a glance. But the Yorandu were well-armed and trained, and the cultists fell before their sorcery, spears, and arrows.

I weaved around the clashes where I could and buffeted back any who attempted to come after me. Twice, flying missiles nearly caught me, and I barely knocked them aside in time. I rounded the descent and came into the basin — and there it spread before me, sickening to behold.

The blood lake.

I gagged as I stumbled toward the bodies ringing its edge. Cultists swarmed here. They lunged at me as I neared, eyes wide and bloodshot. Something possessed them, be it daemon or drug, for they acted with no regard for their safety.

I screamed and blasted them back.

The cultists sailed away, blackened and smoking. It was as mighty an offensive as I'd ever put forth, yet I barely felt the strain. I was intoxicated, drunk on violence and sorrow. My balance pitched as I turned my head up to the sky.

Death choked me with its putrid stench. Death filled my ears with shrieks and sobs. Death was everywhere I looked.

Yet as I opened my eyes to the Pyrthae, I saw a more terrifying sight.

Famine cavorted in the sky, twisting and slithering in what could only be called ecstasy. Through our connection, his pleasure became my own. I fought down a smile as he sucked in the souls of those dying around me. I tried to deny my growing invigoration as the battle raged on.

He did not see or notice me, even now. I bared my teeth, then let the word tear free of my throat.

"*FAMINE!*"

In this plane, my command became something else, a white wave that cascaded from me. As it touched the daemon god, his movements jerked to a halt, and his vast head swiveled around to peer at me with one eye. I'd forgotten how black and cold his gaze was until it settled on me. There was no end to the darkness in those eyes, their own brand of oblivion.

I fought not to be lost, blinking and shaking my head. The words — what were the words I was supposed to say?

But though my mind had gone blank, my hand hadn't forgotten its duty. Instinctively, I'd drawn Aika's knife and now clutched it in both hands. I held it out, the blade pointing toward my chest. It had never seemed so sharp as it did then.

Something about this drew Famine's interest, for he turned fully toward me. His mouth still hung open, and in

J.D.L. ROSELL

that chasm, I saw the glimmer of souls being forever consumed.

He'll devour the world. All you love. All you hate. Everything.

It was the last push I needed. I drew in a breath, then shouted out the words.

"Famine, I offer myself as Sacri—"

Before I could finish, I fell crashing to the ground.

The Pyrthae faded from my vision as I fought against the one restraining me. They were strong; a warden, with kinesis-strengthened limbs. I swelled with force to counter theirs, but stopped just short of releasing as I glimpsed their face.

"Don't!" Talan grunted with the effort of holding me. My knife had scored a cut on his shoulder, red staining the white. As I watched, the dagger absorbed the blood, leaving it as untouched as before.

Then I snapped out of my daze and let my magic flow back out of me.

Talan collapsed atop me, but he didn't allow himself time to rest. Stumbling to his feet, I watched him disperse one kinetic attack, then shred a radiant plume. The battle sounded as if it waned, but still it limped on.

I came to my feet, barely feeling as if I were there. I was supposed to be dead. I'd come here to die.

Why am I still alive?

But though Talan had interrupted me, I still had a chance. He was distracted. Perhaps now—

His hand closed over my hand, then he pried Aika's knife away.

"Talan!" I grabbed at his arm, but I didn't fight him for it. I couldn't take it back from him without hurting him. Even amid the battle, words were my best weapon. "I have to, don't you see? I have to die!"

He shoved me away, countering another attack. Against all reason, his lips curved upward.

"If you think I'll allow that," he yelled as he spun around me, blocking another blow, "you don't know me at all, my Finch!"

I stared at him, trying to sort through what I should do. Part of me knew I should help keep him alive, and myself for that matter. I was going to die anyway, but I had to die in the right way.

Yet I felt a curious lack of concern for my own well-being. Death was death, in some ways. It was difficult to accept it, only now to push it away.

But slowly, the stupor faded. As a kinetic wave charged toward Talan, I channeled to counter it, meeting it with greater force.

I whirled to ward against other attacks, but found that the battle had abruptly ceased. Those cultists who weren't dead either lay too injured to fight or had surrendered and were being tied up by Yorandu warriors. We had won, and better still, survived. Even those of us who weren't supposed to.

Turning, I channeled quintessence and stared up again, only to lurch to a halt.

Famine soared away. The cloud of quintessence he'd feasted on had thinned to almost nothing, too thin to hold his attention, especially since he'd grown. His satiation was already fading; it was time to seek the next feast. The daemon god's long, sinuous body undulated as he sped off through the air, back toward the ishakas.

I could do nothing but watch him leave.

"No." My knees gave way. I barely noticed the pain of the impact as I stared after Famine, already obscured by the rise in the land.

We'd come close, so close to ending it.

But once more, I had failed.

I felt Talan nearby, and the others gathering around, for their quintessence blazed in my senses. All the wardens, at least, had survived. I couldn't look at them, couldn't bear to see the horror, the disappointment, the anger. It would only amplify the feelings simmering inside me.

"Airene."

I squeezed my eyes shut, releasing my hold on quintessence and trying not to tremble. I couldn't kneel forever. Eventually, I had to face this.

Face him.

I opened my eyes and found him crouched before me. His mouth smiled; his eyes did anything but. He looked as if he were shivering.

"Why?" It came out as a whisper. "Why did you...?"

I shook my head, then tried to rise to my feet. Nomusa and Xaron were there to help me, and I gave each of them a grateful look before turning back to Talan. The former Guilder stood as well, looking as if he were trying to stand before an angry ocean, wave after wave crashing against him.

"I'll explain it all," I murmured. "But we have other messes to clean up first."

With that, I numbed myself to pain and carried on.

INTERLUDE II

JIHU

She had just set the flask to boil when the knock came at the door.

Jihu stiffened. Nearly three decades of hiding, and still she had never grown used to it. But her nerves quickly hardened again, and she quickly set to hiding any evidence of her work: peeling off the heavy leather gloves, dampening the fires, ensuring nothing would explode in her absence.

Closing the door behind her, she peered into a looking glass, hung next to the laboratory for just such an occasion as this. And a good thing — as usual, ash dotted her hair. She combed it out with her fingers, grimacing as she pulled hair loose from its tight bun.

There was no time to fix it. The knock came again, polite but insistent. If it was whom she suspected, they would not soon turn away.

She eyed the front door. Her husband was out, scrounging up any food he could find to purchase with the last of their savings. She was aged and scarred, and though she hated to acknowledge it, becoming frailer by the year.

Yet Jihu had never been defenseless. More than a few men had discovered that to their regret.

Smoothing her expression, she approached the door, took in a breath, then opened it.

Armored guards stood there. Worse, a quick glance showed them to be from the Laurel Palace, telling by the insignia engraved into their helms and breastplates. Behind them stood aqua cowls and shadowed faces, undeniable signs of Shepherds.

Jihu felt too warm, and in a way that had nothing to do with aging.

The soldier who had knocked stepped aside, speaking as she did. "You have been graced by a visit from the Despot himself, His Radiance Jaxas Wreath. Bow before your ruler."

Jihu's eyes flickered past the woman, and only then did she see him. She didn't know his face, but she would have known him for the Despot by his clothes and appearance. Jaxas Wreath was as thin as everyone said; "a skeleton in robes," her crassest neighbors called him. His gold-and-green robes were voluminous around his spare frame. He had a slight hunch to his posture, though his head was held high. The Evergreen Wreath, eternally verdant, sat atop his brow.

Seeing him, she didn't hesitate longer, but bent her protesting body over itself.

"Thank you, but that is not necessary. Please, Jihu, rise and speak with me. Time is not a luxury we can waste."

His voice had a whispering quality to it, like he was confiding a secret in her, just between the two of them. Even more ensnaring were his eyes, burning like coals with an inner fire. That fire was familiar, for a similar one fueled herself.

"Please, Your Radiance, be welcome," she said, picking up the address from the guard. "My home is humble, but—"

"No apologies necessary." The Despot was already sweeping forward, and Jihu had to step hastily aside to make way for him. The soldier who had spoken looked annoyed, perhaps at her charge entering a house without her first inspecting it, but she only wordlessly followed. To Jihu's relief, the other laurel guards and the Shepherds remained on her stoop.

Jihu's back trickled with sweat, but she kept her expression stony. They wouldn't suspect her of any misdoings. The Despot of Oedija didn't make house visits for arrests. And though she hadn't expected him personally, she *had* expected someone to come knocking.

It was inevitable after her son's request at the beginning of the season.

She took the opportunity to calm herself by offering tea, which the Despot politely accepted. Fetching the last of the oolong leaves from her home jaitin, Jihu set a pot to boil and sprinkled the dried leaves in the cups. When she could delay no longer, she turned back to the monarch and waited.

The Despot studied her with his feverish eyes for a long moment. She wondered if he'd taken ill, or if the stress of all he faced was overcoming him. She hoped not. However illegitimate the way he'd claimed power, Oedija needed a leader now if it was to survive the army knocking at its gates.

Jaxas Wreath shifted in his chair, but before she could apologize for its meanness, he spoke. "I assume you know why I have come here, Jihu."

She decided to play it safe. "I am sorry, Your Radiance. But I do not."

A slight crease appeared on his brow, and a thrill of fear shot through her. Displeasing this man was not likely to end well if half the things spoken about him were true.

"First Watcher Xaron said he'd spoken with you. Though you refused, you must know my request."

There it was; the truth, baldly stated. Terror rattled through her as she realized the power he possessed over her. But instead of weakening, Jihu found her resolve set. She'd always thrived under adversity.

"Ah." She gave a perfunctory bow. "Of course, Your Radiance. You mean my experiments."

"They are more than experiments, by your son's report. 'Catalysm' — that is what you call it, your brand of magic?"

Jihu tilted her chin up. "Yes, Your Radiance. It is my invention."

To her surprise, the Despot sniffed the air. "Unless I am mistaken, we have just interrupted you."

That rocked her back. What had he smelled? Her nose was growing dull if she'd missed that. Rumors had put Jaxas Wreath as being devious, but he was even sharper than she'd counted on.

She gave a stiff nod. "It is no concern, Your Radiance. Nothing that will endanger you."

"And here I was hoping it would." Jaxas leaned forward on her rickety table, the wood creaking as it bore his weight. "Danger to myself is not my concern, Jihu. I have a nation to protect."

Before she could answer, the Despot nodded at the fireplace. "But it seems our water is boiling?"

She scrambled after the excuse. By the time she had poured the water to allow the tea to steep, Jihu had collected and calmed herself again. She turned to face her unusual guest.

"With the humblest respect, Your Radiance, I am not sure you understand what you ask. Catalysm is volatile and dangerous. It is not a thing to be trifled with."

Jaxas Wreath scrutinized her in silence, long enough to make her want to squirm. When he spoke, it seemed an abrupt change in topic.

"Have you seen the Avvadin army outside our walls, Jihu?"

She shook her head, though she'd dreamed of it often enough that it seemed like she had.

"It is vast, unassailable. They are as numerous as fish in the Lighted Sea. They have warden priests, enslaved spirits, and the deadly Damask Esir. And what do we have?" The Despot spread his arms, eyebrows quirked, as if to show her. "A few groups of militiamen, a small collection of wardens, my palace guard. Hardly enough to withstand a siege."

Jihu knew what he was asking. Knew she should deny him if she could. But with each fresh reminder of how doomed Oedija was, she felt herself drawn into his plight. Her resolve, built over decades, crumbled further, just as it had when her son had made the request.

But she'd always been able to say no to Xaron. The Despot was another matter entirely.

Jaxas Wreath smiled, but it was a sad, limp thing. "We need you, Jihu. We cannot hope to last a day without your expertise. If what Xaron has said is true, you could give Oedija a fighting chance."

She should say no. Explain how many it could kill. How it could harm their own soldiers as easily as the enemy. She opened her mouth to say just that.

Her tongue betrayed her.

"I have already begun the concoctions, Your Radiance."

His eyes widened. "Then you did not refuse your son."

"I did." She grimaced, then wondered if such an expression was appropriate before one as high as him. "But I have always believed in caution, Your Radiance. I thought this request possible and prepared for it."

"If you were ready for a visit from the Ruling Wreath, then you are just the woman I've been looking for."

With a wry smile, Jaxas Wreath rose. It might have been her imagination, but he seemed to stand a fraction taller.

"First Laurel Syrne here will discuss the details with you. I'm afraid I must depart myself. But know, Jihu, that anything you need is at your disposal. Anything at all."

She meant to let him depart as he strode toward the door. But she had been a mother too long to allow that, even of her monarch.

"Protect Xaron," she said to his back. "Please, Your Radiance. Protect my son."

Jaxas Wreath turned back, and she flinched at the sadness in his eyes.

"I'm not sure I can protect anyone. But I promise to try."

With that, the Despot of Oedija swept from her home.

Jihu stared after him, but the female guard had remained behind, so she shook out of her stupor and went to the cups of steeping tea, abandoned before she could serve them.

"Drink," she told the guard as she set the cup before her. "Then we may proceed."

First Laurel Synne eyed her with something like respect, then took a sip.

Jihu repressed a sigh. She had always known it would come back to this. Magic could not be long suppressed. It hadn't worked for Xaron, nor for herself.

Now, it was time to embrace it, and hope it was not too late.

19

THE THIRD FOLD

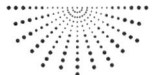

The bold witch becomes lost
If she rises too high
Or falls too low
They are not places for mortals
The gods guard their claim
Beware, beware

- A scribestone of Jolduun; estimated 300 SLP

We fled before Ayize could stop us.

Though my spirits were low, I brimmed with power spilled over from my enemy, and it was a simple matter of cutting open a rift into the Pyrthae and stepping through. I caught a last glimpse of Ayize's resigned expression before sealing it closed behind my party.

"What was that?" Talan hovered near me, anger radiating from him in a scarlet cloud. "Airene, what in the 'Thae's depths happened back there? Why were you—?"

"We have to go," I interrupted, turning my back on him. I doubted my shame was hidden, exposed as we all were in the spirit realm. "We have to reach our camp and figure out our next steps before we can stop and chat."

"If you think I'll let you—"

"Guilder," Xaron interjected, "she's right. We're not exactly safe yet."

I turned back to watch as Talan rounded on my former loftmate. But our companions stood firm beside Xaron, and after a moment, the former Guilder sighed and took a step back.

"Fine," he conceded. "I'll wait for now. But once we're through this..."

I only began walking away. That was one conversation I would happily put off forever if I could. But as long as he held Aika's knife, there was little chance of finding an end beforehand. I'd seen the way he clutched it, like he was afraid it would stab me of its own accord if he let it go.

As our party set off, I took stock of my companions' conditions. We'd sustained blessedly few injuries. Nomusa had a burned shoulder from a stray ray of radiance. Kari had a bruised lip, though I couldn't figure out how she'd received it. Talan was in worse shape. Having thrown himself into the fighting to pursue me, he'd received cuts and burns that left his coat in tatters, but seemed to hurt little. A pack, however, would make the injuries more uncomfortable.

I wanted to thank him for saving my life, but considering what still lay ahead, the words felt too ironic to utter.

By traveling through the Pyrthae, we easily reached our camp before Ayize could, loaded up our packs again, and reentered the spirit realm. Only when we were safely away did we turn to one another and realize the obvious.

"What do we do now?" Xaron took off his pack and set it down on the shimmering ground. A smile quirked his lips, though by how his eyes flared, I could tell it wasn't from humor.

I felt Talan's stare and avoided looking at him. "We follow."

"No. We must move ahead of Taozu."

Only as Azhi spoke did I realize what a state he was in. His fury was palpable, radiating off him in an orange mist. It didn't take much effort to guess why.

"I'm sorry." My head fell, shame making it feel too heavy to keep upright.

"Sorry?" Talan barked a bitter laugh and turned away.

Azhi turned his glare on him, while the rest of my companions wore various expressions ranging from sorrowful to confused. None spoke up before our guide continued.

"As you no doubt sense, Airene, our quarry moves southwest. I have a guess where he is headed, and why."

Nomusa answered before I could. "Avvad."

"Avvad?" Isidora frowned. "What is there for him?"

Azhi spoke in a sigh. "Valem."

A shiver ran through me. The others seemed to feel it as well.

"*Valem?*" Xaron shook his head. "Don't tell me he exists, too."

The daemon-possessed man smiled, and I saw more than a shimmer of the pyr around him. "He does. Long has Valem slumbered, as have many of his fellow great spirits. But he has always exerted influence over the world. Part of his essence resides in the volcano that bears his name, feeding the rage he craves."

Even knowing of the existence of the Quintyr, it was a shock to hear of yet another god who was more than myth. But the epiphany that came after was more troubling still.

"Has he grown so powerful as to challenge him?" I said. "A fellow Quintyr?"

Azhi looked back at me. "You know he has. This was our best chance to stop him while he was distracted by feeding.

Now he flies to war, to finish the slaughter of his fellow gods he started long ago."

I'd been so focused on keeping Famine from our world I'd forgotten the damage he could do in his. "Eidola above..."

"They won't save us." Azhi smiled then, and I found I preferred his scowl. "Some have tried. But none have ever been as powerful as Famine after he has feasted so much."

"How can we do anything?" Nomusa demanded. "Even gods are inept! We're just human." Her arms pressed tight against her belly. I guessed she was still on edge from her encounters with her kinsmen.

"We are. But we have Airene." Azhi looked at me, and I read more in his eyes: *If she will do as she should have done.*

I turned away. My own shame was a heavy enough burden to bear without adding his.

No one responded to that. They had an inkling of the methods upon which we relied to defeat our enemy, but they had never truly understood. I wouldn't have been able to in their position, either. I scarcely believed myself, and I'd witnessed Vusu use them.

But he didn't truly succeed, a part of me whispered, *nor has anyone before him. Famine always comes back. The cycle continues.*

I hugged my arms about me, wishing I wasn't filled to the brim with Famine-born energy. I wanted to feel too tired to go on. As it was, I tried to focus back on what we knew and could do, not all that we could not.

"Whether or not he's challenging Valem, he's going in that direction." I turned my gaze over my small party, looking each of them in the eye — except for Talan. "Azhi's right; we need to get ahead. But how?"

Kari spoke, surprising us all. "The third fold."

We stared at her.

"What's that?" I asked, wondering if it was worth the

bother. She had rarely given straight answers before, and I doubted that would change now.

The witch glanced from one of us to another, her brow drawn. "The world above." She gestured with a hand to the mirror image of Telae hanging above us.

Corin laid a hand on her sister's shoulder, their images shimmering with the contact. "You must explain, Sister. We do not know this third fold."

Kari stared at Corin for a moment longer before a smile blossomed on her face. "Ah. Then I shall—"

Before she finished speaking, a silvery cloud erupted from her form. I flinched, but couldn't avoid it as it passed over me.

Images exploded into my mind.

They passed by swiftly, a whirlwind of the senses. I smelled vinegar and saltwater, peered into a depthless cave and then the bright sun; then a woman appeared, and she felt familiar and warm. Enough of my wits remained to recognize her as an outlander, and that her features were etched in Kari's face, and Corin's. Blonde hair. Kind eyes. Strong jaw.

Their mother.

No sooner had I figured it out than the woman spoke. "Listen, Kari, and listen well. Long ago, the gods sundered the spirit world to protect witches who visited it. We call these sections 'folds,' like wrinkles in fabric, for they are but pieces of the same cloth."

As she spoke, the scene around the woman filled out, adding texture and detail. It was a fine summer day, judging by the sun and warmth. The grass of the fields surrounding us was yellow, and bird calls filled the air. Kari was remembering more, I guessed, and thus strengthening the memory's picture.

"The first fold," her mother continued, "is a reflection of our world, a place humans can understand. Have you seen it in your dreams, sweet-blossom? It looks as if a second world hangs above you, but neither is truly there. They are created, and never to be trusted — yet as long as you stay within these reflections, you will not be lost.

"But there are folds above and below. The second fold is under your feet, through the ground. Never go there, sweet-blossom — you must promise me! Time is fickle in the spirit world. In the second fold, years will seem moments to you. I may be gone by the time you return. Would you want that?"

Kari, as she remembered herself, gave a muddled response. I couldn't see her clearly, perhaps because she didn't see herself in that moment. Yet she remembered well the touch of her mother's hand on her head, stroking her hair to counter the frightening words.

"There is also a world above the first fold, through the hanging world — the third fold. This is a safer place to go, sweet-blossom, but nowhere in the spirit world is safe. Time slows the higher you go, so spans would be only days in our world, and distance warps as well. But it lacks the familiar surroundings of the first fold, and many witches have become lost there.

"If you find yourself in the spirit world, and need to escape the first fold, ascend to the third fold. All that is needed to break through it is to believe. Wraiths who have forgotten themselves will not follow you there. So long as you do not wander, you will be safe."

The scenes dissolved into mist. I blinked, and the Pyrthae reasserted itself.

So Kari hadn't been the first witch in her family. My mind drifted past the thought to what I'd learned from the visions. *The first fold*, I thought as I gazed around me. The words echoed things Eltris had told me long ago, but were conveyed in a clearer way than the augur had ever bothered with."Stoneward" and "skyward" had been the most she explained of the places beyond the initial staging ground of the Pyrthae. But it seemed they were as distinctive of realms as that which now surrounded us.

"Tyurn's balls, what *was* that?" Xaron shook his head as if to clear it.

Kari looked puzzled again, so I spoke up. "Her memories. She shared them with quintessence."

Isidora nodded, while Xaron grimaced. "Why not just say it," he grumbled.

I smiled at that. But with Talan still glowering my way, my amusement didn't last long.

"So this third fold is dangerous, but will make travel even quicker." I glanced at Azhi. "Will it work?"

He nodded, the motion blurring his image for a moment. "It is our only choice."

I was tired of ultimatums, yet I muttered my agreement.

"And how will we get up there?" Nomusa pointed out.

I craned back my neck to look up. Hundreds of cubits stretched between us and the hanging world. *All that is needed to break through is belief,* Kari's mother had said. Belief had carried us far before; it had allowed us to defy the natural laws, to weigh less and jump higher. Perhaps, if we believed hard enough, we could even soar.

Kari was already demonstrating this. Her chin tilted up, a smile on her lips, she began to float, her feet leaving the ground. Corin stepped toward her, seeming about to pull her back down, but she stopped short and watched with the rest of us as the witch ascended higher and higher. My stomach clenched when she went high enough for a fall to kill her. I suspected it wouldn't, but I'd too often followed my instincts to silence them now.

"We should follow her," Azhi said. Then he, too, started to drift upward. "Believe, and you can," he added before he picked up speed and went out of earshot.

I found my gaze falling to Talan. His silhouette, all shades of darkness, still shimmered with anger. Yet he said nothing as he glided upward.

"*Fareshi* wardens," Nomusa muttered. She shot me a look. "And what are Corin and I supposed to do?"

"The same thing," I countered. "This doesn't have to do with channeling. It's force of will."

Xaron suddenly grinned and spread his arms. "Exactly! See? All in your head, so to speak!"

I saw then that he ascended with the others. A moment later, Isidora followed suit, a wondering smile on her lips.

That left Corin, Nomusa, and me. I was certain I could follow, having more experience than most in the Pyrthae, but I was reluctant to attempt it until the other two had succeeded. Corin looked even more dubious than Nomusa. I wondered if she was too grounded in good sense to be able to believe in anything not of the material world.

I approached her. "If it's easier, pretend that you believe it. It might work the same way."

The cartwoman's brow was still furrowed, but she nodded, trusting me as she always had. Yet a minute passed, and still nothing changed.

"Airene!"

I looked over and found Nomusa floating above the ground, a mixture of bafflement and delight making her expression childlike. A laugh bubbled out of me, taking me by surprise. I hadn't thought I could laugh after what we had just witnessed.

I looked back to Corin, hoping she had also succeeded, but her feet remained firmly on the ground. The smile slipped away as I contemplated what to do.

Then an idea came to me.

"Hold my hands. I want to try something."

We clasped hands, and a feeling like channeling magnesis buzzed through me. I *felt* Corin in a way that went beyond words or senses. It was like how Kari had shared her memory. Our quintessences touched; I delved inside her, and she inside me.

With an effort, I reinforced the boundaries of myself, and the feeling faded. Looking into Corin's shadowy face, I saw I was not the only one disturbed by it.

"Hold tight," I muttered, then closed my eyes and focused all my mind on one thing:

The sky weighs nothing. I weigh nothing. I am weightless.

I repeated the phrases, again and again, binding and reinforcing them. Each time doubts seeded in, memories of how heavy the sky pressed down on us to keep mortals to the ground, I let them drift past and away. They could only weigh me down.

I almost spoiled it as the feeling of the ground beneath my shoes disappeared, my natural skepticism reasserting itself. But doing it only served to reinforce my belief rather than undermine it. Opening my eyes, I saw Corin still hadn't succeeded herself. A smile played on my lips as I floated to the edge of her reach, then became anchored down by her.

But I knew I didn't have to be.

Corin weighs nothing, I thought, and barely a moment passed before she, too, lifted off the ground. I wanted to laugh. I'd flown in the Pyrthae when visiting as a spirit, but in my actual body, it had seemed impossible. Now, all boundaries had been broken.

What could hold us down?

Corin's hands were tight on my own, though I knew she wouldn't fall so long as I believed for both of us. The ground fell away, and the reflected world above grew nearer. I saw Kari reach it and press her hands against it, then look down. After a moment, she lifted her head again, and before my eyes, she sank into it.

I blinked, this feat stretching the limits of my belief. Then I took it as inspiration.

The sky is not solid. I can pass through it. Corin can pass through it.

By the time we reached the edge of the first fold, almost all my companions had passed through. Nomusa still pressed her hands against it, wearing a look of consternation. I took pity on her.

"Come here — I think I can help."

I tried prying loose one hand free of Corin's panicked grasp, but she clung on until I gave her an exasperated look. When at last she released me, only to hold with both hands to my other one, I reached out to my fellow Finch. Nomusa looked skeptical, but she took hold of it just as my head brushed the suspended ground. I closed my eyes and added to my belief, then dragged my friends up into the world above.

Darkness for a moment, then light pressed on my eyelids. I felt the differences of the third fold even before I saw them. A cold, incessant wind blew, piercing my spirit and sapping my strength. I wondered how long I could endure it. Opening my eyes, I noticed it looked much different from the first fold. The world was cast in a dusky blue light that seemed to come from everywhere and nowhere. A thin mist slithered through the sky, and I resolved to stay away from it, for it reminded me too much of pyr. Below our feet was an unnaturally flat surface that resembled tiles, but lacked the texture to make them real. They seemed more like the concept of floor rather than floor itself.

Already, I didn't much care for the third fold.

Yet there was nothing for it. I set my jaw, firmed my belief, and released my friends' hands. "Stay close, and we'll be alright," I said.

They both nodded, fear shining from their shimmering forms. I hoped they couldn't see my own as I tried to bury it deep inside me.

"Come," Azhi called from ahead. "Keep your feet on the

floor, and you will not become lost." The two halves of him, human and pyr, seemed on the verge of splitting apart up here. Light and shadow leaned away from each other. I wondered if it was due to ascending higher in the Pyrthae, or if Eazal strove against his captor.

Though it disturbed me to think about it, I put it from my mind. We'd trusted him this far. We could do it a little longer.

The daemon led, and we followed.

THE FINAL SOLUTION

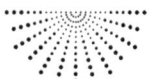

How long have I searched for another solution? But there is no other way. Death, blood, and sacrifice are what he craves, and they are what will bind him.

But it is not death of only the body that I will suffer, but the soul. Annihilation... If I accept this burden, never again will I fly through the forest. Never again will I see my brother, if he has lingered all these long cycles.

Condemn myself, or condemn all... Men were not made for such dilemmas.

- The journal of Vusumuzi; date unknown

Not long into our journey through the third fold of the Pyrthae, Talan fell in beside me.

By silent consent, Nomusa and Corin drifted away, granting us privacy. I wasn't sure that I wanted it. In the journey since the battle at the blood lake, I had dreaded this moment, and would have put it off longer if I could have.

But Talan deserved the truth. No matter how much it hurt us both.

He didn't speak for several strides, yet I heard murmurs

of his thoughts. I tried to hold my own close, afraid of what he would sense from me.

"Why?"

I closed my eyes, wishing I could drift up and become lost in the endless blue space above us. *Why.* The only question he needed answered. The very one I wished I didn't have to.

"It's the only way to stop Famine," I answered at last.

"By suicide?"

I winced. "By sacrifice. I don't want to die, Talan."

"Then don't."

His obstinacy was beginning to grate on me. "I told you, it's the only way."

Our features had become murkier this high in the Pyrthae, but I knew he wore his usual smirk as he responded. "How do you know that? Because a few dusty old tomes said so?"

Now I plainly radiated my frustration. It drew glances from the others, but no one intervened. I wondered if they could hear every word we spoke. Sound didn't always work as expected here. Even whispers might be heard over miles.

"Vusu held Famine at bay by acting as a Sacrifice. Aika, whose knife you stole from me, did the same during the first Hunger War. It's how Seeds of Famine have always caged him. It's the *only* way. He's a 'Thae-cursed god, Talan. We're fortunate there's any way to defy him at all."

He was shaking his head even before I'd finished speaking. "Vusu stopped him for a day. Even this Aika only held him for so long before he returned. It doesn't last, Airene. Why not search for a different way? Why die, when he'll only return years or days later?"

I burned with fury, and in response, the radiance in my form gathered heat. He didn't mean to insult me by implying I could only hold Famine for days, but I couldn't help but take it that way.

Still, I needed him, and not only for the artifact. Talan had always been there for me. He'd saved my life more times than I could count. That he might turn his back on me now, when I needed him more than ever, was a thought I could not bear.

So I took the only avenue left to me. I seized his arm and spliced our souls.

We'd done it before, when Talan was dying to Silks in the Underguild tunnels, and I'd given him the strength to live. This time, I pushed not energy into him, but knowledge. I held all the memories I had of learning how to defeat Famine, the certitude with which I held them, and thrust them into his mind. He resisted, trying to twist out of my grasp, but I was the stronger one here. I didn't let him go until he sagged, all that I could share with him exhausted.

When I released him, Talan backed away a step and stared at me. I felt it more than saw it, for his body had become murkier, and his eyes were nothing more than shadowed pits. Still, I held his gaze, willing him to believe, to understand, to support me as I needed him to.

He took another step back, shook his head, then walked away. I stared after him, trying not to shatter.

WE CONTINUED ON.

Our company grew morose. Morale had already been low after the fight with the cultists, but Talan and my falling out lowered it further still. Perhaps even more impactful was the third fold itself. The wind never ceased to blow, and our strength and resolve were carried away on its current. Each step became laborious, and no matter how I told myself I was weightless, my legs felt like anvils.

But I still sensed Famine. His hunger pulled me forward.

Mostly, we were silent. All that needed to be discussed had been. We had hopes more than plans, yet could make nothing more concrete until we found Famine again.

Yet in the changeless landscape, something shifted. Where only cold had reigned, an inkling of warmth seeped through me, like the first touch of dawn reaching over the horizon. I thought I imagined it, but it grew with each passing moment, the effect rapidly amplifying.

"Something is coming," Azhi said. "Something is here..."

I barely heeded him, for another thing caught my attention. The directionless light had turned from blue to darker hues. From yellow to red, then to angry violet.

Before I could feel alarmed, the Pyrthae split apart.

Lightning flashed. I screamed as I threw myself flat to the tiled floor. Around me, my companions sank through it, fleeing the third fold for the safety below: Xaron, Isidora, Azhi, Talan. I would have fled as well, but I couldn't abandon the others. Corin and Nomusa needed me.

Kari had taken hold of her sister and rapidly passed through, so I lunged toward Nomusa. Her features had almost entirely dissipated, leaving an amorphous spirit trembling with terror. I was so close to her, mere inches away, my fingers reaching—

A tidal wave crashed over me.

Pain and emotion rode the lightning that ravaged my spirit. Rage, it seemed, but of a particular kind. Like when I saw Feiyan succeed and wished for it myself.

An envious anger, but without bounds or control.

I fought to stay above it, but how could I fight a feeling? I pulsed quintessence, but if it had any effect, I couldn't detect it.

The magnetic attack didn't last forever, though; perhaps it was only a moment. As it released me, I sagged against the tile, exhausted and in agony. Nomusa was speaking beside me, but I couldn't understand her words. The booming presence had filled my mind and scoured it clean of willpower.

But self-preservation is difficult to kill. As Nomusa seized my hand, I knew what to do. *It is not real,* I thought, then sank through the floor.

Then we were falling.

Weightless, I thought, but the first measure of belief had sapped my scant strength. Nomusa clung to me, winding around me with all of her being. Without meaning to, she seeped into me as well. Fragments of memories bit at me, all the times she'd been afraid. Hearing her family murdered when she hid in a cupboard. Fleeing into the jungle, afraid of the dark and all it held. Entering Oedija's gates and quailing at all the foreign humanity amassing around her.

Each wound provoked my protective instincts, honed over years of employing them on Linos. I wrapped myself around Nomusa and thought, *The sky weighs nothing.*

Our fall abruptly slowed.

We hovered there for a long time as I recovered enough to control our descent. When we finally touched down on the ground of the first fold, Nomusa and I fell apart and sprawled upon it. Our companions were there around us, worry in all their voices. But I could only heed one.

"Airene." Talan cupped my neck, supporting my head. "Are you hurt?"

I shook my head. I was in pain, but it didn't feel permanent. "Just need to rest," I murmured.

But already, I felt better. I closed my eyes, knowing I should not fall asleep in the Pyrthae, unable to help it.

He cared for me still. He would never stop caring. It was all the comfort I needed.

I felt my friends pull me out of the Pyrthae and reenter Telae just before darkness entirely claimed me.

21
PRINCIPLE

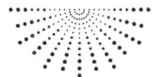

Gods are no more free than men. They are bound by themselves, the rules by which they dictate their lives. Each possesses a calling to which they dedicate their existence — some for the good of humanity, some for evil.

Understand these principles well, and know how they can be exploited, and you may survive your encounter with them.

- Scroll fragment; origin unknown; estimated 31 PLP

"What in the Lighted hells happened up there?"

I opened my eyes to Isidora's question. Shadowed greenery surrounded me, solid and natural in its appearance. A forest.

We're in Telae.

Only then did I remember exiting the Pyrthae just before I fell unconscious. How long had it been? Not long enough for them to discover the answer to what had just occurred.

A groan escaped me as I sat up.

Talan was by my side in a moment, as was Nomusa. "Easy," my fellow Finch muttered. "You were struck hard up there."

The former Guilder spoke at the same time. "You're certain you're not hurt?"

"I'm fine." I wasn't, but it felt better to not have them hovering over me like hens about a chick. Easing them back, I breathed through the nausea that stole over me, then looked up at Isidora. She wore a frown until she noticed my gaze, then smoothed it away.

"It wasn't just a storm," I said. "When the lightning hit me, I felt something behind it. Emotion undiluted. It was anger, but there was more to it." I reached for the hazy memories, trying to capture the right words to describe the feeling. "Like the anger at seeing someone with something you want to have."

"Envy?" Xaron guessed.

"Does it matter?" Isidora had always had a great capacity for patience, but it seemed to finally be depleted. "It doesn't answer *what* that was."

"It does matter." Azhi leaned against a nearby tree. "If the storm was sentient, that makes it a very different thing."

"Sentient." I met his gaze. "You think it was... a pyr?"

He shook his head. "A great spirit. A Quintyr."

My skin rose in gooseflesh. It made a certain sense. The storm had been implacable and single-minded, yet there had been something conscious behind it. And simple pyr were never that powerful.

"Another one?" Xaron shook his head. "They're sprouting all around us!"

"Not precisely," Azhi said. "This one has likely wandered the third fold for millennia, not touching the mortal realm or its inhabitants. After all, how many have entered the Pyrthae, much less the level above the first?"

I sat with the thought. The daemon was right once more; there was so much we didn't know of the Pyrthae, despite traveling through it for many days. Could far more Quintyr exist than we knew, just beyond our reach? Were there more stoneward or skyward?

Isidora spoke up again. "If there are more up there, then we cannot travel through it. It's too great a risk."

Azhi frowned, but didn't respond. No one else objected. I grimaced, knowing I had to speak.

"Famine's still ahead of us. If anything, he's gained ground. I don't know that we have a choice."

"No." Talan put his hand on my shoulder, softening the denial. "Better we reach him whole than not at all."

I suspected his ulterior motives, but only sighed. My body felt heavy with all I'd put it through. Traveling the Pyrthae for long already took its toll; being attacked by a savage Quintyr only made matters worse.

Yet even as I sat there, vitality swept through me. My spirits lifted, and my apprehension grew in proportion. Famine had found a fresh source of quintessence to feast on. I hoped we weren't already too late.

I stood, surprising everyone. "We should keep going. Famine has arrived wherever he was headed. I don't think he's far. If we can reach him before we rest, we might still stand a chance."

The others nodded, though most with heavy resignation. Isidora's frustration had not abated, telling from her scowl, but she only sighed without further protest. I wondered if they knew the reason behind my sudden revival. Talan, at least, watched me with narrowed eyes and a sharp smirk.

I bent and retrieved my pack from where they'd lain it next to me and shouldered it once more. Then, as Azhi cut into the spirit realm, I followed the others in.

"THE GREAT SPIRITS," Azhi said a short way into our walk, "or the Quintyr, if you prefer, are governed by their driving principles.

They are different beings than mortals, with their own brands of reason and logic. In some ways, their minds are more limited than ours; in other ways, they are unimaginably expansive."

The daemon had begun the lecture at a prompting question from Xaron as he mulled aloud over the magnetic storm. I remained silent, content to listen. Eltris had spoken of this once, but she had always kept secrets. And there was the likelihood that this spirit had learned something in his two centuries of existence that the augur had not.

"Famine," he continued, "is driven by hunger — a desire for quintessence, specifically. This is partly what makes him so powerful; it is in his nature to accumulate it and destroy any who could challenge him."

Xaron frowned. Though Eazal had once been familiar to him, he'd grown used to Azhi in a way I could never manage. "And Valem? He's powerful as well. What's his principle?"

"Rage," Talan answered before Azhi could.

The daemon turned back and eyed him thoughtfully. "Yes. That is why he imbued part of himself in the volcano. I believe it fuels him in a similar way as Famine's feasting. That is why he remains perhaps the most powerful spirit in either world."

A thought occurred to me. "Quintyr can influence the material world, even if they cannot enter it."

My words drew Azhi's eye to me now. "Yes. They cannot help but radiate their principle, and no being with quintessence is entirely separate from the spirit realm."

I nodded, wondering how it had never occurred to me before. "Maybe that's how Vusu created the Manifest so swiftly, and why it dismantled so soon after Famine left Oedija. Their hunger for more — it was born of him."

Azhi drifted back to walk next to me, and though I preferred to keep my distance, I allowed it.

"Not born," he corrected gently. "Amplified. Those drawn

to the movement were the worst off. The poor. The hungry. The daemonized." He glanced at Xaron, who only shrugged.

My thoughts turned inward again as I contemplated my own actions. I'd been driven by a hunger of my own, hadn't I? The desire to understand, to pull the secrets surrounding me into the light, and thus achieve fame and fortune. Had that been Famine's influence all along?

Was he why I'd sacrificed everything to come to this point?

I didn't know, and I wasn't sure I wanted to know. If it was Famine, it would make me his pawn. But it somehow would be worse if it was solely my own. If it was my hubris and ambition that had brought ruin to so many I loved.

Linos. I hoped he still lived, that Oedija stood against Avvad. But just as before, I could do nothing for him. Nothing at all to protect my little brother.

"Avvad," Talan spoke up again. "My people are also influenced. Valem seeds hate in their hearts…"

As he trailed off, something in his voice drew me from my misery. I stared at him, puzzled for several moments before I recognized the emotions vibrating from his spirit. *Relief.*

Only then did I understand. For as long as I'd known him, Talan had resented his home country. The Avvadin Imperium had taken everything from him, ground him down to a shadow, until he had to leave or lose himself entirely.

But it was still his home, his people. He wanted to love them. Now, he'd found a way to rationalize why he still did.

I smiled at him, and he returned it. For once, the interaction was devoid of irony.

"What of Clepsammia?" Nomusa asked into the silence that had fallen.

I glanced at her, curious why she had thought about it. She only shrugged in response.

Azhi, too, seemed intrigued by her question, head cocked

to one side. "As with many of the Eidolan gods, the answer is in her stories. Fate is her principle, Nomusa. The guiding of mortals along the paths she has determined to be best, or correct, or inevitable." He shook his head. "I have never known her intentions, if they are helpful or harmful to those of the material plane. Only what drives her."

Fate. I thought over my interactions with the Quintyr, or at least the spirit I believed to be her. She seemed to have been well-intentioned; she had saved me twice, after all. But none of the Quintyr seemed good or evil on their face. They fulfilled their principles; that was that. Just as a storm or natural disaster couldn't be moral in their actions, neither could they.

Not even Famine was truly evil. Though that fact didn't change what we had to do.

"And Harvest… she is growth? Or perhaps life?"

This came again from Talan, once more surprising me. I wondered how he even knew to ask of her when I remembered how I'd pushed my memories onto him. His smile had faded, and the impressions of his eyes narrowed. I mulled over what he might have in mind.

Azhi smiled, and there seemed something knowing in it. "Yes — vitality is how I think of it. She is, or was, Famine's antithesis, for her principle was to help quintessence flourish. But she is dead, consumed by her enemy in the last Hunger War. Life cannot triumph over death, in the end."

That put an end to the conversation. But as we carried on our journey, I glanced often at Talan. He seemed to mull over something, and come to conclusions that didn't altogether displease him.

I only stopped when he caught me looking and flashed me a smirk. It didn't stop me from wondering what he was planning.

22
WHIRLING WORLD

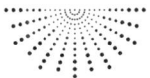

"The Buyujinn of all sects are welcome, so long as allegiance to the Molten God is foremost and absolute. In variety, there is violence, for a difference of opinion must eventually be resolved."

- Father Tarik, a priest of Valem; date unknown

T he light was fading when the first signs of civilization came into view. I'd long ago felt that we neared our destination. Famine's presence pulled at me strongly now, and his hunger had waxed. I guessed that his present feast was running thin. But it didn't feel as if he was leaving. Something kept him tethered in place.

As homesteads appeared, then a city and volcano beyond, I saw my enemy and understood.

The volcano named for Valem rose above the city of Erimis. Lava trickled down its sides, and smoke billowed out of its top in a thin black plume. Impressive as it was, it was the Quintyr curled around its sides that caught my attention.

Famine was now long and large enough that he encircled the volcano's peak twice. The dragon god had his teeth sunk into the rock, and by the working of his jaw, he was trying to gnaw his way in. Around where he chewed, more lava spewed out, and Famine flinched back as it splashed on his snout. As he shook his great head free of it, I wondered if it was lava we actually saw. We were in the Pyrthae, and whatever it was had hurt a Quintyr. More likely Valem fought back against the intrusion, though lazily.

"Valem still sleeps," Azhi murmured.

"Not for long, by the look of it," Nomusa noted.

I wondered what would happen if Valem awakened. The thought drew my attention to the city sprawled below. Erimis was fortunate to have survived this long at the foot of an active volcano. I'd heard of eruptions occurring in the past, lava flooding the streets and killing people by the thousands. Yet the Avvadin considered this a holy and powerful place. No matter how many times Valem drove them out, they always came crawling back.

We were still outside Erimis's walls when Azhi turned back to face us. "We must agree this time," he said. I knew his words were meant for me, though he didn't look my way. "I believe our best chance is to awaken Valem and provoke battle between him and Taozu. Then, while he is distracted, Airene will cage him."

Everyone glanced at me — or past me. Condemning a friend to death could not be an easy thing.

I nodded, trying not to let my fear show. "Yes. I will."

Talan shifted as if about to speak, and I braced myself for his objections. But none came.

"We should rest before the attempt," the former Guilder said. "I know a man who will grant us shelter, no matter how many years have passed since I last saw him." He gestured, and when Azhi followed, the others filed behind the men.

I stared at Talan's back, unable to move. He'd been willing to doom Telae to save me before. Had that changed? Was he now ready to let me die? I was glad I brought up the rear of our party, for I was sure I did a poor job of hiding my feelings.

In the Pyrthaen version of Erimis, the outer gates were open, so we entered the city without issue. Its foreign buildings rose around us. I wasn't unused to Avvadin architecture, Oedija being plenty influenced by it, but it still felt strange to be surrounded by it.

Sandstone and volcanic rock adorned the domiciles and walkways. As we traveled the main promenade, I looked up to see people thronging the streets. Resentment twisted in my gut. They looked almost normal here, their lives unaffected by war, while my people suffered.

But it wouldn't be long before they knew Oedija's pain. We would make sure of that.

I only caught myself for the nasty thought afterward. Was it Valem's influence or my anger that spawned it? I hated doubting even my own mind. Not knowing which was the source, I tried numbing emotion altogether and focusing on putting one foot before the other.

We came ever nearer to Valem's base. Famine's hunger hollowed me out so I felt as empty as a cloud, drifting through the streets. *Eat*, the nagging thoughts came. *Drink*. Unable to do anything for it, I tried my best to ignore it.

At last, we stopped before a building that could only be a temple. It was large and formed of sandstone, with a dome in the middle and wings extending out from it. Its bricks and gilding were aged, but seemed to have once been built at great expense. I wondered if a Kahin-Shah had once favored it, and when it had fallen out of the ruling family's good graces.

Talan turned, conflicting emotions radiating from him. "My home," he said with a twist of his lips. "The temple of the Hortum Kor."

How odd, to see the place he'd so often spoken of. My gaze lingered on the facade as I followed Talan and the

187

others around to the alley next to it. Hidden there, Talan cut a rift back into Telae, then led the way through. I exited last. My natural senses reemerged in a flood, the stenches in particular overwhelming. It was quieter than I expected, though the crowds had been fading above us in the Pyrthae as we traveled.

The disorientation only took a moment to adjust to, but I was glad when Talan reached out a hand to steady me. My eyes alighted on his, then darted away. Doubt still seeped through me. His brow creased slightly, but he said nothing before drawing back.

"This way," he said. "We shouldn't linger outdoors past nightfall. The Silks enforce the curfew."

He led us to the front of the temple. Passing through the doors, I saw we weren't alone. The foyer was dark, but ahead of us was a rotunda illuminated by the fading sunlight and the rising moons. A single figure occupied the space between the columns, an older man by his graying hair. I was astonished to see him occupied by the strangest practice.

The man was spinning.

He whirled in place, around and around, with such balance and grace I wouldn't have believed it possible was it not before my eyes. I'd heard Talan describe the dances of the temple he'd once been part of, and the effect to which he'd employed them against Silks. But to see one play out before me was another matter altogether.

As we approached, the man stopped turning and faced us. He had thick and wild hair, grayed with dark strands throughout. Deep furrows worked into his skin, and many of them seemed to be lines from smiles and laughter. His eyes were arresting, the color of honey, and his skin was a deep bronze.

He seemed to have been aware of us, for he didn't startle. Yet his eyes widened as his gaze fell upon Talan.

"I would think you a ghost, had you come alone," the grizzled man murmured in the ash-tongue.

Talan grinned as fully as I'd ever witnessed. "I'm here in the flesh, you old lion."

Then they were striding toward each other and embracing, laughing and smiling all the while. Tears were in the older man's eyes; I couldn't see Talan as he faced away, but I guessed he was in much the same state. My chest felt full at the sight. Until I saw him so happy, I'd never known how lonely Talan must have always felt in Oedija. The thought brought a tinge of bittersweet with it.

After several moments, they broke apart, and the priest wiped at his eyes before smiling apologetically. "It's been five years," he said by way of explanation. "But don't leave your companions as strangers, Talan. All are welcome here."

Corin and Kari's brows were furrowed, unable to follow along in the Avvadin language. I spoke in the sea-tongue instead. "Do you know Oedijan speech?"

The priest started, then chuckled as he responded in the same tongue. "I do. My apologies — I should have known where you were from."

"Some of them are," Talan conceded. "But if you don't mind, Osman, we have urgent business here. Perhaps we might make introductions while having refreshments…?"

The priest, Osman, loosed another laugh. "You never were shy about asking for food!"

We followed the grizzled man and Talan deeper into the temple, where they turned into a cozy room just large enough to fit us all. It boasted a thin mattress, full bookshelves, and a merrily burning hearth that warmed the space. A glass window looked out over Erimis and let in a little more illumination.

Once we were all settled on the bed and the few chairs available, Osman sent Talan to fetch the food, and to my amazement, the former Guilder complied with a single quip.

The two had fallen back into roles of mentor and mentee so easily I wondered if I'd underestimated just how close they were. It was more like how a father and son interacted.

As Talan's footsteps faded, the priest peered at each of us. Though he still wore a friendly smile, a hint of shrewdness entered his eyes.

"Now," he said, still speaking in the sea-tongue, "why don't you tell me who all I've just allowed into my temple."

We gave brief introductions, and Osman returned the favor. He was apparently called the "Hodja" here — a head priest, I gathered from his description. A silence fell for a moment, then the priest asked the inevitable question.

"Why are you here? What trouble have you dragged Talan into?"

I looked at Azhi, and he looked at me. As the others turned to one of the two of us, Osman did the same. I was quickly discovering where Talan had gathered much of his mannerisms and his sharp wit. The priest's stare was difficult to endure.

I was on the verge of admitting our mission when Talan returned. He bore platters filled with pita bread, hard cheese that had a ripe stench and was tinged green, and plump, purple grapes. A veritable feast; reports had been of drought in Avvad as well as Oedija, and I was grateful we wouldn't starve here.

We set to soothing our aching bellies while Talan took charge of the explanations. He painted in broad, bold strokes all we battled against: the Manifest, Avvad, and even Famine. The Hodja didn't seem to begrudge us for the war our leaders had brought us to; to the contrary, he seemed against war entirely and sympathetic to the Oedijan cause. I also thought he would balk at the insinuation that the dragon god existed in actuality, but he only nodded. Only after did it occur to me that he *was* a priest; belief was his expertise.

When Talan finished, I dared to hope the interrogation

was over. Then Osman smiled and said quietly, "So you have pursued Famine here to Erimis. Now what do you mean to do?"

A knife could have cut the silence. My companions all glanced at me, so Osman followed suit. His eyes narrowed minutely, even as the smile never left his lips.

"Airene, wasn't it?"

I nodded. "Airene the Finch, to some."

He smiled wider. "It seems my answer lies with you, by how your friends are trying not to look at you."

I glanced at Talan, but no aid was forthcoming from him. He seemed almost amused as he watched me flail with the decision of how much to reveal. He clearly trusted this priest, and we had put our lives in his hands already. Yet it remained that he was Avvadin, and a worshipper of Valem. I doubted I could ever fully trust him.

But the truth had long been my best weapon. I employed it now.

"We mean to awaken Valem and challenge Famine — to cage him, if we can."

Osman stiffened. His eyes shifted to Talan, who showed no amusement of his own.

"Is this true?" the priest asked quietly. "You want to awaken him?"

Talan's shoulders bowed. "It's the only way."

"It's the wrong way." I saw now why Talan called the Hodja an "old lion" as he leaned his elbows onto his knees, his eyes bright with the firelight. "When Valem awakens, he erupts. You know this. Would you kill thousands, Talan? Thousands of your kinsmen?"

I flinched, though I'd known the price all along. But to put it in such bald terms placed it in a new and disturbing light.

Talan bowed his head and spoke to the floor. "If we do

not, hundreds of thousands more will die. The whole of the Four Realms, and the world besides."

Osman stared at him, then turned his eyes across the others around the room. "You all believe this?" He sounded incredulous. "That you must do this, or the world will end?"

"We *know* this, Hodja Osman," Azhi said, as calm and composed as ever. "It is in Famine's nature to devour, and he will do so until there is nothing left."

The priest seemed slow to anger, but his temper was rising now, telling by the scowl stealing over it. I gripped my seat, half a loaf abandoned on my lap, hoping that coming to the temple hadn't been a mistake.

"I would not hear massacre preached by you, *Qarin*," Osman all but spat. "You, who steals the body of another!"

All of us startled at the accusation, all but Talan and Azhi himself. The daemon only gave a small smile, while the former Guilder shook his head, as if he'd been expecting this.

Perhaps he had. In a rush, I realized Talan had set a trap for us to stop my sacrifice. A trap for *me*. Anger flared within me, and when he glanced my way, I didn't bother hiding it. Talan grimaced and looked away again.

"Yes," Azhi spoke into the silence. "This body is not my own, as my companions know. But I do it only out of necessity, Hodja Osman. I will go to any lengths to stop Taozu, for his tyranny is the guilt I have borne for far longer than you have been alive. Telae must survive, and for that to happen, a sacrifice must be made."

With unerring intuition, Osman looked at me. My temper sputtered out as quickly as it had come, cold fear replacing it.

"Blood and spirit," he muttered. "The same cost, I expect."

Though my feelings of hurt toward Talan had not changed, I looked at him then. How could Osman know this? The priest was far more knowledgeable in these matters than I'd thought possible. By Talan's expression, he wasn't surprised.

The Hodja calmed as he looked at me again. "You do not need to awaken Valem, Airene and company; not yet. As my onetime pupil no doubt believes by bringing you here." He cast a sidelong glance at Talan, who flashed an innocent smile, before continuing. "Even Buyujinn have always been enticed and susceptible to sacrifice. Perhaps, if we work together, we can come up with a different plan."

A different plan. One that did not involve me dying. It sounded too good to be true.

It *was* too good to be true. If it wasn't, someone across the ages would have discovered it before now, and Famine's cycle would have been broken.

But they hadn't. This was the way. The only way.

My hands had tightened into fists. As Talan's eyes flickered down to them, I loosened my muscles and smoothed my face. Neither of us was deceived.

Osman watched the exchange, but he only rose with a sigh. "Stay here the night; rest and think over it. We'll speak more in the morning." He addressed Talan then. "The north dormitory is open. We've had fewer recruits than normal in recent years."

Talan nodded and gestured us out. We thanked our host, but as I met his eyes, I could tell neither of us trusted the other.

Just as well. I already knew I wouldn't be relying on his hospitality for long.

23
THE ONLY WAY

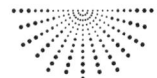

I have betrayed many. I will betray many more. But is it truly betrayal when I do so for the greater good?

- The journal of Vusumuzi; date unknown

While I waited for my companions' breathing to even out in sleep, I drifted into the Pyrthae.

My thoughts had been circling it, so I wasn't surprised to find myself there. The landscape always appeared differently than when I entered the spirit realm in the flesh, and this occasion proved no different.

Erimis had turned into a volcanic wasteland. Lava flowed through the city streets. I could tell where wardens lay by concentrated swirls of cinders, a variation on the cyclones and flames they'd appeared as before. The heat was intense and uncomfortable; radiance dominated the energetic elements here.

It was no mystery why. My gaze traveled to the volcano in which Valem slumbered, ablaze with fire and lava and so bright it hurt to look at. More frightening still was the beast entwining its peak, from whom I felt a hunger that hollowed out my soul.

Famine had a similar form as upon my company's arrival, except he was now wreathed in flames. He'd made progress gnawing through the stone, his head disappearing into the mountainside.

How far did he have to go to feast on Valem's quintessence? I feared it wouldn't be long. Perhaps this new form of his protected him from the volcano's defenses; perhaps it was just a feature of this variant of the Pyrthae. Either way, it didn't bode well for my party's present plans.

I hadn't entered the Pyrthae with any particular intention, but now that I laid eyes on my enemy once more, I felt one crystalize in my mind.

We couldn't afford to delay. If I had to die, I didn't want to live with the fear of it any longer.

Facing the heat below, I dove back into my body. The world turned dark and cool as I opened my eyes in Telae, gasping for air. For a moment, it had seemed I breathed in the fumes exuded by Valem, but in truth, it was only the scent of hot stone. I waited until I'd calmed, then gazed around at my companions.

And froze. A silhouette stood in the open doorway.

As it approached, I opened my locus wide and sucked in energy. This close to Famine, my abilities were as great as they ever were, far surpassing anything another warden could amass. But I couldn't unleash it all without hurting my companions. I had to be careful.

Then a dim glow appeared on the figure's fingers, illuminating their face. I stifled a groan as I repressed my magic and frowned. It was only Talan.

He wore a smirk as he neared, though it lacked some of its usual bite. Maybe it was how shadowed his eyes looked, almost malevolent in the darkness, if I didn't know better.

"Sorry to startle you," he murmured as he kneeled next to my cot.

"Who says you did?"

His smile widened briefly, then disappeared. "Can we talk?"

I nodded, then rose and followed him from the dormitory. I was still dressed, being in the habit from our journey. He had found clean clothes himself, and much more in the Avvadin style than I was used to seeing him wear, with a sash instead of a belt and shoes with pointed toes. Somehow, they suited him.

Talan led me to the rotunda where we'd first seen Osman spinning. When he reached its center, he looked up at the ceiling.

"This is where it happened," he said, his back still to me. "Where I became attuned."

I nodded. He'd told me the story before, though it hit differently to see the place where it had occurred. "When the Buyujinni visited you."

Talan turned to look at me over his shoulder. "The Shrouded Mother, patroness of the Hortum Kor. I thought it a gift. But it turns out she only wanted to steal my soul."

A prickling ran through me. "What did you really want to talk about, Talan?"

He fully faced me then, his stance set like he readied for me to charge him. Seeing him like that, even suspecting his ulterior motives, I wanted to fold him into my arms and be enveloped in his. We'd never had a proper courtship like either of us wanted or deserved. Of all my regrets for my life, it ranked high on the list.

But he was going to try convincing me why Osman was right; I was sure of it. I hardened myself and waited for the attack.

He drew in a breath, then exhaled it slowly. "I've been thinking about all you shared with me, up there. About what you have to do. And there are some things that are just beginning to line up."

"Like?" My interest was piqued, but I tried not to show it, sure he would take advantage of any vulnerability he could.

"That tree in the Wumofu, that Azhi showed you — the Chains. And the one you read about, the one that grew from Aika of the Green."

I nodded, letting the silence draw him out.

One corner of his lips quirked. He wasn't fooled, but he continued all the same. "You've talked about being a Seed of Famine. But Aika also claimed to be a Seed of Harvest. What if that's the important piece, Airene? A tree as a symbol for the Goddess of Bounty — what could be better suited?"

I frowned. It wasn't a poor point; its logic intrigued me. But I didn't see how it would support his argument.

"That doesn't change what I have to do, Talan. The sacrifice I have to make."

He took several steps closer, but stopped just beyond reach. "The temple that Buyujinni lured me to — do you remember how I described it?"

I played along with the tangent, though I remained cautious. "It was like an underground city, all of white stone."

"But it wasn't stone; they were souls, solidified and manifest. I have never forgotten how the city felt alive, and I finally realized that's why this felt so familiar."

Talan's hand went to his waist, and he withdrew the bone-white knife to hold it out before him. I stared at it with fresh eyes, then raised my gaze to meet his.

"You think this knife is made of quintessence as well. The quintessence of Harvest."

He nodded, eyes bright in the moon-lifted darkness. "And not only that. I've been studying that scepter Azhi carries. It looks to be made of the same material as this dagger. And since it was used for a similar purpose, to bind Famine—"

"—maybe it's Harvest's soul."

My head reeled. As with most epiphanies, I found a smile claiming my lips.

Talan grinned as he drew nearer still. "We feared that she was dead, but she's not. Harvest still lives and has for thousands of years. There's hope, Airene. We just have to figure out how to reach her."

My smile faded as I took his assumptions to their conclusion. "I know how to reach her, Talan. It's like Osman says: 'spirit and blood.' Only through sacrifice—"

"*Airene.*" He tucked the knife back into his sash and took my hands in his. "You're thinking too narrowly. What if there's a different way, one that doesn't kill you? What if... I don't know, we sacrificed pigs instead? Every animal has quintessence, right? Maybe that would be enough."

I didn't pull away, but only just. Objections brimmed on my tongue. *It has to be a Seed of Famine*, I wanted to say. *It has to be me.*

But I couldn't speak the words, couldn't extinguish this spark flaring in him. Talan, once made bitter and cynical by the world, had found a reason to hope.

His eyes darted between each of my own, searching for something. "We're close to understanding this. Too close to throw it away by doing the same thing that's been done before and perpetuating the cycle. Swear to me, Airene. Swear to me you won't do anything until we figure this out."

I hesitated. Then I whispered, "I promise."

He seemed taken aback for a moment, then his lopsided smile returned. I ached to see it, for soon it would slip away entirely.

Talan asked for time, but time was precisely what we didn't have. He had meant to convince me of his way of thinking, but the revelations only solidified my own resolutions. It provided rationale to the ritual that would take my life. It helped me make peace with it.

I gazed into his eyes, those belonging to a man I'd come to

care deeply for over these past three years, and my old resolve reemerged. I would do anything to save him. To protect him.

I would die, since that was what it would take.

I freed my hands, wrapped them around the back of his neck, and drew him closer. His breath was warm on my face.

"I love you," I murmured, then channeled as our lips touched.

Quintessence had always had a stronger influence when I touched my target. I was at the height of my power, with Famine having grown strong and being nearby.

Even Talan, as clever and talented as he was, stood no chance.

Sleep, I commanded him, and his eyes widened for a moment. The next, his eyelids drooped closed, and his body went slack. I clung to him, making sure he would not come to harm in the fall. But he surprised me by struggling back upright.

"Airene..." he said thickly, his eyelids fluttering as he tried to focus on my face.

I smiled sadly back at him. *Sleep,* I repeated the command, more forcefully.

He sagged in my arms, dragging me to the floor as I cradled his limp body.

I lingered for a moment after he fell unconscious, loathe to leave him. But he would be safe there, even sprawled in the middle of the floor. Our companions or Osman would discover him come morning, or perhaps before that, if I succeeded in my aim.

I abandoned him for his own safety.

I took Aika's knife from him and clutched it as I stood. I would need nothing else. Not with what I intended.

Only my grasp on quintessence alerted me to the presence of someone behind me.

Spinning around, I readied myself to fight, but saw it was

again unnecessary. Osman stood there, his hair wilder than usual so it truly resembled a lion's mane. I was surprised he was a warden, but only just. It made a certain sense, considering his bond with Talan. But it was his expression that made me truly wary.

"He cares for you," the Hodja said. "As he has cared for no one else."

I clenched my jaw. He knew precisely where to strike, this priest.

"That's why I'm doing this."

"Is it? Or do you want revenge on my country for what it has done to yours?"

The accusation startled me. I opened my mouth to deny it, then paused. Could that be part of why I sought to awaken Valem? For revenge? It bothered me that I couldn't fully say.

But I couldn't show doubt before him, not now. "It's the only way. Please move aside, Osman."

He shook his head. "Don't do this, Airene the Finch. Please. You will kill innocents, thousands of them. I know you must hate my people, but there is much good among us, too. Do not destroy it all."

I tried shutting out the words. What choice did I have? It was one city or the world. I'd already surrendered my home; what was my enemy's capital next to that?

Yet my response came out in a whisper. "I have to."

I didn't hesitate any longer. Calling upon quintessence, I cut a rift into the Pyrthae with the white knife, then leaped inside. Osman's wide eyes were the last I saw of the world.

24
THE FIRES BELOW

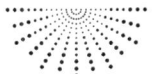

The young are plentiful, their knowledge is shallow, and their desire for glory is great. Send forth one, no younger than fourteen, to the Chains each generation, and name them Yusishu, Savior. Heap honor upon them even after their passing, for thus will children crave to be chosen.

It is not a barbaric practice, as foreigners claim. It is the Savior's duty, and one of the utmost importance. What better purpose for one's life, what greater glory, than to give oneself to save one's people?

- The Ancestors' Path; by Matriarch Yin Shengton of Daodo-Yuan; estimated 900 SLP

The world burned around me.

I almost stepped back into the rift as the heat rolled over my being. Radiance shimmered violet in the air, unbalancing the energies and throwing them into chaos. I had no flesh here, but I was pained as if I did.

But Famine had made me strong enough to endure. Hardening the borders of my soul, I closed the portal between the planes, then exited the temple. Erimis now reflected the true one I'd left behind in Telae, but for the searing air.

My gaze was drawn upward, and there my quarry lay still: Famine, burrowing into the volcano. He was not aflame now, and as lava flowed around his head, his scales blackened beneath it. Still, if it caused him injury, it wasn't enough to stop him.

I looked down at my hand, still clutching the impression of Aika's knife. I didn't know precisely what I had to do, but I knew where it ended.

I walked toward the volcano and the dragon atop it.

Maybe I could have flown to him, freed of Telae's natural laws as I was, but there was a comfort in walking. It delayed the inevitable, and I treasured that small luxury.

I barely noticed the city as I moved through it. My chest was heavy with regret. I would never say goodbye to Linos or the rest of my family. My last act toward Jaxas was to abandon him and his city, my home. And there were my friends, of course: Nomusa, Xaron, Corin. Talan. I had to put them from my mind before I fled back the way I'd come.

But maybe I would see Thero soon, after so many years apart. I smiled and hoped it was true.

Before I knew it, I'd passed beyond the city walls and begun ascending the side of the mountain. In Telae, such exercise would have left me out of breath before I'd taken a dozen steps. Here, with Famine's power fueling me and his hunger driving me on, I was relentless.

The heat increased with every step. Radiance dominated the air, almost to the exclusion of any other element. It was all I could do to endure it.

Yet it was better than what simmered under my feet. This also resembled heat, but one that bludgeoned my spirit. Pressure built inside me as I fought against the intrusion. My resolve weakened, and something else leaked in.

Rage roared to life in my chest.

I stopped where I was, struck by the force of it. I should not have to sacrifice everything! Why should I die when no one else did? It wasn't *fair*, wasn't *right*. So I wouldn't do it. They could damn well save themselves if they wanted to! I would show them, show all of them—

I mended my fragile walls and collapsed onto the searing ground.

The sudden wrath that had swept over me still pressed at my mind, undiminished in its strength, but it no longer dominated me. The force of it left me trembling. In a moment, I'd almost abandoned everything I'd been working toward.

But Valem would not be put off for long.

I would have wept for fear and frustration had I been able to. As it was, there was only one thing I could do. I drew upon the deep reservoirs of vigor Famine had connected me to, rose to my feet, and kept climbing.

The caldera atop the volcano drew near. Lava flowed around me now, rivers of fire that would eat through skin and bone in seconds. Famine was close as well. In Telae, it might have been only a hundred cubits before me that his first coil lay; here, distance was more fickle, less easy to pin down. I stared at his scaled body, twenty times my height and dark as a moonless night, and tried unsuccessfully to banish my fear.

At fifty paces away, I stopped. It was close enough; it had to be, for I could make myself go no farther. Now came the first of my uncertainties.

How would I awaken Valem?

I raised Aika's knife again, wondering if it was up to the task. Did it only work to cage Famine because I was his Seed? Or because Harvest was his antithesis? Or perhaps there was another reason I didn't know.

But it wasn't to cage the Avvadin god that I acted now,

but only to awaken him. For that, all I needed was within me: spirit and blood.

Blood required a body, however, and that meant returning to Telae. I didn't know what Valem's sides would be like so high up, but judging by the lava spilling around me, it would be far from hospitable. Hoping I would live long enough for the task, I lifted my hand to cut open the rift.

"Airene, *wait!*"

I startled and spun around to see someone hurrying up the mountain behind me. I barely recognized him, for his shape was cloudy and amorphous under the strain of with-standing the Quintyr. But as I saw two spirits separating from each other, I knew who it was.

"What are you doing here?" I demanded of Azhi. I wanted to ask if Eazal was breaking free, but didn't. Part of me hoped he would manage it. Even though he'd tried to kill me, his enslavement had never sat easy with me.

Azhi stopped and crumpled to the ground. But though he looked spent, his voice reverberated within me.

"Aiding you. You should have told me you were going. I would have come."

I ignored the reprimand. There was no time for it. "How can you help? You're barely staying together."

"I am sufficient for this." His blurred form rose a little, as if he straightened on his knees, while the half of him I guessed to be Eazal strained back down the slope. "I have brought the Binding Ruyi to awaken Valem."

That finally piqued my interest. "We don't want to cage him, just awaken him."

"It will. Through it, I will give of myself to him. A sacrifice of spirit."

Spirit and blood, Osman had said. But I decided Azhi stood as good a chance of knowing what would work as the priest did.

"Fine. Can you do it here, in the Pyrthae?"

"Yes. If I let go…"

Before I could ask what he meant, Azhi split apart.

I took a step toward him, hand outstretched, shock shivering through me. I'd seen it coming, yet still, I wasn't ready for it. As the front half of his spirit collapsed, the back half flowed swiftly down the volcano. The farther away they went, the more solidified their form became, until I could clearly see it was Eazal who fled his captor.

In a single smooth motion, Azhi rose to hover in the air. Once again, he wore the form of the Qao Fu boy he'd been before he'd died. Free from chaining Eazal, his poise had returned and his force multiplied.

"He will survive," the pyr said at my lingering look. His voice was a boy's too, higher-pitched and prone to cracking. "He knows many of my tricks now."

I hoped he was right. Eazal had tried to kill me, but only because he was under duress. I'd forgiven Corin for her betrayal under the same circumstances. Could I do any less for the apothecary?

But he couldn't be my concern now. I turned back to look uphill, at the massive, sinuous body, and the gouts of flame and smoke beyond. I was ready.

Ready to die.

"Awaken him."

I felt Azhi comply before I saw it. His quintessence was like a cool breeze amid the fiery terrain. I glanced back and saw him slowly walking on the slope behind me, the scepter dragging along the stone. A trail of white mist billowed out from behind it to settle on the black rock. The boy spirit wore a solemn expression, and I wondered at how young he must have been when he first set out to do this. No older than thirteen, by his look.

But he was a child no longer. He had a right to make his own sacrifices.

Azhi channeled his spirit into the mountain, and the

stone lapped it up like a thirsty hound. He wandered away from my position, making a revolution of the volcano, never moving the scepter's head from the stone. I began to follow, the need to bear witness too strong to ignore. It wouldn't take me away from Famine, for he was always just above, writhing in anticipation. Besides, I had to know if he faded before Valem awakened, in case I needed to finish the job.

Erimis disappeared from view as we went around the far side of the volcano. Where lava flowed in our path, Azhi hovered above it, dragging the scepter through, while I hopped with unnatural buoyancy. My daemon guide was being worn down, but he kept moving and channeling, never stopping for more than a moment. Despite myself, I wanted to reach out and help him, but I knew what his answer would be, the only answer it could be.

This was his burden to bear. My own would come soon.

As I walked, my mind wandered into dangerous fantasies. Talan charging up the mountainside and dissuading me from this course of action, having found a different way to deal with Famine. Xaron and Nomusa restraining me and convincing me to run far away from all of this. Corin still attempting to repay the debt she felt she owed me by offering to be the Sacrifice in my stead. Even Eazal, running back up the mountain and throwing himself at Azhi to stop him from waking Valem.

But none of them came; I'd evaded or subdued them too well. I was alone with the daemon.

Azhi tripped and fell to one knee, and I startled out of my daydreams. Before I could speak, he used the scepter to pry himself up and limp on. Only then did I wonder what the cost of this act would be for him. If he gave of himself as fully as I soon would.

Only then did I trust him, and was sorry that it had taken me so long.

Had nothing happened thus far, I would have stopped

him. But the volcano below us, always alive, became increasingly violent. Radiance was not the only thing to burn now. From deep in the ground, a distant presence welled up, building with every passing moment. I knew it was sentient just as I felt Azhi to be, its quintessence resonating with mine. But this was a foreign mind, strange in its workings, both too simple and too vast to comprehend. I could barely focus on it, or even endure it, for it was painful to behold.

Valem was awakening.

My heart ached for Azhi, stumbling now with each step, but I turned my face skyward. Famine had noticed the rousing of the Quintyr he meant to feast upon, judging by the savage vibrations of his folds. Whether he would fight or flee, I couldn't tell. I had to be ready to act swiftly, to see the moment he was weakest and take advantage of it.

The ground rumbled beneath me, and a new feeling roused in me.

Though it seemed like little time had passed, we had nearly completed a circuit around the volcano, and Erimis came back into view. As the lava gushed from the top and sides of Valem, I thought of all the people Talan and Osman had pleaded on behalf of. This god would not come gently; he would wipe out half the city before they rose from their beds. Perhaps even my friends would be caught in the destruction.

I'd known this would happen, all of it. But until that moment, I hadn't felt it.

This was what Vusu would do, what he *had* done. Spending lives like coins.

I would willingly give my life to defeat Famine. But I had to do it without becoming the man who stole my brothers from me.

"*Azhi!*" I shouted in a way beyond words. "*Stop! We cannot do this!*"

The spirit boy paused, turned back. He barely kept his

shape anymore, his essence leaking in a cloud around him, so I couldn't tell if he met my eyes or not. Yet I sensed something in him understood me.

"*All those people!*" I continued. "*They'll die, Azhi! They won't escape!*"

His head fell so his gaze was on the scepter, still touching the stone. As he looked back up at me, I mimed lifting my arm, then realized I might have to do it for him; he didn't seem to have the strength anymore. I lurched into a fast walk, though it was difficult even to move.

I was half a dozen strides away when lava spewed up from beneath his feet.

"*No!*"

I fell to my knees as I stared at where the boy had been. The lava blinded me, yet I couldn't look away.

The volcano had swallowed him whole.

Once more, I was too late.

Valem rumbled alive, and fresh lava spilled up from behind. I began to fear the same fate awaited me. I couldn't stop what Azhi had begun. Now, I had to press forward. If I wasn't to waste Azhi and Erimis's sacrifices, I had to act now.

I looked up at Famine, muttered a half-hearted prayer, and cut back into Telae.

Then stopped and stared.

The eruption was not just happening in the Pyrthae. In my plane as well, Valem spilled forth lava. Through the rift, I saw it flowing beneath where I would step out, as well as for a score of paces to either side. And telling from what was happening in the spiritual plane, the entire mountainside might explode at any moment.

I sealed the rift shut, but I didn't relent. This was my last chance. I ran up the volcano, rivers of fire drawing ever nearer on either side. When I judged I'd moved to a clear spot from my brief glimpse, I cut a rift again. Lava lay before me still, but I was closer. I almost didn't bother sealing it, but

I was trying to mend the world, not break it further. I braved ever nearer the lava and tried again.

Stone, as hot as all the hells, lay before me.

I didn't stop for doubt — I threw myself out of the rift. And was nearly knocked flat by the heat.

A scream worked free of my throat, but I couldn't hear it. Roaring filled my ears. My flesh felt aflame; perhaps it was. I was dying, and not slowly.

I had to do it now.

Somehow, I mustered the concentration to channel quintessence. The Pyrthae came back into view, as did Famine. To my surprise and horror, the daemon god no longer tried to feast on the volcanic Quintyr, but had drawn out. His dragon countenance was marred with oozing burns, and his size had lessened. His quintessence shone half as bright.

He was injured and diminished. So far, the plan was working.

Valem rumbled, and fresh lava spurted up, splashing over Famine, weakening him further.

This was my chance. My last chance.

"*Famine!*" I shouted in both realms. My body was failing, but my soul clung on.

The daemon god swiveled his immense head to stare at me, death-black eyes set among the charred scales.

I held up Aika's knife trembling before my chest. *"I offer myself as Sacrifice!"*

I drove the knife toward my flesh.

I waited for the pain. The cold. The darkness.

But there was nothing.

With my vision in the Pyrthae, it took me a long time to realize why. Only as I opened my real eyes did I discover I'd been knocked off my feet. I looked at my hands, red and blistered, only to find they were empty. I looked around me; only black stone and orange, sweltering air.

Then I saw the knife. Burning in lava.

I didn't even have the breath to scream. I watched as the only thing that could bind Famine swiftly smoldered into ashes. Did I imagine the shriek as Harvest's soul disappeared into the aether? Perhaps it was only in my head.

I raised my gaze and found Famine had turned away from me, my hold over him lost. Then, with Valem still lashing after him, he turned and flew away.

I watched him go, my body dying, my soul fractured. Perhaps I would have stayed there, but for what happened next.

The volcano erupted.

25

RAGE, HOPE, DESPAIR

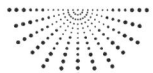

Rage, hope, despair
The Lord laments, the Lord laments
Fear, awe, prepare
The worthy ascend, the worthy ascend

- Prayer to Valem, origin unknown

A s the sky rained stone and fire, I fled.
Instinct saved me. I didn't will myself upright; my body acted on its own initiative. I didn't consciously cut into the Pyrthae; my hand and mind conspired against me.

I didn't want to live, but I couldn't help but keep on doing just that.

Even as I escaped into the spirit realm, I found little relief. Radiance churned all around me, as dangerous as the lava in Telae. The need to survive numbed all else, so I easily imposed beliefs on my mind.

The sky is weightless, I thought, and lifted from the ground to float over the volcano.

I didn't look down until the heat had begun to fade. When I finally did, the sight that greeted me was too bizarre to understand. The mountain was red and black, smoke and fire billowing out of it like a sea of daemons. I felt Valem, too, and his earth-shaking rage. The city suffered for it; the ground cracked, the lava flowed, and the stones fell upon the rooftops.

My fault, I reminded myself, then descended.

I didn't care about my life, but I still cared for my friends. Already, I feared I was too late. With dangerous speed, I dove toward the temple of the Hortum Kor, too near the feet of the volcano. Horror grew as the heat of Valem's fury blazed about me again. *I cannot be hurt*, I willed to myself, and as I crashed into the rotunda, it was so.

Slipping in a window and falling to the floor, I finally cut my way back into the material world. Stepping free, the injuries I had suffered announced themselves with screaming urgency. I gasped and choked, noxious gases having nearly suffocated me upon Valem's slope. My skin was in agony, and more with each movement as it pulled and tore. I lumbered forward, feeling a corpse somehow still standing, and went to the dormitory where I'd left them.

There they were, shouting and pulling together their things, arguing over something that my mind couldn't parse.

Then they saw me.

At once, they collapsed about me, touching me until I flinched back in pain. Did they know the emergency? I tried to tell them, yet couldn't form coherent words. But I could show them with my actions, and I did, cutting back into the Pyrthae and gesturing them inside.

Though hesitant, Xaron obeyed first, dragging Isidora with him into the rift. Corin ushered Kari in next, and Nomusa came after. They all looked at me, but I could barely meet their gazes. My vision was hazy, yet I could still read what was behind their eyes.

Talan shouldered my pack along with his own, but he

didn't follow the others. His eyes smoldered on me; there was no hint of a smile now.

I gestured to the portal, hoping he would understand. He glanced to the side, toward Osman's chamber, then hung his head as he strode forward into the Pyrthae.

I entered last, sealing the tear behind me. Only then did I realize I hadn't done so atop Valem. I wondered what the consequences of that would be. Surely no worse than what had already befallen Erimis.

No sooner had I turned back to my companions than did Talan seize my arm. With the touch came all he wished to convey to me, and I reeled under the onslaught: the anger, the betrayal, the fear.

He released me a moment later, but the knowledge lingered, burning in a different way than my wounds. Talan turned his back on me and faced the others.

"We head for the outside of the city," he announced, then led the way.

The others looked at me, but the situation was clear. Escape first; questions later. I shambled after them, bringing up the rear.

We didn't make it far into Erimis's streets before we had to will ourselves into the air. In this realm, at least, lava flowed in rivers down the stones. We'd seen the path of past fire rivers on our way in, but Valem didn't content himself to that avenue this time. It was everywhere, destroying and all-consuming. None of his worshippers were spared his fury.

In the air, we were safe. I found it easiest to move, for I kept few of my beliefs now, and my mind latched onto any I provided it. Almost, I flew as I did when I entered the Pyrthae as spirit alone. The others floated to the reflection and entered the third fold, coming out again ahead of me from the bend in time. I could have followed, but something in me didn't allow it.

When Erimis's walls lay behind us, Talan gestured to

descend. I followed, though fear had returned, seeping through my stupefaction. We landed in a forest clearing, then Talan opened a path back into Telae.

No sooner had I set foot on real earth did I collapse. My body shrieked in protest, but I couldn't muster up the will to care as I sprawled on the grass. The sky glowed red above, Valem's fires lighting up the night. I wanted to sleep and never wake, but my companions crowded around me, hounding me with questions.

"Airene, oh Airene... How did you get those burns?" Nomusa reached out a hand, but stopped short of touching me.

"How can we help?" Xaron wrung his hands. He kept glancing at Isidora, but the First Watcher only frowned.

"Where is Azhi?" she asked.

I only shook my head. I couldn't muster any other answer.

Corin watched on with evident concern, while Kari looked curious. And Talan... My gaze wandered up to him, willing him to look at me, but he only scowled off into the woods. My head fell, unable to keep upright any longer.

After silence fell, I tried speaking and found I could whisper. "I'm sorry."

Xaron and Nomusa leaned in close. "Sorry?" Xaron queried. He gave Nomusa a look. "For what, Airene?"

"For killing all those people." Talan didn't look around as he spoke the damning words.

I tried to speak, but couldn't again. My throat had swelled up, and not only from inhaling smoke.

"Did you...?" Isidora's eyes widened. "You did, didn't you?"

I nodded, unable to look at her.

"Did what?" Xaron threw a hand toward the fire-wreathed mountain. Even miles away, ash rained down on us from Valem. "You're saying she did *this*?"

"Yes," I whispered. "Azhi, too."

My companions shared a silent conversation. When they turned back to me, I saw their consensus was not falling in my favor.

"Airene..." Nomusa bit her lip. "You cannot be serious."

I cleared my throat, to no avail. "I am."

"*That?* How could you do that? Tyurn's balls, it's a volcano! You can't make a volcano erupt on your own!"

"But he's not just a volcano," Talan interjected. "He's a god. And she made a sacrifice to him."

I shook my head. "Azhi did. He gave his life. I wanted to..." *Stop him*, I almost said, but cut myself short. Excuses didn't matter now; I was complicit, and all knew it.

"And Famine?" Isidora watched me with narrowed eyes. "Did you stop him?"

"No." I held up my empty, scarred hands. "I lost them. The knife. The scepter. They're gone."

Everyone went still as the implications set in.

"The scepter *and* the knife..." Xaron let loose a joyless laugh. "But Airene, those were the tools we needed to—"

"I know." An edge had returned to my voice, though he didn't deserve it.

Isidora looked between the others. "Those were to be used to cage Famine, weren't they? So it's impossible now?"

I nodded, but couldn't speak the affirmation. It was too terrible to utter aloud.

My companions reeled, each in their own way. Xaron laughed. Nomusa stalked off to the edge of the clearing. Isidora kneeled where she stood. Corin frowned, reacting so little I wondered if she understood. Talan didn't move a muscle.

Yet Kari's response was most curious of all, for she smiled with what seemed genuine amusement.

"It is not," she said. "The same is in you, Airene. In all of us, but you most of all."

I stared dully at her, not bothering to try and understand.

She was mad; no one else could be undeterred by what I'd just confessed.

Without warning, Talan turned and brought the focus of the group on him. His eyes were only for me, though.

"She's right. It's not done. Not yet."

His words were cold, but fire blazed within them. I found it hard to meet his gaze, but forced myself to all the same.

"What do you mean?" I asked, voice rasping.

No warmth radiated from him as he spoke. "You shared all you knew with me, Airene. And I believe I've figured out something that you overlooked. As I would have done eventually, had you given me more time."

I winced, but didn't look away. I'd done too much of that lately.

"Don't leave us in suspense." Xaron crossed his arms.

Talan glanced at him, then turned back to me. "Those items — the knife, the scepter. We guessed them to be shards of Harvest, her soul made material."

I nodded. The others stared, surprise written into their expressions. He didn't pause to explain, but only continued.

"But there's a reason they felt familiar to you." His eyes bore into me. "A reason Vusu targeted your family. And I think a part of you has known why for a while."

I stilled but for the shivering brought about by my burns. I couldn't have turned away from him had I tried. My silence drew him out.

"Harvest lives in you, Airene. You carry a piece of her spirit. You're her 'seed,' just as surely as you're Famine's."

The declaration fell upon me like a droplet in still water. It rippled through my being, changing everywhere it touched. I didn't know what to make of it, but I felt the resonance of the truth.

"Like Aika," I muttered. "A Seed of Harvest and Famine."

Talan nodded. His smile had returned, but I wish it

hadn't. It was bitter and cold and biting, and all for my benefit.

"I felt her when you surrendered your memories. I didn't know what she was, but she is a distinct part of you." His voice fell softer. Our companions were frozen around us, transfixed by what he said. "Hope isn't lost. Not as long as Harvest lives within you."

Hope. Did I still have hope after all I'd witnessed, all I'd done? I hung my head. Though I felt dry of all moisture, tears squeezed from my eyes.

A hand touched my shoulder, then a second. Next I knew, my companions surrounded me, comforting, mourning. I looked up and stared at them through blurred vision, and though every touch was agony, the consolation was greater.

Only Talan remained apart. I looked at him and knew what lay between us couldn't be ignored.

"I'm sorry, Talan. Sorry I woke Valem. Sorry I betrayed you. Is... is Osman alright? His priests, and the children?"

As if they were the words he'd been waiting to hear, Talan deflated with a sigh. "They should be fine. Osman has places to hide, and no small power of his own. He'll protect them."

I tried to smile, but my lips wouldn't comply. As soon as Talan saw it, his face hardened again, even as he kneeled behind the others.

"But Airene, if we're to do this, to defeat Famine, you must trust us, all of us. We won't let you fail. We all need this to succeed. You aren't fighting this war alone."

Before, I wouldn't have believed him. I thought that since I had to die, I alone carried the burden of the world.

But I wasn't the only one to have made sacrifices. All of them had lost something or someone. And Azhi's absence was a reminder that some might even have to give their own lives.

I wiped gingerly at my tears and nodded. "I know that now."

Quiet reigned for a time before Xaron broke it.

"So... what now? Do we chase after Famine again?" His expression turned sour. "What are we supposed to do when we find him this time?"

"That depends on her." Talan scooted closer to sit cross-legged before me. "You said before that the knife was the only way to access Harvest. But I don't think that's true. I touched her through your spirit. Perhaps, if you try, you can as well." He paused, his eyes flickering around our group before settling back on me. "Reach for Harvest, Airene. You must be able to touch her. I suspect you already have, on some level. We need you to now. Reach for her."

I didn't protest or ask how. I'd made catastrophic mistakes and betrayed his trust; now was my chance to atone. Closing my eyes, I cleared my mind, then let her name fill it.

Harvest?

No response. I didn't give up. Talan had felt her within me, within my spirit. Perhaps by accessing it, I could reach her.

I opened my locus, channeled quintessence, and drifted halfway into the Pyrthae. Valem's awakening buffeted me from his distant mountain, while Famine's hunger pulled me in the opposite direction. I tried to ignore both as I reached not outward with my spirit, but within. Was there a similar presence to the other Quintyr there? I couldn't detect anything. Doubt seeded through me. Yet Talan was right: I had to trust him, or I would fail once more.

Harvest. I fixed her name in my mind. Perhaps it wasn't her true name, but on this plane, it was never about words. Intention, will, and belief were the organizing principles here, the laws by which the spirit realm was formed. Those would have to be enough.

Harvest, I called again. *Hear me, Harvest. Do you sleep in me? Have you been with me my entire life?*

I thought of the ways she might have impacted me. Perhaps she had insulated me from my childhood; the loss of my brother and the scorn of my mother could have easily scarred me, as they had Linos. Perhaps it hadn't been Famine or Clepsammia who spawned my ambition, but the sliver of Harvest's soul living within me. After all, the need to strive for ever greater things could be more than a hunger; it could be growth as well.

But there were other events where I could infer her direct interference. I hadn't perished when Famine struck me and made me his own, opening my locus to channeling, nor when fire blossomed from me during Eazal's attempted assassination. I had healed.

Was that you, Harvest? Did you heal me?

All those days and nights of seeking the truth about Famine — something had sustained me and kept me going. Though I suffered failure again and again, I didn't yield. There was a well within me, depthless, that had never yet run out.

Are you that well? Answer me, Harvest, please!

I delved into myself, memories manifesting around me, then fading in turn. I sifted through them, but could never find more than a trace of the goddess. If Harvest had to do with any of those events, there was no explicit link.

Then an idea occurred to me. If Harvest had ever appeared, it had been in my time of need. Where Famine desired the sacrifice of others, Harvest longed to sacrifice herself.

I hesitated, then took the plunge. I broke down the walls I'd erected to keep at bay all the hurts, fears, and doubts that plagued me and let them inundate my mind, filling it to the exclusion of all else. It felt as if I would die, floundering among them, drowning in the flood of despair. I treaded water, while the Pyrthae twisted around me, molding to the onslaught of emotion so it became a waking nightmare.

Harvest, please... I need you...

Something changed.

At first, it was a gentle warmth, like morning sunlight grazing an eyelid. With that first contact, my awareness expanded, the feeling spreading throughout my mind, then my body. She didn't force her way anywhere, but gently touched until I invited her further in. I didn't resist or fight back. I didn't give in to the apprehension at what I attempted. I trusted her as I trusted Talan, and Nomusa and Xaron, and all the friends and allies I'd gathered along the way. And with it came a blossoming that didn't banish my fears, but filled me with hope and invigoration so no room remained for them.

Harvest. Her name filled my mind as her presence filled my soul. She pulsed in recognition, and I smiled.

"Airene!"

I didn't want to leave her, but with my needs fulfilled, she was already departing. Reluctantly, I felt her glow fade, her warmth cool, until I almost shivered in her absence.

But I didn't, not quite. For now, I held the truth. She *was* in me; she always had been.

Harvest was alive in my soul.

I ceased to channel, closed my locus, and opened my eyes. And found my companions crowded around me, squawking in amazement.

As I comprehended what had caught their fascination, I looked down at my hands and blinked. My hands had been red and chapped before, burned by the nearness of the lava and heat in the air. Now, they were whole, my skin beige and unblemished. I lifted my sleeves and found the same; looked at my sandaled feet and it was no different. I touched my face, and all was as if the events of the night had never occurred.

"What happened?" I expected the question to come out as a croak, but my throat had mended as well.

"You healed." Nomusa tentatively brushed her fingertips over my cheek, her eyes wide. "You were burned, then you started to heal."

"Like before," Corin added. She leaned over the others. "After you became a warden."

Kari glanced up at her sister, her brow scrunched. "Of course she did. Why would she not?"

Corin only shook her head.

"Was it her?" The question came from Talan, who kneeled next to Nomusa. "Was it Harvest?"

I nodded. Then, though it seemed impossible after everything that had occurred, I smiled.

"You were right, Talan. She *was* within me. She is still. And I know how to reach her. She'll come when I need her."

Thinking of Famine and the coming confrontation dampened my elation, but it didn't smother it. She'd driven away too many of my fears for that now.

He nodded, and even gave me a small smile. But no more. I didn't begrudge him that. I still owed him much, and was prepared to continue to pay my debt for as long as I could.

"Time to go." Talan paused, looking at me. "Which way did he fly?"

At his words, the others seemed to rouse from their reveries, and they looked to me for an answer. I didn't need to ask whom he meant.

"Due north."

"North." Xaron frowned as he looked north. "Only one thing lies in that direction."

I'd guessed the same thing. "Yes. He's returning to Oedija."

Silence descended once more, suspended for a long moment.

"Why?" Nomusa's voice was heavy with resignation. "After traveling the length of the Four Realms, why return now?"

I think she knew even as she asked. But I spoke the conclusion aloud.

"There is war there, which means souls to devour. But I think it's more. I think he feels it's time. Time to break through."

Despite the gift Harvest had given me, fresh horror awoke in me then. *Linos*. I didn't know how Famine could force his way into Telae, but I suspected my brother had something to do with it. I'd failed him too much already to allow that to happen.

"To Oedija, then." Talan sounded almost wistful.

To Oedija. It was far from the homecoming any of us wished for.

But still, we were homeward bound.

26

THE ENDLESS STAIR

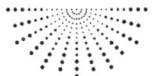

They watch from great heights. They wait, though we know not for what. Sometimes, they grow restless...
   Dare not venture near, lest you are lost to their whims.

- Scroll fragment; origin unknown; estimated 84 SLP

With our path clear before us, we wasted no time in setting upon it.

Everyone was tired. Hungry. Exhausted in both spirit and body. But no one complained as I opened a rift back into the Pyrthae, nor faltered as I instructed everyone to lift themselves up to the reflected world hanging overhead.

We had hope again. And after so long without it, it sustained us as nothing else could.

I alone felt truly revitalized. Harvest had cleansed me of many of the ills plaguing me; not entirely, but enough to gift me strength. Famine fed me more. Through our ill-fated connection, I felt small spurts of pleasure. He was feasting, which likely meant he had already reached our city. The sands were running out, and we were still so far away.

"We have to rise," I called to the others. "To the third fold."

They stared back at me, terror plain in their expressions and in the color emanating from their spirits. I understood it and shared it. This was a desperate act. But now I knew I was strong enough for it.

"The storm!" Nomusa objected. "What if it finds us again?"

"Then we'll flee it. But we have to try, Nomusa. It's our only chance of arriving in time. Famine will use Linos if he can; I know he will. I cannot allow it, nor can the world afford it."

She stared at me for a long moment, then nodded. With her capitulation, the others began to fall. I looked last at Talan, willing him to understand. Then I realized it wasn't resistance I saw in him, but determination. He would stay with me to the last.

Gratitude washed through me, and as I smiled at him, he returned it with one of his own.

The feeling was short-lived as we ascended. Kari had the presence of mind to assist her sister this time. I went to Nomusa, but she lifted off the ground of her own will, scowling as she stared at the reflected world above.

As we rose through the air, Valem and Erimis came into clearer view. The city had become a wasteland. Its streets were orange and bright with the molten fire flowing through them. Yet there was something beautiful to it, if I forgot the suffering of those within it. Something that inspired awe and humbled me.

I looked away as the reflected land above drew nearer. With trees hanging upside down around me, I pressed my hands against the grass and dirt, then willed myself through.

I'd hoped the third fold of the Pyrthae would feel warmer than the last time, but as I emerged and stood on the feature-less tile floor, the chilling winds proved to be unabated. Girding myself against them, I waited for my companions to gather around.

"We have to go as high as we can!" I had to shout to be heard over the gale. "I'll build a staircase so we don't get lost!"

"Build a staircase?" Xaron narrowed his eyes, and from more than the knifing wind. "Out of what?"

I only closed my eyes in answer and imagined it. There was a resonance to the Pyrthae, and all the more in the relative emptiness of the third fold. I knew my will had been enacted even before I opened my eyes.

The mist that swirled and danced through the sky had coalesced into stairs, rising as far as I could see. I smiled. The sight of them doubly reinforced my belief; they would hold during our flight.

Looking back at Xaron, I found him emanating amazement as he stared up at it. The others were in much the same state. I suspected their belief would also work to maintain the stairs.

A sliver of doubt remained. If this didn't work, we'd be lost in the Pyrthae, perhaps for good. But now wasn't the moment for hesitation.

"No time to waste," I called to my companions, then set my foot on the misty staircase. The first step held, as did the second. Soon, the tiled floor was falling away below me, and all my companions followed behind.

We climbed. The third fold was never-changing. The wind blew; the mist swirled; the light shone with cool, diffused light. Only the disappearance of the floor below showed any sign of progress, and then for only a moment.

I only just kept my doubts at bay. My belief had to be absolute if we were to make it through. I resolved to climb as high as we could, then build the stairs back down. No use in questioning whether it would build the right way down, or lose our sense of direction entirely. Belief was our salvation now.

We climbed, and climbed, and climbed, and the others soon wearied. Not in limb or body, for they had none; their souls themselves were eroded by the numbing winds. I felt much the same, though whenever I tired, I thought of Harvest slumbering within me and took heart in her. I wouldn't falter so long as she was with me.

"Should we turn back?"

I didn't look around at Talan, worried staring down at the staircase fading into the mist would break my belief. "Soon."

No sooner had I spoken than I felt them.

They appeared as light, glowing like distant suns above. The sensation came closer with each step, crowding in like the heat of a lit hearth. I almost felt I could reach out and touch it; then I tried, stretching my arms overhead.

Something brushed my hands.

I should have been startled, but the presence behind that touch was calm, reassuring. I knew they meant me no harm, not when their assurances whispered in my head. They didn't speak in words, but in feelings.

They promised an unchanging existence. They promised solace, respite. Oblivion, the final rest.

Why fight against that?

"Airene, I feel something." Talan spoke again, as if from a great distance. It was difficult for me to focus on his words. "There's a change in the air."

I paused in my questing after the vast minds above. Only then did I sense it: a distant agitation that jangled through me like I'd drank one cup of coffee too many.

The realization struck me just as Talan announced it: "Another storm!"

I withdrew from whatever beings I'd touched souls with. I didn't want to; I longed to throw myself after them, to accept all they offered. But my companions needed me, as did everyone else remaining in the world below. I couldn't rest yet.

"We'll descend as quickly as we can." I adjusted my will, and the stairs rearranged themselves. Opening my eyes, I saw the staircase now went down, fading into the mist. I felt off balance for a moment. How did I know it would lead back to Telae and the first fold? That the direction truly was down?

I shook my head, then stepped forward, holding to hope.

The storm was coming, and quickly. Magnesis resonated within me, the elements that my soul had gathered around it sparking. Yet it was not the only unfamiliar sensation. A slight pressure came from above, like the weight of the sky in the material plane, but a fraction of its strength. Sensations stirred inside me, like a churning in my belly, one thing spawning another in a chain of energy. I couldn't associate these elements with anything I'd felt before. Were they different combinations, or entirely new energies, like the catalysm Xaron's mother used?

But such ideas wouldn't save us from the storm. I pressed the notions away, firmed my will, and hurried my pace.

We ran down the steps, taking them two at a time. I contemplated leaping off and attempting to fall back to Telae. But it was too risky; there was no sensation for orientation up here but for the staircase and the mild sky-weight, and both would disappear as soon as we drew away from them.

We had to stay the course. It was the only sure way.

The storm overtook us, as I'd known it would. But it wasn't above us like the previous time; now, it surged to life all around. My companions cried out as the air became charged. I felt my soul shriek its terror. But the staircase held, and our descent continued. If we could keep going, could only endure...

The first strike boomed behind me.

Stopping mid-stride, I whirled around and saw a body falling slowly into the mist by the stairs.

"*Talan!*"

I threw myself after him.

Propelled by terror, I caught Talan in moments and

wrapped myself around him. Belief was sufficient to rise back to the staircase, still faintly above us. I reached it and collapsed upon it, setting him down roughly. The stairs were only so wide, so his body, as much as it still resembled one, dangled off either end. Our companions were nowhere to be seen.

"Airene, Talan! Where are you?"

Their cries came from above; the fools must have stopped. Growling in frustration, I lifted Talan onto my shoulders, then set back up. I wouldn't have been able to carry him in Telae, but here, my strength was sufficient. The air had turned violet. I could see the impressions of lightning all around me, just waiting to be unleashed.

But what if I believed they couldn't hurt us? A desperate gambit perhaps, but it was worth a shot. It was our only possible defense.

The rest of our party came into view above. As soon as they saw me laden with Talan, they hurried down. I waited, trying not to expect lightning to strike, but denying it instead. Doubt would get us killed.

They reached us, but even as they babbled questions, I turned with barely an acknowledgement and ran downward. *It cannot hurt us*, I thought, I hoped, I pleaded. *The lightning will not strike me.*

A bolt flashed down three stairs below. I flinched, then scolded myself for it. Belief couldn't be a shield if it cracked. I firmed it.

Then the world shattered.

I was falling, a thousand shards of glass tinkling to the ground. But there was no ground — only pain and air and endless wind. I was lost among it.

It was some time before I could see. Even as my vision cleared, the pain stayed. I bore it as I took in my surroundings. Nothing but blue air all around. I'd fallen free of the storm, at least.

Then I noticed I wasn't alone; somehow, I still clung to Talan. *Magnesis*, I realized; we'd been charged to stick to one another. A lucky stroke.

But there, our luck ran out. The stairs were gone from sight. We could not know up from down. In every direction hovered the same mist, the same blue light, the same chilling wind.

We were lost in the third fold.

"Talan?" I reached for him in a way beyond words. Our spirits were touching, so I could feel his lack of awareness. I could only hope it wasn't a permanent state.

I would have to get out of this on my own.

I racked my mind. I delved into my senses for any change in the environment. There was nothing, nothing at all. Harvest couldn't save me here.

Then I realized another Quintyr could.

Famine's hunger had become so much a part of me I had forgotten it for a moment. Still, it tugged, pulling me toward the daemon god who had connected me to this world. I smiled and willed myself after it.

The irony of my salvation was too rich.

Assured Talan and I would survive, I turned my thoughts to the others. It was possible that, even without me there, the stairs would hold, for all had believed in them. My fears that it wouldn't could only hurt their chances. I pushed them from my mind, concentrating instead on reaching safety ourselves.

Talan stirred before I saw any sign of progress. "Airene…" he muttered, or I thought he did. With our souls intertwined, he could have thought my name and I would have known.

"You're safe." I pressed feelings of warmth and home upon him, hoping to reassure him. Memories of Canopy, I recognized them afterward. "We'll reach the floor soon."

"Lightning…?"

"It struck you twice."

Muddled surprise at that. "Damn... The others?"

I didn't want to answer, but knew I had to. "We lost them. Hopefully, they're still descending by the stairs."

He went quiet, but we couldn't conceal our fears from one another.

At last, the tiled floor loomed into view. I slowed our free fall to land lightly upon it. We hadn't come straight down; drawn by Famine, our drop had been angled. Part of me had hoped to find the bottom of the staircase, but that was just as improbable now as before. We could only trust our friends would find their own way out.

A shudder of pleasure ran through me. I tried not to take satisfaction in it, knowing what it meant. The daemon god felt near now, very near.

"I think we're there," I said. "I think we're above Oedija."

Talan's spirit still felt ravaged, his form nebulous and torn. But I felt his assent. "So we must go," he whispered.

I made to move through the floor and back into the first fold, but Talan seized my arm. I waited, feeling he had something to say.

"Remember," he said at last, his voice stronger than it had been a moment before. "What you've learned of Harvest. What you know of Famine. Use that knowledge. And if you can..."

"...I'll come back to you."

He nodded. I tried to hide the feelings roiling through me and knew I did a poor job of it. Even if I succeeded, I doubted this was a mission I could come back from. Talan was too practical to have delusions about it either.

For a moment, we were silent together, sharing a quiet union. It spoke loudly enough.

"Are you ready?" he asked at length.

"Yes." And I was. Ready as I ever would be.

"Then we go."

Hand in hand, we descended through the tiled floor.

And emerged into chaos.

Figures swarmed around us, marching and fighting and dying as they hung upside down from the reflected world. A storm was raging, for radiance fell upward like rain upon the scene. I jerked down, away from what I realized was a battle.

And if there was battle, then this could only be...

I looked below, and Oedija spread beneath us, burning and broken.

And soaring between the mirror lands, swallowing the souls pouring into the Pyrthae, was Famine.

27

CATALYST

We do not know all the energies that flow through the gods' realms.
Witches may use some, yet others resist manipulation. Perhaps
they are not for mortals, but reserved for the gods.

Yet I wonder what has been locked away. What heavenly
powers we might still touch...

- A scribestone of Jolduun; estimated 300 SLP

For a long moment, I hovered above Famine, watching his long, dark form slither through the quintessence, thick as fog from men and women dying on the battlefield. Already, he had grown since attacking Valem, though not as great as he had been before Erimis. We had gained ground, but were quickly losing it.

Talan jerked my arm, rousing me from my stupor.

"We have to leave!" he cried, pulling me toward the city walls. "Famine will take us!"

I wanted this to end here and now, but I knew he was right. I'd reached Harvest midway between the worlds before; reason dictated I had to be at least partially within Telae to reach her again. And here, with a battle underway and Famine growing fat on dead souls, it would be just as foolish as when I'd collapsed upon Valem's slope.

So we headed for Oedija's walls, or what remained of them. The stone had shattered under the barrage of Avvadin artillery, the gate pounded inward into a mess of shattered wood. Soldiers fought at the entrance, but even my untrained eyes could see my countrymen were swiftly folding. As we watched, Avvadin cavalry charged in, and even slowed by our view from the Pyrthae, they seemed a deadly wave of hooves, swords, and spears.

Death was everywhere around us. Even when their bodies fell, their spirits wouldn't find peace. I wished I could close my eyes to it, but each killing was like a barb in my soul.

"Airene!" Talan urged, and I peeled my eyes away.

We willed ourselves forward with renewed speed. As we entered Oedija, we dipped lower, for while Famine remained over the battle outside the walls, it was safe to do so. Midway between the mirror cities, I couldn't help but see how we fared again.

There was fighting in the streets. In Port, red-clothed soldiers fought against those set against them. Damask Esir; I knew them by the Qarin that controlled them and were visible to me here in the Pyrthae. They were supposed to be the supreme warriors of Avvad, yet those they faced seemed to match them. I understood why as I took in the strangeness of their battle garb, feathers and bone and bronze, and the styles of fighting I'd seen Nomusa practice in Canopy.

Komo and his warriors fought down there. I was glad they still held their own.

Other areas were less contested. Spirits lurked in Bazaar: Silks, sweeping upon any soldier they found and enwrapping them. No trace of quintessence rose from them, for their souls were devoured by the bound pyr. I wondered what could be done to stop them.

Not all the fighting was between Oedija and Avvad. Dirty, thin men stormed a granary in deme Hull, though I doubted much food remained inside it. Just outside the Laurel Palace, there looked to be riots at the gates, people only just held back by the laurel guards. I hadn't thought my heart could break further. Here we were, losing and dying to invaders, and we still couldn't unite against them.

Talan's next words pulled my attention back. "Where to?"

I tried to focus. *Famine.* As badly as the battle proceeded, he remained a worse threat. I could feel how powerful he'd become; his presence was distorting even this layer of the Pyrthae, a wasteland spreading across the fields where he soared. It wouldn't be long before he resolved to break free.

I needed to be ready.

The answer came to me. "Linos. We have to find Linos."

Famine would come for my brother before me; I knew it as I knew the daemon god's nature. Linos was defenseless, yet could likely still serve as a conduit into Telae. I had to find him and protect him.

Talan didn't argue. "Where is he?"

Only then did I realize I didn't know. At a calmer time, I might have been able to sense him by his connection to the Pyrthae. But amid this chaos, there was little prospect of that happening.

One spot remained likely, however. "The Laurel Palace — we'll check there first."

Talan clasped my hand, sending strength and hope into me, though he could ill afford to lose any. I expressed my gratitude back, then we sped down to the palace. I aimed for Jaxas's solar, which faced out over the city. If I knew the Despot, that was where he would be, commanding the defenses where the Stratechons fell short.

As we approached, I found Jaxas wasn't on the balcony as I had supposed, but on the broad stairs leading up to the Laurel Palace. Wondering what he was thinking by exposing himself unnecessarily to danger, I directed Talan down. We landed around where I could see the Despot and his followers milling.

I exchanged a look with Talan, then cut open a rift.

As we stepped out into the real world, pain pelted my face, and lightning flashed, blinding me. Shouts sounded around us, and I recovered my vision in time to see spears bristling toward us. Kinesis sprang to my fingertips and pulsed outward. Vaguely, I noticed the pillars rising around me crack and scatter dust, but my eyes were set on the man surrounded by his staggering guards.

Jaxas held up one bony hand. "Stand down. You know these two."

The laurel guards, one of them First Laurel Synne, the other one I didn't know, obeyed at once. Synne wore a scowl, not bothering to disguise her hate. I could hardly blame her. She probably thought me a deserter still.

The Despot's eyes were no less difficult to meet. His robes were drenched, revealing just how thin he'd become under them, yet he stood taller than when I'd left him. Jaxas thrived during conflict; it was the anticipation that made him wilt away.

"So," he spoke into the tumult. "You return at the fall."

I hardened my expression, blinking against the rain running into my eyes. "Famine is here."

His facial muscles twitched, and his frown deepened. "Then you have failed."

"Not yet," Talan said. He slouched, exhausted from our journey to this point, and looked miserable as rain plastered his clothes to his lithe frame. Yet, impossibly, a smile curled his lips. "Help us, and Airene can still succeed."

"To what end?" The Despot's eyes drifted over my shoulder to the burning city beyond. "Will there be anything left to save?"

"Jaxas." The word came out sharp enough that Synne took

a threatening step forward. I didn't spare her a look; there wasn't time. "You've never lost hope before. Don't lose it now. Help me, and we might still help Oedija."

For a moment, I thought he'd refuse. The Despot's face was furrowed with sorrow and anger. Yet he nodded.

"Tell me what you need, and I will do what I can."

I flashed him a grateful smile. "Linos — I need to find him."

"Your brother?" Jaxas frowned again, but he didn't question me. "He's not here."

My chest grew tight. "What? Where is he?"

"The Master Augur came and took him. Said she could help him."

I stared in disbelief. Then red-hot anger blossomed through me. *Eltris*. She'd stolen my brother. I knew what she intended for him. She'd nearly let him become a Sacrifice to Famine before.

She would doom us all if she had her way.

I took a step forward, and the laurel guards' spears lowered a fraction. I didn't care. "Where did she take him?" I demanded. "Where is that 'Thae-damned woman?"

Jaxas didn't quail before my anger, but drew up straighter. "I do not know, Airene. I would tell you if I did."

Talan gripped my arm, and though his touch seemed to burn, I didn't shake him off. "The Acadium!" he said, a thunderclap almost drowning him out. "Perhaps she took him to her tower!"

Before I could respond, I felt a tear in the world open at my back.

I whirled around in time to see five figures emerge from the Pyrthae. My chest leaped with recognition. Xaron, Nomusa, Corin, Kari, Isidora. They'd survived the storm of the third fold.

I threw my arms around my fellow Finches, and they embraced me tightly back. "We thought you died," Xaron said, his voice choked. "When Talan fell and you jumped after him…"

"I didn't." I pulled back and flashed a grin. "And neither did you."

Nomusa held me by the back of my neck, staring intently into my eyes. "You'll have to explain yourself later."

I shrugged. "There will have to be a later for that."

The joy of our reunion was short-lived. Jaxas stepped forward and, in a hoarse but commanding voice, said, "I am glad you've returned, but we have dire need of you now, First Watcher and First Warden."

Xaron and Isidora straightened at the Despot's address. "Yes, Your Radiance," Isidora said formally. "We will fight wherever we're needed." Xaron nodded, though a bit of his apprehension of old had returned.

"Good." Jaxas looked to the demes to the east, and my stomach sank as I suspected what he had in mind. His words a moment later confirmed it.

"Silks run rampant through Bazaar. I know you do not know how to stop them, but if they can be delayed…"

"We'll try, Your Radiance." The First Watcher didn't show the least bit of hesitancy. Glancing at Xaron, she gave him a small smile, and he seemed to take heart in it.

"Perhaps burying them in rubble?" Xaron suggested. "If they're chained by the fabric, perhaps obstructing it will restrict their movements."

Talan shrugged. "Worth a try. But be warned: their most potent weapon is against your mind. They will tempt you to go to their embrace. Resist it at all costs." He paused, then continued. "If you have to fight them, try to use quintessence. It's the only thing I've found effective against them."

The two nodded, though I didn't know either of them to have consciously used quintessence before. As they glanced at the Despot. Jaxas waved a dismissal. "May the Eidola watch over you," he murmured.

Xaron looked at me, and I tried for a smile. He failed to return one.

Corin surprised me by kneeling at Jaxas's feet. "I would fight for you, Your Radiance. Send me where I am needed."

Nomusa did not kneel, but stepped forward as well. "And me. I can fight as my people do."

I longed to tell them to stay, that it was too dangerous. But with the risks I would soon take, how could I speak against theirs?

Jaxas looked from one woman to the other, then nodded. "The fighting will find us soon enough. Stay by my side and you will have your moment."

Jaxas's eyes flickered to me, and I suspected he had placed them purposefully. Gratitude flooded me. But before I could find the words to express it, something boomed from afar.

Whirling around, I stared toward the noise, not knowing what to expect. A part of me feared it was Famine, already breaking through the veil between the realms.

The sight that greeted me was stranger still.

Between the broken doors of the eastern gate, green flames rose in a plume, almost too bright to look at directly. Even as I watched, the flames spread in a tsunami that crested the walls. The resulting crashes thundered in my ears even across the distance, and the ground shook beneath my feet. I grabbed for a column, and stone crumbled beneath my fingertips as I fought for balance.

Blinking against the flashing afterimages, I stared at the black smoke that rose from the fey fires, then turned back to the Despot. Jaxas wore a grim smile now. Almost, I felt I could see the flames in his eyes.

"Catalysm!" he answered my unspoken question. "Our last defense!"

"Mother came through!" Xaron sounded dazed, as if it was the last thing he had expected. From all I had heard of his mother, I wouldn't have blamed him if it was.

"Not quite your last!" Talan called, and I looked where he pointed. In Port, flashes of what could only be radiance flared against the invaders, who looked like little more than red smudges in the distance. Wardens, *our* wardens, were fighting back. I'd feared them all dead.

"Did you think Kyros would yield so easily?" Jaxas nodded to Bazaar, and I saw a wall of violet flames burn down the street. The Archmaster had always been prodigious in his strength; I hoped that, with Xaron and Isidora's aid, it would be enough to overcome even Silks. By Talan's pursed lips, he kept his doubts.

But I couldn't be distracted; none of this was my immediate concern. I had to find Linos.

I turned to Jaxas again, meaning to say something, when a second roar sounded behind me. But this was not an explosion, but human voices raised in challenge.

I whirled back to see red-clad people surging up the steps of the Laurel Palace, steel flashing in their hands. There were two dozen, and each with a snarl on their lips. As I watched, one soared through the air, leaping twenty cubits in the air before landing on a step above and continuing their sprint up. Others followed his lead. At their pace, they would be upon us in moments.

Yet for a split second, I could only stare, unable to believe it. But my eyes knew the truth.

The Damask Esir had found us.

2 8

TO THE LAST BREATH

"Foreign states are like chickens: chop off the head, and the body will continue to flail. But eventually, both must fall.

To kill the heads of state, send the Damask Esir to clear a path, then the priests and their leashed spirits to finish it."

- Aasjuqal Kahin-Shah, the First Prophet King of the Avvadin Imperium; date unknown

Shouting rang around me, but I ignored it, pulling on the energetic elements until they stormed inside me, then loosing it upon the advancing enemies.

Fire erupted from my fingers, growing and forming into a wall a dozen cubits high, then flying down the wide stairs. Rain sizzled in the heat as it pattered against it, but it blazed too hot to be dampened. I trembled with the force of it, yet with Famine so near and at the height of his power, I could endure the pressure.

As the fiery avalanche crashed upon the Damask Esir, I maintained it a moment longer, then released, blinking through the black spots left on my vision to see the results of my attack. Expecting to see mangled black corpses lying prone on the stairs, it took me a moment to understand what the oncoming shapes were.

The attack had barely slowed the Esir. Except for one fallen to the ground, screaming and writhing as he burned, the others had repelled the flames.

Wardens. In the confusion, I had forgotten every one of them could channel, and had been trained in its use their entire lives.

I had no time for a follow-up, for in mere strides, they were upon us. My companions and Jaxas's guards met the charge.

I stumbled back a step, conjuring kinesis and throwing it at the two closest to me in a desperate ploy. They shredded through it, whirling and bringing about their curved swords to slice at me in perfect coordination. I screamed a denial, but even as I summoned radiance to blast at them, I feared it was too little.

Mid-swing, one of the enemy soldiers collapsed, while the other went flying as Talan crashed into him.

There was a flurry of motion, then Talan was staggering back, a line in his shirt dripping red as rain washed the blood away. Whipping his head up, he caught my gaze and yelled, "The Qarin! Sever their connections!"

I nodded, cursing myself for not remembering earlier, and channeled quintessence. As magic laid their spirits bare, so were the connections to the beings by which Avvad leashed them, resembling long candle wicks, flames burning at the top.

As another Esir lunged at me, I lashed out with an invisible weapon of my own, and the connection frayed under it like string. The woman collapsed with a bloodcurdling cry, then lay twitching on the stairs.

Skirting farther back, I tripped over a stair and fell on my rump. I scrambled back to my feet, jaw clenched, resolve tight, then found my next targets: two Esir sparring against

Corin. The former cartwoman proved as handy with a blade as she always claimed, and though outnumbered and bleeding, she had so far defended her sister cowering behind her.

I struck at one Esir, and as the Qarin's connection frayed, the woman toppled. But before I could reach the second, the soldier found a gap in the cartwoman's defenses. A blade slashed across Corin's chest, and she jerked back, a surprised look on her face.

"*CORIN!*"

I was running toward her, heedless of my safety, slipping and sliding on the rain-slicked stones and knowing I was already too late. I cut the Esir free of his daemon, then ignored him as I skidded to a halt before my fallen friend. Kari was already there, cradling her sister's head and rocking back and forth. She looked up at me, eyes wide and pleading.

"Heal her!" she cried. "You must heal her!"

"I don't know how!" My thoughts raced as I kneeled and hovered my hands over the wound. It spurted forth blood, faster than I had ever seen before. "Corin, Eidola above, Corin…"

I knew no way to stop it. But I had to try.

Harvest! Harvest, please help her!

I was halfway between realms, just as I had been before. I pressed my need inward, resonating through my soul.

The goddess did not rise within me.

Bracing myself, I placed my hands on Corin's chest like I could stem the wound, gagged as blood poured through my fingers, warm and reeking.

"Harvest, *please!*" I begged aloud.

Corin's heart was beating too fast. I looked into my friend's eyes and saw the life fading. It would not be long now.

Still, Harvest did not come.

"I'm sorry." I withdrew my hands and sat back on my feet, shoulders sagging. "I'm so sorry."

Corin wasn't a warden, so I couldn't feel her quintessence in the Pyrthae. Yet I still knew the moment she left.

Kari wailed into the battle surrounding us. "*CORINNA!*"

"Airene!"

A hand tugged on my arm, heaving me to my feet. Mind numb, I looked around and saw it was Xaron, long hair plastered against his face, shallow wounds bleeding across his body. He shook me, and I abruptly came back to my senses.

"More are coming!" He turned me to face down the palace stairs, pointing. "Silks!"

I saw them at once. There were about ten of them, each little more than knotted bands of silken cloth, twisted around a body invisible to my eyes. But they were not hidden in the Pyrthae. There, they blazed, their quintessence bright and powerful.

They glided across the ground, the ends of the cloth reaching like an ant's antennae, feeling the air for their next victims. The blood of those they had already claimed soaked the silk so it was dyed pink, blood dripping from the ends as rain poured down.

Behind the bound spirits came their masters, the Tefra, priests of Valem. They wore the gold-and-jade masks I had glimpsed before, hiding the burns inflicted upon them in a demonstration of their faith. Red cowls covered their heads, and black robes their bodies. Chains hung from their arms as they held them up, commanding the daemons before them.

I looked back to the Silks sweeping up the stairs, and only then did I notice the feeling rising in me. Having experienced the spirits' allure through Talan's memories, it felt familiar, and the desire was not unlike the hunger Famine awoke in me. I had yearned to be consumed by the daemon god when he first broke free of Vusu. The feeling stirring in me now paled in comparison.

Yet they could kill us with an embrace. And unlike the Damask Esir, I knew no effective way to deal with them.

"Airene, we need to go!" Talan was by my side, shouting in my ear, a hand protectively on my shoulder. "We must face Famine!"

I looked up to see the dragon god swooping through the Pyrthae over the field. His wounds looked to have healed, and he was close to the size he had been before Valem. I gritted my teeth, knowing Talan was right, wishing he was wrong.

Still, I pleaded. "I can't leave them! The Silks will take them all!" I glanced at Corin, and a surge of emotion lapped at me, trying to swallow me down. "I won't let them die!"

"Go, Airene!" Xaron spoke now, eyes shining, fear etched into his face, though he tried not to show it. "We'll make it through!"

I stared at him, then looked to find my other companions. Isidora had just cut down a Damask Esir with a well-timed slash of kinesis, and she retreated to put her back to Xaron, panting and sagging with exhaustion. Nomusa, pressed against one of the Laurel Palace's columns, looked mostly unharmed, yet she huddled on the ground, clutching at the stone and staring down at the Silks with wide eyes. Their influence must be worst for her, and unattuned as she was, she had no defenses against them. Kari still huddled by her sister's body near the front of the fighting, ignoring the advancing spirits and priests as if they couldn't harm her. Jaxas had retreated within the palace with his messengers and some of his protectors, while a dozen laurel guards fought against the Damask Esir still standing.

They might die here, just as Corin had. If I stayed, I might save them. But if Famine broke free of the Pyrthae, we would all die.

There was only one choice.

I looked back at Talan, then, with teeth clenched together, I nodded.

He smiled bitterly, then glanced at Xaron. "Keep them alive. Remember to use quintessence."

Xaron grimaced and nodded. I knew as well as he did that he'd never been a deft hand at it. I had to hope he would learn quickly.

I tried to say a goodbye, but the words stuck in my throat. "Don't be a hero," was all I could think to say. My eyes stung with more than the rain splashing into them.

Xaron tried to smile and failed. "Could say the same for you."

Talan cut us short by slashing down. I felt him channel quintessence as he split the fabric of reality open.

"No more delays," he said, directing me toward the tear.

With one last look at the friends I was abandoning, I turned to the rift and stepped in. The strangeness seized me at once, then I shuddered and adjusted. Talan came through a moment afterward, then turned and sealed it behind us.

I looked around at the scene, now distorted with the Pyrthaen touch: colors eschew and shifting, the very air seeming to shimmer with the energies coursing through it. The quintessence of the wardens and spirits shone, while a glance up revealed their corporeal bodies hanging from the reflected world overhead.

"Airene."

At Talan's urging, I moved forward and left them behind.

29
CHAOS

Each battle is controlled chaos. Wars are won by small measures of will.

- On the formation of a standing army; by Stratechon Bion, 1086 SLP

We ran past our enemies — the remaining Damask Esir, the Tefra, the Silks — leaving them to overrun our friends, then threw off the sky to launch into the air. I wished I could as easily shed my guilt, but it remained a heavy weight within me.

The Acadium was not far, especially when soaring, and soon, its sprawl of buildings appeared below us. But Famine had drifted closer, consuming the souls that drifted up from the city now. As he spiraled through the air, his presence pulled at me, beckoning toward him, a dozen times the strength of the clothbound spirits. Between his influence and my burning guilt, I had to fight hard to concentrate on the matter at hand.

Swooping down to the world below, I searched for signs of my brother or Eltris. I looked to her tower first, but it lay dark and empty. Panic rising in me, I swept my gaze over the rest of the campus. Could she be hiding somewhere here? Perhaps she'd returned Linos to the Ward, where he'd spent several spans before. Would that mean he'd taken a turn for the worse? Would they have a bed for him amid a war?

But even as I studied the building, I sensed something beyond it. My gaze was drawn to the tower of Kyros Brighteyed, then up to the very top of it. There, at its broken apex, stood two wardens. Could it be Eltris and Linos? It seemed impossible that she could have brought my brother so high, but it was the best lead I had.

I ascended to the top of the black tower, Talan by my side. Famine was drawing dangerously near now. I tried to ignore him and sped toward my destination.

We had almost reached the tower's peak when a figure materialized before us, arresting our path. I braced myself to fight and almost bowled through before I recognized them. For a moment, I could only stare.

Against all odds, Clepsammia had appeared.

The Maiden of the Sands looked much the same as I'd seen her before. Her shape was the approximation of a woman's, but with distorted proportions: legs and arms of different lengths, her face oddly asymmetrical. Her coloring was as flat and gray as the ocean at night. Her silver hair and tattered robes streamed about her. A wide smile dominated her face, and even her angled eyes seemed to share in it.

I reached out to Talan, warning him with a touch. His soul bunched tight beneath my hand, but he refrained from an attack.

"Who is she?" he whispered.

I didn't answer him, my eyes glued to her lips. Why did she smile? What plan did she have for us, for me?

But it wasn't her lips that moved, but her hand. The one that didn't hold the sandglass pointed upward, toward the Oedija hanging above us.

I frowned, uncomprehending. "What?" I shouted at her. "What do you want?"

The gray ribbons of her robe trailed lazily about her, unaffected by the movements of the massive dragon nearby or the war below. She only turned her head upward, as if to emphasize the direction of her hand.

"Why up?" I tried to think of what she could intend. "What does that mean?"

Clepsammia gave no answer. With one last amused glance, the goddess turned and dissolved into mist.

Talan tugged at my hand as he rose. "Airene!"

He was right. Putting the enigma from my mind, I followed him up to the top of the tower. It appeared much as I remembered it, the room burned and the ceiling broken from the Seekers who had stolen Aika's knife from the Archmaster. The two wardens appeared to be in the center of the chamber, judging by the swirling flames of their Pyrthaen connection.

I glanced at Talan, and he shrugged. Then something loomed behind him.

Shouting wordlessly, I grabbed at the former Guilder and drew him back, staring up in horror at the one approaching.

Famine had seen me. Famine was coming.

I didn't hesitate to wonder why, but fled at once. Talan flew with me, darting for the tower to land on the uneven floor. Famine was fast, slicing through the air as if it took no effort. His mouth gaped wide behind us, and an endless, dark chasm showed within.

Temptation stole over me to fling myself toward him, but I'd been ready for it and fought it down. With an agonized cry, I cut open a rift, then lurched through it.

My entrance was far from graceful as I fell to the rain-slicked stones. Talan was a step behind me, though he remained on his feet. While I failed to rise, he kept the presence of mind to pivot and run his fingertips along the seams between the realities. Through the shifting light, I saw the darkness closing in as Famine sought still to swallow us. Fear choked me. Could he escape through the rift? Did he even need a conduit?

Talan yelped as he mended the last of the rift — yet even then, I feared it wasn't enough. The air distorted, the shape of the daemon god's teeth impressed upon it for a moment.

But the next, they faded, and reality resolved as it was supposed to be.

I had no time to breathe a sigh of relief, for fire blazed toward me. On instinct, I whirled toward it and channeled kinesis. Famine's presence roared into me at the opening of my locus, and I rebuffed the flames with a mighty blast as I borrowed his power.

The woman who had attacked me stumbled a step back, but no farther. Only then did I catch a glimpse of her face and recognize her.

"Eltris!" I shouted, and the Master Augur paused in her assault to squint at me from beneath a drenched hood. I could see from her yellow eyes that she recognized me, but her posture remained as tense as before.

"You," was all the greeting I received.

My anger, tightly coiled about me, snapped free. "Where is he?" I demanded. "What have you done with my brother?"

But even as I spoke, my eyes alighted on him. Linos stood a little ways behind her. His head was tilted back, his mouth ajar. A memory darted through my mind: he and I, young and as innocent as we'd ever been, running through River-port's streets catching raindrops on our tongues.

I shook free of it and heaved a sigh. My little brother was still alive, at least. She hadn't killed him.

As Eltris stalked toward me, her expression said she had a fight in mind. Yet instead of attacking, she only said, "About time you came, girl! He'll find him soon!"

Animosity fled before the declaration. No need to ask

whom she meant; I felt his presence swelling within me in a way it never had before. With an effort, I closed my locus, but it only brought a small measure of relief. Famine was too strong now.

Fear trembled through me. I'd hoped that Linos and I would be beyond the daemon god's reach in Telae. But he had attuned us; that was a connection that couldn't be denied. Soon, he would take advantage of it.

Eltris was shouting something at me, but I ignored her, spinning through my thoughts. She was out of her depth now and had nothing to offer. All the while, Famine's presence grew, a sense of bloating around my locus underlying the hunger I was used to.

There was only one thing to do — the final thing.

I closed my eyes, held close my hopes, and opened my locus. But before I could channel, my connection to sorcery burst wide.

My soul split in two as Famine poured through.

30
REQUIEM

Aika of the Green said unto them:
    "Does not a tree sleep within a seed? So shall I become when my
time comes."

- The Seeds of Famine, a translation from the Lighted-tongue; by
Oracle Kalene of deme Hull; 881 SLP

M y spirit broke; my mind split apart. Yet enough of me remained to bear witness.

I drifted apart from my body, yet looked into both planes. In the Pyrthae, Famine, as long as Oedija was wide and as thick around as the tower I lay upon, dove at me, then *into* me. My locus had been corrupted into a portal, and he exploited it.

As he traveled through me, I felt his agony. He was a being unnatural to Telae, not meant for the material world, and his substance was far more difficult to transmute than my own.

But I watched in my world, too, as he burst free of me, reformed and nearly as massive as when he'd entered, then soared into the sky. As his length slithered through, it corkscrewed in the air above the tower. Still, he defied the natural laws, the sky's weight lifting for him alone.

A far corner of myself screamed at me to stop him, to call upon Harvest and trap him, but it was too small to have effect. I was helpless to impede Famine, lacking even the power to move, to think.

If Harvest remained within me, she was silent and offered no help. I waited for a final splitting, the death that must come after such a ravaging.

His tail, layered with impenetrable dark plates and wicked spines, tore free into the air, and then he was gone. I heard his triumphant roar as if from a distance, though I knew it must make my ears bleed with its volume. My spirit settled back into my body, and I saw with dimmed eyes as my enemy unfurled to undulate through the air.

Famine loosed his booming cry again, then dove out of sight.

Figures flitted above me, but I couldn't follow or identify them. Too little of me remained to even close my eyes, yet I was still there. That part of me that had never died fought for control, though it was a battle she couldn't hope to win.

A face neared my own. I knew him as much by his soul as his features. *Talan.* He shone in my mind, brighter than the light that remained to me. He was speaking, but my hearing was lost. Words of encouragement, perhaps, or mourning; I took comfort in them either way.

Here, at the end, I wouldn't die alone.

With that resignation came an exhalation, of body and soul. My vision dimmed to darkness. A strange warmth rose around me. Death was gentle; I hadn't expected it, and was grateful.

Then, silence.

But even in that quiet, there was a song. A requiem for the departed, to carry them to a place beyond. There was no melody or harmony, yet it moved with a music of its own tempo. I listened and was content to pass down its current and into the dark depths at its core.

Yet the warmth grew, and grew, then swelled greater still. Suddenly, I knew it wasn't heat at all, but a soul within my own. The soul I'd been aware of; the soul that had been with me all along. And where it spread its influence, the last night lifted, and the song faded away.

Slowly, inevitably, Harvest pieced me back together.

In a cradle composed of her essence, the goddess healed me. The silence gave way to an incessant clanging, the beating of my heart, then the distinct sounds of the world. I tasted blood from biting my tongue and oily smoke on the air. My nose filled with the nauseating, overpowering stench of a reptile long confined.

Then my vision returned, and Talan's face appeared above me.

"Airene?" His hand cupped my cheek, while tears trailed down his. I reached up to wipe them away before I realized I could move my arms again.

A wondering smile came to Talan's lips. I returned it. But both were fleeting. Harvest remained vital in me, reminding me that my duty had not ceased with my small death.

I was not his. I never could be.

"I'm alive," I murmured, rising from the erratic pavers of the tower floor. "But I must still cage him, Talan. Please, help me."

It was like knives stabbed into me, again and again, as the joy crumpled on his face. A sliver of the smile remained, but only enough to curl one corner.

"Of course," he answered, and though his voice was soft, his eyes screamed.

I ignored it. I had to. "Linos. You must get him away from here. And Eltris, too, if she tries to stay." I couldn't see the aged augur, but suspected she was just out of sight.

Talan's mouth parted, hesitant. "I'm sorry, Airene. Eltris didn't survive."

I stared at him, startled from my purpose for a moment. "What?"

"She saved us. When Famine emerged, his magic would have torn us apart but for her. She shielded us at the cost of her own life."

He looked over, and I followed his gaze to her body. She was on her back, eyes staring sightlessly above. Violet burns ran jagged along her body, too similar to the scars around Linos's eyes. She seemed smaller now, the force of her personality having made her seem larger.

I was surprised by the tears prickling my eyes. I had never gotten along with the woman, nor even much liked her. But she had been my teacher once, and she and I had shared the same goal, and sacrificed everything to reach it.

In the end, she had hesitated to give up my brother, and saved his life as well as Talan's.

"Rest at last, Eltris," I muttered, lowering my gaze.

A trumpeting that shook the very tower stones blared through the sky, pulling me from my thoughts. I knew what I would see even before I turned to look.

Famine.

His exultation at this greatest feast sent sickening pleasure through my soul. Our connection felt stronger than ever since his passage through me. In making me his conduit into Telae, he had bound us tighter together.

I looked back at Talan and pushed away my fresh grief for Eltris. I wished I could comfort him, knew that I couldn't. Yet I'd always found that as powerful as truth obscured could be, truth revealed was still more potent.

"I love you, Talan. I have for a long time now. I only wish I'd told you sooner."

His expression softened. His hands found mine and clung

to them. I almost felt his quintessence through the touching of our shifts.

"I've never kept my feelings a secret." He bit his lip, eyes darting away, then drawing back to mine. "Must you die now? When we finally have what we always should have?"

"Talan." I closed my eyes. I was strong again, but it was a fragile strength. I couldn't continue to refuse him. "I need you to help me. In every way."

I felt his answer through our hands. Then his lips brushed upon my forehead. I opened my eyes to see him rising, our fingers falling away from one another.

"I'll save your brother," he said. "Make sure you save yourself."

I nodded. It was the only answer I could give.

Another cry crashed against my ears. Talan held my gaze a moment longer, then grimaced and turned back to the other two. I rose to my feet, still vaguely surprised to find myself whole, and tottered to an opening in the chamber's walls.

There, I looked upon Famine.

I hadn't thought he could appear more terrifying than he had in the Pyrthae, but the sight of him now proved me wrong. With his powerful body made flesh, it gathered a weight that was apparent with every turn through the air. Dark clouds obscured the sky, yet his aubergine scales seemed to gather an unholy light. Horns curled from his head, and spines bristled from his mane and along his back. But his eyes remained the same, dark pits that swallowed souls.

His physical embodiment, however, posed the least of the danger. Sorcery crackled around him, the mastery and use of it as inherent to him as breathing to mortals. Storms formed and broke as he dove into the dark ranks of the Avvadin army, blue lightning killing the soldiers as surely as his crushing jaws. Magnesis was not the only element running amok; kinesis blasted men, horses, and siege machines to the ground, leaving them in pieces. Radiance blossomed into angry plumes, spinning through yet more of the dissolving troops.

At other passes, energies of which I understood nothing activated. Some made men rise into the air, as if freed of that force that kept them to the ground. When it released them, they fell and didn't rise again. I thought I recognized catalysm, however, when a tide of explosions erupted in violet light.

In the short time since he'd broken free, Famine had devastated the armies of our enemy. Yet I couldn't find any celebration in my heart.

He was my only enemy now. Impossible as it promised to be, I had to try to defeat him.

I closed my eyes, holding both my awareness of Famine and Harvest in my mind. They were there, both of them. I was their Seed, and now I would unveil the promise that held.

I opened my locus to the Pyrthae and flung my challenge through both planes.

"*Famine!*"

If he heard me, he didn't show it. The daemon god swooped down to decimate another phalanx before rising again.

I sought after our connection, that thing that had lodged in my spirit and twisted our fates together. Holding it firmly in my grasp, I shouted again, directing all my force of thought at it.

"*Famine, heed me!*"

This time, my cry reached him. The great dragon writhed around so his head faced me. His dark eyes found me at once, and all my doubts flooded through me again. I clung to my courage and pressed on.

"Come, Devourer! I am your weakness, your final flaw! Come and kill me and be free!"

He didn't know speech, but he must have felt some level of my truth. Famine surged into the sky, cutting through the cloud layer, and Telae fractured at his passage. Lightning rippled across the bellies of the clouds, charging the air so my hair stood on end.

He wasn't fleeing. He'd tasted what this world offered, and he wasn't capable of stopping until he'd consumed all of it. Such was his nature.

I had mere moments.

From the corner of my eye, I saw Talan drag Linos, as mindlessly compliant as before, into a Pyrthaen rift. I put them from my mind. They were safe, as much as they could be, and I needed all of my wherewithal for what came next.

Famine was rapidly nearing, but I ignored him, reaching instead after that other celestial being who lodged in my soul. *Harvest,* I thought, and she glowed brighter in response.

I didn't know if it would work. But it was the only thing I had.

I need of you again. We all do. But I won't ask and not give something in return. Perhaps it's what you need.

In my fear, I'd begun rambling. Famine's presence grew urgent. Even Harvest seemed to radiate alarm.

I tried again. *Save us as you saved us before. I don't have the knife, but I must have the tree. So I give to you my life to grow it. Harvest, I am your Sacrifice. Please—*

But the time for words, even unspoken, came to a sudden end. The sky split open, and Famine ripped free of it. He was a blur overhead as he dove toward me. His mouth open, I almost believed he could swallow the world.

I braced myself, waiting for the end.

ZENITH

The gods wait at death's gates. They hold in their hands potential without end.

- Scroll fragment; origin unknown; estimated 212 PLP

Before Famine could reach the tower, Harvest and I grew together as one.

The boundaries between myself and the goddess eroded so I didn't know where she ended and I began. It didn't matter. Our mission was the same, and together, we found the strength to do it.

We grew, and grew, and grew, and we stood strong against our enemy's charge.

My limbs were no longer limited to arms and legs. A tree, the mortal part of my mind recognized, yet that fragment which touched divinity knew this to be only an interpretation. Our trunk used the stone tower to spread and broaden. Our roots pressed through the rock and dove deep into the earth below. Our branches reached up, but not for the rain and light. They were weapons, sharp and stalwart, and a thousand rose to greet our enemy with a killing embrace.

Yet Famine was no feeble adversary. He'd grown fat on souls, and he commanded the Pyrthae even in this realm. Fire blistered our branches, and pure force broke them. His hard scales repelled our attacks, and his teeth gnawed through us. Harvest screamed at the destruction, but death had always been part of growth's cycle. It did not dissuade her.

Yet it wasn't enough. Miraculous as her emergence had been, Harvest couldn't match her ancient foe.

But maybe she didn't have to.

Though I'd merged with Harvest, I kept my connection to Famine. It had made me feel his hunger, but also his satiation. I'd detested the link and never plumbed its depths before, yet it had always lent me power.

What prevented me from reaching for more?

I followed the ravenous appetite now and dove into it. In my mortal mind, I saw myself entering his mouth and plunging down his throat. Even entwined with a deity, I wasn't prepared for what awaited me.

There was no end to Famine's hunger, and in that moment, I felt all of it. It threatened to devour me.

I fought for sanity and sensed something more. Famine was not his drive alone; he was also the substance that fueled his body. It was the same as every spirit was made of, what filled humans and elevated our intellects.

I reached forward, and quintessence met my touch, silken and warm.

I had to push down my revulsion. These were the souls of those he'd consumed, people robbed even of an afterlife. I hated touching them, using them.

But to save them, I had to do just that.

I reached for the quintessence and channeled it. I hadn't known if it would respond, and yet it did. What was Famine's was mine to command, now that I seized it.

So I pulled it into myself, then funneled it into Harvest.

Even in the dragon's gullet, I felt the goddess weave it into herself. Our tree grew again, and Famine's assault slowed.

Then the daemon god roared, and I became lost to the world.

Next I knew, I was vomited up and flung back into my tree-body. When I recovered, I reached again for Famine's quintessence and found myself blocked. He roared a warning; he knew my trick and would not fall for it again.

But it had been enough. Harvest no longer faltered before the dragon's attacks, but rebuffed them and pushed him back. It was Famine on the defensive now, lashing and biting at branches grown sharp enough to pierce his scales. Harvest had a hundred spears, a thousand arrows, and they all sought our enemy's heart.

The first snuck through his counteroffensive, then a second. Famine roared, but it was too late. He hung impaled on our branches, and we were pitiless.

A dozen more branches broke through his armor, but even that wasn't enough. I knew it with Harvest's knowing: Famine would not die, not truly. Just as the goddess had survived for millennia, her seeds scattered across the world, he was ever-encompassing as well. Hunger could never be vanquished, but only kept at bay, in an ever-renewing cycle.

He has consumed too much. I pressed my assertion on Harvest, and she grew a score more branches in agreement. If he couldn't be killed, we would do everything in our power to bring him as close to death as we could. So we struck him, ensnaring him, staking him with bark and branch. And we grew higher still.

Famine! I threw out the challenge, sending it vibrating down our connection and humming in our blood-strewn branches. *I am your cage now!*

My awareness of Oedija had faded, but I could sense the city falling away with our deep-set roots as our canopy ascended. I smothered the doubt that arose at that and pressed on. I couldn't think of what I was leaving behind. All I had was needed for the fight.

Famine was ailing, but he struggled against us every cubit we rose, breaking our branches and screaming his protests. But for every spine he escaped, we skewered him with three more. Neither Harvest nor I would yield.

I didn't think of where we brought him until I remembered Clepsammia's final, enigmatic suggestion. Up, she'd pointed — skyward, not stoneward. It was contrary to what Vusu had believed we must do to cage Famine, opposite of Eltris's understanding and Aika's actions. But as we took Famine into the sky, I thought I understood. The years passed slowly in the fold below, but those who went there slumbered. Above the third fold, beings still roamed, and I suspected what manner of creatures they were now.

Only then did I realize we weren't fully in Telae anymore, but also the Pyrthae. Had we pierced the layer above to rise among the radiant winds, where we mortals had always believed the Pyrthae existed? Or had Harvest's nature taken us back into the realm she was born of and ruled?

Yet it didn't matter; it felt right. Famine was both spirit and material now. To detain him for good, his chains had to be in both realms as well. He wouldn't fully die, but spread across Telae and the Pyrthae, the dragon would be weak enough to hold for the length of existence.

I felt when we broke free of the first fold and into the third, for even with Harvest's nurturing warmth coursing through my substance, the icy winds seeped in. Famine's resistance grew weaker, and I wondered if the cold sapped his dwindling strength. The goddess, on the other hand, was relentless. Her growth slowed, but only fractionally, and we continued our race ever upward.

Time bent. Before I knew it, we had risen beyond the cold and broken into the place above. Serenity stole over me, as it had before, even as I endeavored with Harvest to keep

Famine confined. Yet the daemon god had ceased to writhe. Had he given up, conceded he could not win?

Yet I was joined with him still, and by it sensed this was something different. Famine couldn't violate his drive anymore than the other Quintyr. But what we brought him to was part of that: oblivion, the cessation of substance. An end to hunger. Nothing but silence surrounded us — then the air filled with them.

The gods had descended.

Some were warm to my mind's touch, and some burned. Others were frigid, chilling me even from afar. With them came a plethora of sensations, each of their drives made manifest.

The storm that had been violent with envy was Odaon. Clepsammia was there, with her touch of inevitability. Other Eidola existed, too: Caradon Night-Veil, cold as the darkness he claimed; Lavvash, electric and whimsical in her moods; Cendaur, steadier in his temperament. Some, I had no names for; perhaps the deities of forgotten lands, robbed of life by Famine long ago.

All gathered around the dragon impaled upon Harvest's branches, and he roused again, but not to fight. Was it the greeting of kin? No, nothing quite so warm. But there was recognition and familiarity. Perhaps that was as close as divine beings came to welcoming their own.

They reached out, not with hands, but the essence of themselves, and enwrapped him. This, I thought, must provoke him, but still he did not struggle. Our branches impaled him, yet they wound around to touch every part of him. He was like a worm in a cocoon, and I wondered if it was a chrysalis or a cage.

Then they melded away, and it was like they had stripped the flesh from the bones. The skeleton of the daemon god remained, but a third part of him had been split off. Divided, he couldn't return to his full power. He would be forever imprisoned.

Their quarry lashed to themselves, the Quintyr ascended, then disappeared.

As suddenly as they'd come, their presence departed. Only Harvest and I remained, along with the inert parts of Famine. I waited, content with my goddess. I knew the moment must pass to another, but as I did not know what that would be, I only listened to the silence. It stirred through my awareness. Death is a silence, yet so is anticipation. The moment before a vital change.

Harvest felt as my thoughts turned ahead, and something changed between us. A gulf had grown, for as things grow together, they also grow apart. We had always been two separate beings, she and I, even as we'd merged as one. She didn't need me any longer; her seed had matured and become its own vessel.

And I — I was the offshoot that must be pruned.

I didn't resent it as she gently but firmly pried me away from herself, then sent me afloat in the void. I knew it was her nature to do so. And what was I now, apart from her?

Was I Airene still?

I didn't know; almost, I didn't care. Yet some things remained, anchoring me to existence. I had left behind people I cared for, tasks left undone.

For them, I held the fraying parts of myself together. I stayed me, Airene.

Then I descended.

3 2

BEAUTY IN THE BROKEN

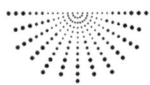

I crave the end, when there are no battles to wage, no people to save, no gods to cage. Then, at last, I will close my eyes, and I will rest.

- The journal of Vusumuzi; date unknown

I fell slowly, inevitably. The fated return.

Yet as I passed through the third fold and into the first, I saw nothing was as I'd hoped it would be.

Oedija lay destroyed, but the first sight that caught my attention was the tree. It dominated the middle of the city, far taller than Kyros's tower, from which it had spawned. Its bark was smooth and a brilliant white, nearly shining amid the smoky haze. It spanned both cityscapes, above and below, the trunk breaking into the third fold and leaving only a few branches behind.

For a moment, I could only look upon what I had, for a moment, become. I marveled at the goddess that had lived within me.

Eventually, my eyes were drawn to one of the lower branches. Something hung there, a dark shape against the shining tree. A premonition struck me as I neared. I knew what I would find, perhaps by the threadbare connection remaining between it and my spirit. Yet still, I had to see.

I hovered there and looked at my body.

The branch had grown through me, centered on my locus. Had it speared me when Harvest first grew, or in the battle afterward?

But it didn't matter. The truth was evident and had been ever since I gave my life to the goddess.

I had died.

I gazed upon my still eyes, my limp hands, my slightly parted mouth. They were all too waxen and pale now. There was no blood, but that made me seem no less a corpse.

I had become the Sacrifice in the end — not to Famine, but to Harvest. That made the difference.

It made facing my death bearable. Only just.

I lingered, but even with it being my own body, it seemed macabre to look overlong. And this was not the reason I'd returned. Other tasks awaited me.

I drifted away, turning my gaze to Oedija. My home, so utterly destroyed: walls toppled, gates twisted, buildings burned, people butchered. It should have crippled me with despair, yet it didn't. A seed of something else had been planted among the ruin, a seed which, I had to hope, would flower and grow.

Oedija would rebuild. My home would be restored. Not soon, nor as it was before. But it would grow.

For me, here and now, that was enough.

I honed my focus, searching for those I sought. It wasn't long before I found them at the Laurel Palace, together and alive. Mostly.

It tore me apart and sewed me together, that sight. I flew to them, yearning to be as near as I could, knowing it wouldn't be near enough.

I went to the reflected cityscape above, for there they all

J.D.L. ROSELL

appeared, pictured in that mirror of the material world. My friends stood at the entrance to the palace, on the stairs where Jaxas had announced himself Despot, where the Damask Esir had cut down Corin. As they gazed over the shattered city, I floated, invisible among them, taking them in one by one.

Xaron leaned on Isidora, lines etched into his face that had nothing to do with laughter. He'd been injured, both in body and spirit, and only stood by his lover's support. Yet he had survived. He, along with the other wardens, had succeeded in driving off the Silks. I wondered if I'd ever been prouder of him.

Isidora had fared better, though a haunted look dominated her eyes. Yet they had each other; my friend would be cared for and loved. I hoped he would soon laugh again.

With a last touch upon Xaron's face, I turned away.

I went to Nomusa next, standing not far from them. Her face was hard, her eyes wide, yet I recognized the set of her jaw. She wasn't broken, nor would she be. Would she stay in Oedija, or return to reclaim her ishaka? Whatever future awaited her, I trusted her determination would see her through it.

I reached out and pressed her hand, hoping some part of her could feel it.

Then I drifted to Kari. She sat by her sister's body, cradling Corin's head, her eyes distant and dry. She did not smile now, but frowned toward the ruined city; her view of the future, perhaps. I could only hope that with time, she would find her smile again, and a place to belong here in Oedija.

My friends weren't alone; Jaxas, Feiyan, and Komo stood among them. I looked over them, wondering if they had been more ally or adversary. For Jaxas, at least, fondness won over. All he'd done, I believed, was in service of the demotism. I hoped he would not become the tyrant I feared, especially with Feiyan as his advisor. But even she, for all her malevolence, had shown she would fight for Oedija, so long as it aligned with her own self-interest. I hoped it would be so, for everyone's sake. Komo, at least, would be a good ruler, so long as the horrors he saw in this war didn't scar him too deeply.

Two others stood with them. I delayed my approach. I feared I might never leave their sides once I looked. Yet still, I drifted closer to hover before them.

Talan and Linos stood side by side. The former Guilder had an arm held out, as if ready to catch Linos at any moment, yet my brother looked steady on his feet. His eyes were as vacant as before, his mouth slack, and the whole of my being cried out for him. Famine and Vusu were gone, yet he carried the scars they'd inflicted upon him. At least he was beyond their reach now.

I cupped his face in both my hands, as I often had when we were children, and planted an insubstantial kiss upon his forehead.

Then I turned to Talan. Fear stirred within me at his expression. I saw little of the hope the others carried. Each of them had a purpose before them; Talan lacked that. Perhaps, had I remained behind...

But that, too, was a future Harvest had pruned away. There was little point in dwelling on it.

I touched his hands, his face, then wrapped myself around him. I willed him to feel me, to hold me, but of course he didn't. He was beyond my reach now, in Telae, while I remained in the Pyrthae.

Then it occurred to me: pyr had crossed the barrier between worlds before. Perhaps, even now, I could as well.

I dove to the Telae reflected below. Though my friends would not appear in image, those attuned I could feel, even though none of them were channeling at the moment. I knew each, and I brushed by Xaron before stopping before

Linos. Other than Kari, he was most present on this plane, for his spirit drifted while the others were anchored in their bodies. I wrapped myself around him, and had I been able to, I would have wept.

He was there, my brother, still there. I pressed my thoughts upon him.

Wake, Little Lion. It's time to awaken.

Perhaps he made some small response; perhaps I imagined it. Still, I didn't give up. Time and determination were all I had now.

Clinging to him, I gathered all the memories we'd shared, the person I knew him to be, and in the same way I'd passed knowledge onto Talan before, I tried to do so with Linos. Perhaps because he wasn't fully in the Pyrthae, there was a barrier to my attempts. I pushed harder against it, made my intentions firm and vivid.

Wake up, Linos! I shouted into the void.

Then the dam broke. Suddenly, he was all around me, and it was *him.*

There were no words, barely fully formed thoughts, yet I knew my brother's mind and treasured every moment. I shared my understanding of him, and he drank greedily of it. A moment later, I became aware what this drained: my quintessence, my soul.

I didn't stop. I was afraid, but my love for him was stronger.

When at last I had no more to give, I separated myself and looked upon him with dimmed senses. His spirit seemed stronger, more anchored. Would it be enough? I could only hope.

There was so little of me left, nothing more than wisps of a cloud. I wouldn't be able to see everyone I'd wished to. My mother, father, and elder sister. Maesos. Other friends and allies, both old and new.

Yet I held onto existence a little longer as I drifted back to

Talan. He was even harder to reach than Linos, yet I tried with all the strength I had left. He was too far; I wouldn't reach him. I felt myself slipping away.

Then he cut into the Pyrthae, and suddenly he was there, all of him.

"*Airene!*" He held me close, and I curled into his embrace. My ability to speak had faded, but my memories remained, so I pressed these upon him. He flinched at first, defying my attempts, then opened up entirely.

I flowed into his soul, and his into mine. Like two rivers joining waters.

Yet a part of me resisted, stubbornly retaining itself. The part that had always lain in the dark, the quiet, the secret places of my soul. Secrets had been the baubles I chased after, that drove me near to madness in their pursuit. They were what allowed me to protect Telae from Famine. Had I not sought after them so ruthlessly, every plane of existence would have been reaped barren.

This wasn't how I imagined my life would turn, when I dreamed of being a Finch as a little girl. It wasn't how I hoped it would end. And so I clung a moment longer to those treasured dreams.

But though there is beauty in cycles, it is also in their breaking.

Nestled into Talan's being, I finally let go of myself. Would Thero be waiting for me in whatever existed beyond? Would I join the gods? Or would I be part of the man I loved for however long he lived, and perhaps even in the time after?

I did not know. Perhaps they were secrets I would discover. But at least Talan and I would keep one last secret between ourselves.

I closed my eyes, listened, and welcomed the song that swallowed me down.

269

33
FROM A SEED

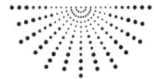

He hovered in the Pyrthae until her presence faded. Only when his soul grew cold did Talan retreat into his own world.

As he set foot onto the steps leading up to the Laurel Palace, the others that had been standing nearby crowded around with questions. Talan ignored them, lost in himself. He had felt her, tugging at him, and had opened the way. He'd thought to find her there, whole and as he'd known her. But there'd been so little of her remaining, a ghost of herself.

She'd folded into him — then, like that, she was gone.

But Airene had left him with more than her absence. Just as she'd shared of her memories before, she had again. He saw her final battle with Famine, her sacrifice to Harvest. He saw the dragon impaled upon the white branches, then lifted away by the gods above. He saw as the goddess that had so sorely used her cut her loose, like a shriveled leaf shed in autumn.

He was filled with anger and love and pride. But most of all, he floundered in pain.

"Are you there?" he muttered, not caring that he spoke

aloud, that he must seem mad to the others. "Are you sleeping inside me?"

But Talan had sensed the manner of slumber she entered. Airene was gone, and all that remained of her, he carried inside him.

Am I worthy of it? He knew the answer all too well.

"Talan. Please, answer me."

Talan roused from his stupor to meet Xaron's eyes. They'd never gotten along, the jester having been protective of Airene and distrusting of him — as well he should have. But Talan liked to think he'd earned his trust now, as Xaron gripped him by the shoulders and gazed into his eyes with unspoken emotion.

"What did you ask?" he murmured.

"What just happened? You entered the Pyrthae, then—" Xaron broke off, turning away for a moment. But he'd found steel inside him over the past season, and he glanced back up. "Was it her?" he continued, quieter. "Did she…?"

Talan hesitated, then stepped back, breaking Xaron's grip. The others crowded around them to hear his answer.

It came out as a sigh. "Yes. It was her. And she did. Famine is gone for good."

They began babbling among each other and asking more of him, but Talan turned away. He didn't want to speak of it, didn't even want to think of it. Airene was as close now as she'd ever been.

Then why does she feel so far away?

He made to leave, intending to find some proprietor of a drinking hole brave or stupid enough to be operating at a time like this. But when he faced the youth standing behind him, all thoughts of it left his mind.

Linos stared at him. But for once, his bright blue eyes were not glazed over.

He *saw* Talan.

Airene's brother blinked, his lips quivering for a moment

before words escaped them. "Who are you?" He slowly turned and looked around him, a bit of the daze returning at the sight. "Where am I? Is this... Oedija?"

Talan stared for a moment, baffled. But he'd always been good at thinking on his feet. Setting his mind, he stepped forward and commanded the youth's attention.

"Yes. You're Linos, right? Linos of Riverport?"

He spoke it as a reminder. Linos hesitated, perhaps trying to decide if it was true, then nodded. "Suppose I am."

Talan smiled, hoping it came off as reassuring. "You've been sick, Linos. A lot of things have changed. There've been tragedies and miracles. I think you being better now is one of them."

Only then did he realize what had truly happened. *Airene.* All of this had started with her trying to save her brother. He doubted she would have rested until she'd given everything to do so.

He looked away as his eyes pricked with moisture.

"Alright." Linos's speech returned stronger with each word. "How do you know me? Why have you been looking after me?"

Talan noticed the others had seen the change in Linos and froze in surprise — all except the Despot and his First Consul, who had returned to governing their broken city. A flurry of messengers, laurel guards, and militiamen streamed up and down the stairs now, none of them unblemished by war.

He ignored them, focusing his attention on Linos. "I'm Talan, a friend of your sister's. There's a lot to catch you up on, but just know, Airene did it all for you..."

Then he told her tale. And as his chest grew warm, Talan wanted to believe some part of her remained to take comfort in her deeds.

But he had never been one to indulge in delusion.

～

TALAN TOLD Linos all there was to tell. In the course of the telling, they went to the kitchens of the Laurel Palace and scrounged whatever food they could find there. The staff, unsure of what else to do in the face of tragedy, had prepared their usual fare. It always felt odd to eat after a day of death, but Talan had endured enough of them to know that memories didn't provide nourishment.

After he'd finished, with embellishments from Nomusa and especially Xaron, who had come along with them, Linos had sat quietly, then excused himself, claiming to be tired. Talan suspected the truth. His sister had just died and his home been destroyed. It was a lot to take in, and not something he wanted to think through in the company of near strangers.

Talan had slunk off himself then, feeling much the same way. He wandered through the Laurel Palace, then beyond it. The guards seemed to know who he was, for they nodded as he passed and didn't stop him. He only smiled back, letting all that burned inside him show through.

He hadn't known where he headed, but he wasn't surprised when he approached the towering white tree. The streets were strewn with bodies and refuse. The fighting had ended, but the wounded and dying still cried out for help. He passed them by, unable to aid them even if he'd had the skill to. Yet others were there, providing comfort and necessities. As much as could be done would be.

At last, he reached the first of the giant roots, then craned his neck back. The tree rose as high as the Chains Azhi had once described, its branches extending into the sky beyond sight, fading to hazy shadows, then nothing at all. He wondered if they reached into the Pyrthae itself, then remembered from Airene's memories that they did, and even beyond that.

Memories, he thought, directing it at Airene like a prayer. *Is that all I have left?*

He kneeled before the root and pressed both hands to it. The bark was smooth and porous, just like the knife Airene had once borne. Like bone. It held an unnatural warmth, a sense of aliveness the knife had lacked. But he couldn't feel Airene, nor any distinct presence.

He opened his locus and channeled quintessence. The aliveness of the tree came into starker view; it was spirit, through and through, a soul grown so great it spanned both worlds. *And binds them*, he mused, wondering what that meant for the future.

With his senses wide open, he noticed the approach of the three others before he faced them. When at last he could ignore them no longer, Talan sighed, closed himself to his gift, then rose and turned.

Nomusa, Xaron, and Linos stood there. Talan wondered for a moment where the others had gone, then let the thought go. There were a dozen things that might occupy them with Oedija in a smoldering ruin and a scattered army on the retreat.

"Figured we'd find you here." Nomusa placed a hand on one hip and tried to smile, but fell short.

Talan shrugged, not caring to respond.

"It's hard to believe." Linos looked up, just as Talan had. "That a goddess lived inside her."

She also lived in you. But Talan couldn't find the energy to form the words.

Nomusa stepped closer. "We should do something. Something to honor her."

Honor her? He couldn't repress a smirk. What did it matter to her, their honor? He'd felt her spirit fade into him. There was nothing left of her separate from himself. Yet at the wariness in their expressions, he sighed and relented. If they needed this, he wouldn't deny it to them.

They each spoke words, recalling loving memories and wishing a good fate upon her. "You never gave up," Nomusa said. "Never lost hope. Even when the rest of us did." Her eyes were dry, but there was a hollowness in her voice and a heaviness in her shoulders that had never been there before.

"All will know your name," Xaron said, smiling as tears trickled down his cheeks. "I think that would make you happy. You always did hanker for attention. Eidola above, I'll miss that."

Linos's eyes were red and shadowed as it came his turn. "You saved me," he murmured. "Saved all of us. You always watched out for others. For me. It's just like you to give your life for the world."

As the youth finished, all three looked to Talan, so he bowed his head and muttered his piece to the ground. "Hope you know what you did. Hope it brought you peace."

They were quiet for several minutes, then Nomusa turned to him. "What do you mean to do now?"

Talan looked up. They waited expectantly; for what, he couldn't say. He shrugged again, and when that didn't seem sufficient, said, "You three make plans then?"

Linos barked a short, bitter laugh. "Find my family, I suppose. And then..." He punctuated it with a shrug.

"You've your life ahead of you." Talan didn't know why he bothered saying the words. *Though I'd be lying if I didn't see myself in him.*

"You'll find a purpose," he continued. "It'll keep you going. Just like with your sister."

"If you say so." The youth looked equally apprehensive and afraid. Talan wondered how quickly he would return to his former ways, the debauchery that had landed him in the Manifest's clutches.

Unless I can stop the slide. He thought he might even have the will to try. It would be like a redemption for his own lost years, if he succeeded.

For Airene's sake, he had to try.

Nomusa broke into his thoughts. "Xaron and I will help Jaxas in his plans, at least for now. To rebuild, and be stronger than before."

Talan snorted a laugh. "Politicians..."

"There was substance there, too," Xaron hurried to say. "He freed the honors, Talan. All of them."

That cut his amusement short. Talan scrutinized the jester, trying to detect any hint of a joke, but he looked utterly serious. A different sort of smile came to Talan then.

"Well," he muttered. "That should be interesting to see."

"There's more." Xaron licked his lips. "Wardens like you and Linos, outside of his employ... he freed you as well. Being attuned is no longer a crime."

For a long moment, the words didn't settle in. When they did, all Talan could do was laugh.

"There won't be much of Oedija left soon, will there?" he said bitingly.

"Probably not." Xaron gave a strained grin. "But it's progress."

Linos snorted a laugh. "I'll make the most of it while it lasts."

Nomusa gave the youth a resigned look, then turned back to Talan. "Jaxas might do some good. You could, too, if you tried."

Talan closed his eyes, letting the laughter slip back into the emptiness that filled him. *Try.* He didn't want to try any longer. But he'd experienced this cycle before; he knew where it ended.

"He claims Oedija is not dead, but will regrow," Nomusa said. "Just like the tree that saved us from Famine."

Talan cracked open his eyes again, sieving his thoughts. He was free: free of the Underguild, of Avvad, of Oedija and its Shepherds. It had been so long since he'd not been hunted for merely existing that he could scarcely comprehend it.

Maybe he didn't have to hide any longer. Maybe he could step out of the shadows and live in the light.

And live without her.

He looked up at the great white tree behind him. "The Harvest Tree," he'd already heard it called, and had no doubt the name would stick.

I won't think of the goddess when I see it, he thought to it. *Only you.*

Then a thought stuck in his mind, and he froze.

"Goddess," Talan murmured before looking at Linos. The youth eyed him strangely, but did not flinch from his stare.

Nomusa frowned at each of them. "What'd you say?"

"Goddess," Linos clarified. "What I want to know is why he said it."

Instead of answering, Talan opened his locus and channeled. His vision doubled, layering upon his eyes the world lit up with glowing quintessence, and he stared at Linos. He didn't know the youth well, but he knew Airene. And when he saw traces of her burning through her brother's soul along with another, his smile grew wide.

Closing his locus, he blinked and adjusted to normality, then spoke to Linos. "They're both in you."

"Both." Linos looked as if he wanted to bolt, but his feet remained rooted where he was. "Who do you mean?"

"Your sister didn't just die for you. She gave the last of her soul to you. And she didn't disappear, but is still within you."

"But she's dead." Linos craned back his neck to stare at her body far above. "What does it matter, if she's still not with us?"

Talan stepped closer to him. "Because she's not the only one alive in your soul. Harvest is, too."

For a moment, none of them moved. Then all three of his companions burst out at once.

"They are?" Nomusa demanded. "You can see them when you channel, can't you?"

"Just like you," Xaron exclaimed, "to only just be mentioning this! If only I could see them, too..."

"What are you saying?" Linos's voice cracked with emotion. "That we can... save her?"

Talan's smile had faded, and something harder remained behind. "I don't know. But if you're willing, I'd like to try something."

Linos had been intractable before being taken by the Manifest, at least in the few instances Talan had met him. Now, however, he moved quickly to Talan's instructions, as eager to help his sister as Talan was. Nomusa and Xaron watched as Talan and Linos stepped closer to the Harvest Tree and placed their hands on it.

"Is there anything we can do?" Nomusa asked tentatively.

"Put your hands on our shoulders," Talan said after a moment's speculation, more to keep them occupied than out of any hope it would help. "You can share your memories of her as well."

After exchanging a glance, Xaron and Nomusa followed his lead, their hands warm against his shoulders. As they became still behind, Talan closed his eyes and concentrated first on the feeling of the smooth bark beneath his palms, then the spirit that inhabited it. This tree was one part of Famine's prison. It stood to reason that not all of Harvest had departed it.

It will work. It must.

I need you.

He couldn't have admitted it aloud, but neither could he deny the truth. Airene had believed in him, helped make him a better man. When he envisioned a brighter future, she was always foremost in it.

He didn't want to guess what he would become otherwise.

So he gathered all the memories they had shared, all the moments both intimate and hard, and he channeled. His spirit quickly found Linos and Xaron's, Nomusa's beyond the sorcery, and with a recklessness that surprised himself, he broke their boundaries to touch upon their souls. Both flinched, but neither recoiled, and soon, their thoughts threaded across the gaps.

Joined, Talan delved both deeper into the tree and into Linos. *Harvest*, he called into the aether, reaching after that presence he had first sensed in Airene; so small, yet so impossibly vast. *Harvest, I need you. Airene needs you!*

The great being still slept.

He didn't relent, but pressed all their recollections upon the goddess. Airene traveling the rooftops with him. The kiss they shared before the Laurel Palace, then the many on the path to the Bali highlands. One of Linos's memories snuck in as well: when she ruffled her little brother's hair and said to him, *I'll always look after you, Little Lion.*

Still, nothing. Minutes carried on. Talan felt the resolve of the other two men waver, but he didn't let them give in. He carried on, dragging them with him, calling for the goddess with mind and memory, pleading for her life.

She needs to be alive! She can't go this way!

Desperate, he reached for another presence, the one that had settled inside him after working her miracle.

Airene, it's time to wake up. No more resting. Come back to us; come back to me.

He wasn't sure any of her was left, yet he felt something stir, little more than a feeble flame. He blew on it, coaxing it to life with his thoughts and emotions, hoping, needing it to be her.

Like a key turning in a lock, Harvest suddenly roared through them.

It was pain and promise as the goddess seized hold of his soul. Talan couldn't have let go if he wanted to now. Ruthlessly, Harvest combed through his being, turning over every memory, both of himself and Airene. He didn't know what she searched for, if it was to judge his worthiness, or Airene's, or something else entirely.

But he endured it. It was the only way.

As swiftly as she came, Harvest departed, and Talan sagged against the tree with her retreat. The others broke off, and he heard their voices from a distance, but he couldn't pay them heed. As the goddess faded into the tree, Talan tried to follow. He wasn't swift or strong enough. Within moments, she evaded his grasp, then was gone.

Gone.

She'd left. He'd failed, failed her again.

I'm sorry, Airene. I tried.

Despair dragged him down, but Xaron's call roused him. "Talan, look! Look up!"

Hope flared back to life as Talan opened his eyes and craned back his neck, looking where the jester pointed to a branch high above them. *Airene's branch.* Only, it looked different from before, shorter, and with the body upon it less obvious.

"It's retreating," Nomusa said, awe in her voice. "She's going into the tree."

"A seed," Linos whispered, and with that word, Talan understood.

He surged back into the Pyrthae, pressing against the tree, expectant now. He didn't have to wait long. Before them, the bark warmed with quintessence, building faster with every moment. He felt Harvest grow in her presence, but within her, something else was evolving.

His eyes had drifted closed again, but as the second presence in the tree moved forward, he opened them. A seam was splitting up the side of the trunk. But instead of darkness beyond it, a person, clad in ragged clothes, was emerging.

Talan staggered to his feet as he left the Pyrthae. His head pounded, but a grin split his face, emotion choking him so he could barely utter her name.

"Airene."

She stepped free of the tree and looked around, eyes glassy. Her gaze slid over each of their faces, then settled on Linos's. She blinked, and her stare sharpened. A smile slowly grew, and she raised her arms.

"Brother."

The youth bolted forward, wrapping his long limbs around her, holding her tight. Talan grinned the wider to see it.

When the siblings released each other, Airene turned and saw him next. Her smile faltered, but she held out her hands to him. He took them, running his hands over her skin. They felt the same as before: smooth but for calloused patches.

Her eyes brought his back up and held them.

"Harvest's seed was in Linos," she murmured, "but you brought me back. Thank you, Talan. You did what I couldn't."

Before he could think of a response, Xaron and Nomusa were there, crowding around and holding her. Talan released her hands, missing her touch as soon as it left. But it wasn't long before her friends stepped back, and Airene reached for him again. He pushed his fingers through hers and wondered if he'd ever felt more complete.

Airene looked around at each of them, then smiled sheepishly. "I feel a bit like Xaron, but I have to say, I'm starving. Think Jaxas's kitchens are still open to us?"

They shared a laugh, then their small group turned toward the Laurel Palace. Talan kept close to Airene's side.

Ash and ruin surrounded them still. Many had suffered, and many more would in the days to come.

But for himself, Talan had never seen a brighter future.

EPILOGUE

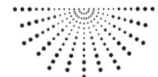

I live.

It is not the ending I expected when I set off in pursuit of Famine. Perhaps not even what I deserve.

Each day, I remember this, and I am grateful.

With Harvest, I defeated Famine. But the cost... that is a specter that haunts me everywhere I look.

The season has turned back to summer, but Oedija still lies in ruin. Between the God of Hunger's feasting and the siege by Avvad's armies, there is much to recover from.

Yet Famine is gone and the Avvadin fled back home, their numbers decimated. And by Kelena's reports, the Kahin-Shah was one of those killed in Valem's fires.

Avvad is another devastated empire. Only this was one I had a hand in razing.

But its fall means our world is safer, and each day, we become a little stronger. The rubble has been cleared from the streets. The fields flourish this season, as if to make up for lost time. Trade and commerce are invigorated, and the ports are busy even at night.

We have suffered. Many lost their lives. But like the great

tree at our city's center, we will grow, and someday become again the Pearl of the Four Realms.

As for myself... I have come to know a secret so plain, yet elusive for so many years, I wonder that I have even claimed it.

I am happy.

I shouldn't be; I know that. Blood stains my hands and soul. Many friends and allies are dead — Corin, Eltris, Azhi. Yet though I often weep for remembering them and all they lost, I cannot deny it. I have too much good in my life not to find joy in it.

My brother is returned to me, whole and as full of trouble as before — or as close as could be expected. Often I catch him staring at nothing, a look in his eyes I recognize well. He catches me doing the same sometimes.

But we are together, and together bear our scars.

The rest of my family rejoined us in Oedija, though reluctantly. Their home destroyed, my mother preferred the fineries of the Wreath estate. Yet even Jaxas's generosity can only be depended on so far, and at my insistence, and that of my father, weak as he's become, they returned. Like the rest of us, they rebuild, and for the first time in my lifespan they are free of their debts, vanished with the Valemish. It is as promising a start as I could hope for them.

My family has, in a way, grown to include others. Kari is now involved in my daily routine. With her sister gone, I felt an obligation to look after her and found her employment suitable to her odd disposition. She is melancholy, but resilient, considering all she lost. I think she will find joy again, given time. With each passing day, I understand her more, and we grow closer.

Nomusa, too, has proven strong, though that is nothing more than I expected. Remaining as Jaxas's Archon, she heads up the rebuilding of the Conclave into a proper governing body, hoping one day, it will rule again without the Despot's supervision. When time allows, we even share a drink or two at Zipho's cafe, which fortunately survived the calamity, and it's like we're back in Canopy, high above the city, our lives full of promise.

But sometimes, she speaks of the home she left behind. I wonder if she will leave us someday to reclaim it, and what that will mean for Komo should she do so.

Xaron and Isidora are receiving a fresh start here in Oedija, for our First Watcher has become pregnant. Everyday, he smiles more with anticipation, and he dotes on Isidora, to her infinite annoyance. I could almost believe him ready to be a father, though it seems like only yesterday he was guzzling down wine, not a care in the world.

And his family has grown in more than one way. Following her miraculous defense of Oedija with catalysm, Jihu reached out to her son, and amends were made between them. Every time I hear of them, they seem to grow closer.

And then there is Talan.

The piece of happiness we found while tailing after Famine? We have reclaimed it in full and more. Finally, we have our chance.

We will not squander it.

But family and friends are not my only preoccupation. Now I have a new purpose. Famine won't return; of that, I am certain. But other threats, be they pyr, Quintyr, or human, might yet assail us.

We can no longer deny our gifts, no longer shun our wardens. We must embrace them, harness them... and protect against them.

And there are more wardens than ever. With Harvest's return came a proliferation of attunements, so now a tenth of Oedija's population manifests magic to some extent. It is a transition that requires a firm hand to not let matters devolve into chaos, one guided by a person who has experience in such matters.

Or two persons, as it happens.

Jaxas appointed me as the First Attuner to oversee this, with Talan as my Second. Though I have my reservations about Jaxas remaining as the Despot of Oedija, the work is too urgent to ignore. Linos and Kari aid the effort as well, as much as their dispositions allow. I finally have a seat at Jaxas's Council — though I make as infrequent use of it as I can. Yet it is the position I require to effect the change I wish to see.

The work is unceasing and thankless. It is not what I imagined myself doing when growing up. Yet I am tired of living in the shadows, and I would only be in Kelena's way as a Verifier.

But once a Finch, a part of me will always remain one. There are those among the fledgling wardens who do not wish to be guided, whom we must seek and convince to come under our sway. Talan in particular is talented at this persuasion.

But in the seeking is where I thrive.

So Famine's cycle came to an end, and a new one was born. One of Harvest, perhaps. Or of humanity.

Only the seasons will tell, and the actions of each one of us. All I know is that I will never cease shaping it.

What can we not grow from a seed?

GLOSSARY

Acadians - The scholarly residents of the Acadium; often, they are wardens. While not all Acadians are wardens, any warden caught are forced to become an Acadian, or face the penalty of death.

The Acadium - Nominally, the center of learning and education within Oedija. The Acadium serves a dual purpose, however: the reeducation and containment of wardens.

Archon - The representative of the Despot or Despoina within the People's Conclave and Demos Council. Their powers are primarily limited to moderation, except when a member is missing on the Demos Council or a tie vote must be broken.

Avvad, or the Avvadin Imperium - The ever-expanding empire that lies to the south of Oedija.

Bali - The people who reside among the plateaus to the east of Oedija.

Buyujinn - The great spirits of the Avvadin people.

The Confessionary Tribunal, or the Tribunal - The judicial branch of Oedija's government, they are responsible for enforcing the rule of law, including the containment and punishment of rogue wardens. They are not elected, but are recruited by their own.

Daemons - Spirits who are considered evil or mean-spirited; also a derogatory term for wardens.

Damask Esir - The elite warriors of Avvad; said to be controlled by daemons called Qarin.

Demes - Districts of the city of Oedija.

Demos Council - The ruling council within the People's Conclave. Traditionally, it numbers eleven Low Consuls, with the Archon acting as a moderator, though often, the eleventh seat is disputed. Their responsibilities largely lie in determining the agenda within the larger Conclave. In times of strife, however, they are granted powers of military action and broad budgetary powers.

Demotism - A system of democratic republicanism in which representative officials are elected by citizens, or landowners, into a legislative ruling body.

The Despot/Despoina - The Ruling Wreath; a symbolic ruler who acts as a figurehead for Oedija. Small powers as the official emissary of Oedija and the nominal leader of Oedija's militia (when marshaled).

Eidola - The gods of the Eidolan religion.

Eidolanism - The religion of the original settlers of Oedija, in Airene's time, it is a fading religion, with many of its beliefs considered antiquated.

Energetic elements - The forms of energy present in the Pyrthae. Three energetic elements are commonly known: radiance, or heat and light; kinesis, or force; and magnesis, or the fields of magnetism. A fourth form of energy, catalysm, is also known to manifest in rare individuals. Other energetic elements are believed to exist, but are unconfirmed.

Finches (as a title) - Hunters and peddlers of secrets. While in purpose, their mission is to expose wrongdoing and uncover hidden truths, in practice they often perform small jobs recovering and threatening others with incriminating information for those who will pay.

First Laurel - The leader of the laurel guard, the soldiers defending the Laurel Palace and other Wreath properties.

The Four Realms - Considered the last bastions of civilization in a backwards world, four nations are united in peace by a concordance. These nations are: Oedija, the Bali ishakas, the Qao Fu jaitin, and the Avvadin Imperium.

Guilders - People who work on behalf of the Underguild.

Hilarion - The jester to the Despot or Despoina. Hilarion is always chosen from among Oedija's male wardens. Traditionally, he wears a crown of wheat, sackcloth clothes, and sandals bound with rope. Hilarion's nominal purpose is to entertain at the whim of the Ruling Wreath, but his true purpose is understood to be to diminish fear that people hold for wardens by making him an object of laughter and ridicule.

Honors - The lowest caste of Oedijan society. They are not permitted to own property, including money, nor choose their own employment, and are often housed and work within the estates of patricians. Honors are the descendants of the Kalthuae, the native inhabitants of the lands Oedija now claims, before settlers sailed from the west to found the nation.

Ishakas - The tribal kingdoms of the Bali people.

Jaitin - The matriarchal groups of the Qao Fu people; grouped by the caves in which they reside.

Low Consuls - The members of the Demos Council. Low Consuls are elected from the Conclave, requiring the support of ten of their fellow Servants to gain a seat.

Oedija - The "Pearl of the Four Realms"; the primary location of the story. A republican society undergoing significant turmoil, with threats from within and without.

Order of Verifiers - A branch of Oedija government tasked with routing out corruption. It was disbanded a few years after its founding, and a century before Airene of Port fashions herself after them.

The People's Conclave, or the Conclave - The legislative body of Oedija. Within their parameters lies the making and governance of laws, the taxing and determination of the treasury, the governance of commerce, and the defense of the nation.

The Peninsula - A rural area of Oedija to the north of the city of Oedija.

Prefectures - Areas of governance across Oedija's countryside.

Pyr - Spirits who are considered either benevolent or innocuous.

Pyrkin - A moss-like substance that is considered somewhere between plant and animal, it is supposed to have a connection to the Pyrthae, on account of its bioluminescence.

The Pyrthae - The plane of spirits, which is said to run parallel to the material plane, Telae.

Qao Fu - The people who reside among the desert caves to the northeast of Oedija.

Quintessence - The soul when it is used by channeling as an energetic element.

Servants - The elected leaders of Oedija, with semi-proportional representation from across Oedija's ten demes. They number one-hundred and twenty-one, minus those Servants who are elected to the Demos Council. They are responsible for legislative actions.

Shepherds - Members of the Confessionary Tribunal, they act under the guidance of a Tribune to contain or punish any rogue warden.

Stratechons - The five permanent military leaders of Oedija. Responsible for the city guard and the taxoi (when they are gathered).

Taxoi (s. taxos) - The militia of Oedija. As Oedija has no standing army, the taxoi are organized and financed by patrician households whenever the need arises.

Tefra - Priests of Avvad who use Silks, or bound spirits, to fight on their behalf.

Telae - The material plane; or, the world as it is known, including The Four Realms.

Tribunes - Members of the Confessionary Tribunal, they act as arbiters of Oedija's justice.

The Underguild - A semi-legitimized criminal organization. Overseen by five Guildmasters, the Underguild has a great hold over criminal activity in Oedija, and is largely responsible for its relatively low crime.

Verifiers of Truth, or Verifiers - Members of the Order of Verifiers, who were tasked with routing out corruption in Oedija's government, and were met with often violent resistance.

Wardens - People who are attuned to the Pyrthae and are able to manipulate forms of energy as magic. Across the Four Realms, they are forced into hiding, killed, lauded, and enslaved, depending on the nation. In Oedija, they are feared and kept to specific roles, such as Acadians or Shepherds, that suppresses their freedom and use of their abilities.

The Wreaths - The royal family of Oedija, formerly the true rulers of the nation when it was a monarchy.

Valemism / The Valemish - Worshippers of the volcanic god Valem, the religion of Valemism began in Avvad. It is considered a strict religion with a heavy emphasis on subjugation and obedience to authority, and the punishments for disobedience.

OEDIJAN SOCIETY

SOCIAL HIERARCHY

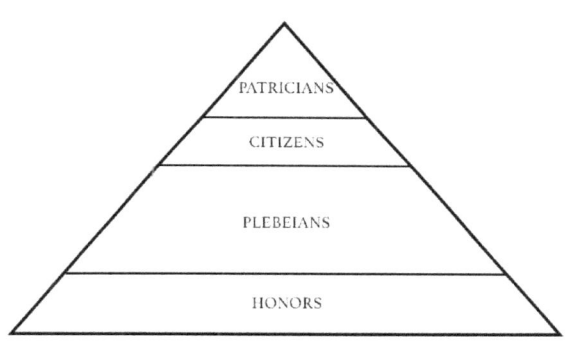

POLITICAL ORGANIZATION

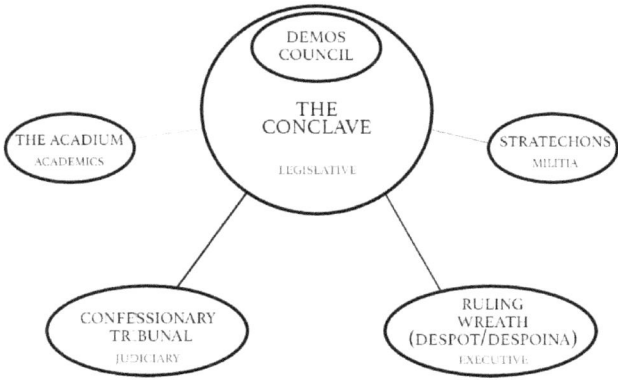

ACKNOWLEDGMENTS

This conclusion to the series has been a long time coming, and many eyes and brains have contributed to what it's become.

So if you didn't like it, be sure to blame those who follow!

In all seriousness, a huge thank you to all of you who left your mark on a Famine Cycle book. This includes my friend Nick, who did the initial proofreading for *Whispers of Ruin*; the original editor of *Whispers of Ruin*, Sylvia Cottrell; and my other friends and family, who are relentlessly supportive of my odd career choice.

More specifically for this book, I must thank:

Kaitlyn, my wife and first reader, who has encouraged me on this journey since I first began scribbling novels back when we were both still in college. Your kind words and cutting criticisms will forever be appreciated.

Shawn Sharrah, who provided swift and excellent proof-reading.

René Aigner, for a truly jaw-dropping illustration.

And finally, thank you, dear reader, for seeing this series of mine through to its end.

BOOKS BY J.D.L. ROSELL

Sign up for future releases at jdlrosell.com.

THE FAMINE CYCLE
1. Whispers of Ruin
2. Echoes of Chaos
3. Requiem of Silence
Secret Seller *(Prequel)*
The Phantom Heist *(Novella)*

LEGEND OF TAL
1. A King's Bargain
2. A Queen's Command
3. An Emperor's Gamble
4. A God's Plea

THE RUNEWAR SAGA
1. The Throne of Ice & Ash
2. The Crown of Fire & Fury
3. The Stone of Iron & Omen

GODSLAYER RISING
1. Catalyst

2. Champion

3. Heretic

ABOUT THE AUTHOR

J.D.L. Rosell is the author of the Legend of Tal series, The Runewar Saga, The Famine Cycle series, and the Godslayer Rising trilogy. He has earned an MA in creative writing and has previously written as a ghostwriter.

Always drawn to the outdoors, he ventures out into nature whenever he can to indulge in his hobbies of hiking and photography. Most of the time, he can be found curled up with a good book at home with his wife and two cats, Zelda and Abenthy.

Follow along with his occasional author updates and serializations at www.jdlrosell.com or contact him at authorjdlrosell@gmail.com.